CW00402869

GEOFF WIGHTMAN

GEOFF WIGHTMAN was born in Dartford in 1960. He was educated at Dartford Grammar School, Bristol University (LLB) and Edinburgh University (MBA), qualifying as a solicitor in 1987. He finished 8th in the Commonwealth Games Marathon and 6th in the European Championship Marathon, both in 1990. He works as a Sports Marketing Manager at Puma UK, and commentates for Eurosport. In an honorary capacity, he is also Head of Road Running Policy and Support Team for UK Athletics, and is a life member of Dartford Harriers.

He lives with his wife Susan and three children in Surrey.

SPORT ARMAGEDDON

BY

GEOFF WIGHTMAN

© 2001 G. WIGHTMAN

The right of Geoff Wightman to be identified as the author of the Work has been asserted by him in accordance with the Copyright, Designs and Patents Act 1988.

A CIP catalogue record of this book is available at the British Library

First published in 2001 by Descartes Publishing Ltd

All rights reserved. No part of this publication may be reproduced, stored in a retrieval system, or transmitted in any form or by any means without the prior written permission from the publisher, nor be otherwise circulated in any form of binding or cover other than that in which it is published and without a similar condition being imposed on the subsequent purchaser.

Words and Music by Neil Diamond taken from the song 'America'.
© Stonebridge Music. By kind permission Sony/ATV Music Publishing.

All characters in this publication are fictitious and any resemblance to real persons, living or dead, is purely coincidental.

ISBN 0 9541718 0 2

Typeset by Designpoint; Cover by Karen Johnson; Editors: Liz Morrell, Sheila Harding. Printed and bound in Great Britain by Omnia Books Limited. Published by Descartes Publishing Ltd, 83 Park Road, Peterborough, Cambridgeshire PE1 2TN

For Susan, Jake, Sam and Martha

With grateful thanks to Liz Morrell for all her guidance and hard work.

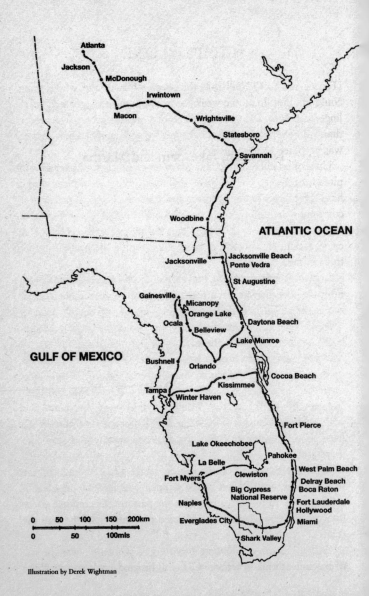

Atlanta
Jackson
McDonough
Irwintown
Macon
Wrightsville
Statesboro
Savannah

Woodbine

ATLANTIC OCEAN

Jacksonville
Jacksonville Beach
Ponte Vedra
St Augustine

Gainesville
Micanopy
Orange Lake
Ocala
Belleview
Daytona Beach
Lake Munroe

GULF OF MEXICO

Bushnell
Orlando
Cocoa Beach
Tampa
Kissimmee
Winter Haven

Fort Pierce

Lake Okeechobee
Pahokee
La Belle
West Palm Beach
Fort Myers
Clewiston
Delray Beach
Boca Raton
Big Cypress
National Reserve
Fort Lauderdale
Naples
Hollywood
Everglades City
Miami
Shark Valley

0   50   100   150   200km
0   50   100mls

Illustration by Derek Wightman

vi

CHAPTER ONE

IT occurred to O'Neill that the sheer effort of the whole thing could kill him. In all the weeks of training, this thought had never lingered before. Dying for the sake of a sports event? It was more than your average sporting challenge, for sure, and he knew that he was prepared to push himself to the limit. But die?

How often did that happen? Every now and then a boxer died in pursuit of his art. Occasionally the big city marathon races would have a fatality. Tommy Simpson had paid the ultimate penalty for combining drug abuse with the Tour de France but the prospect of checking out had never clouded his thinking previously. A swim. A cycle. A run. Hard work, extremely hard work in fact but not life threatening.

Perhaps it was something that should have concerned him before now, but then he was not a fearful man and there had been times, recent times, when he had valued his own life very cheaply indeed.

Besides, people never died swimming, did they? Bike crashes could be grisly. He had suffered a couple of those but always with sufficient warning to protect himself from serious injury. Runners often operated near their limits but could not usually go right over the edge. The body had its own safety valves. If he was in real trouble with the heat, surely he would first feel dizzy and faint? But what if he was on the bike when that happened and banged his head as he toppled off? No, the crash helmet would save him there.

What if it happened on the running stage when he had nothing to protect his head? What would happen if he had the presence of mind to sink to his knees but then the paramedics couldn't get to him quickly enough and he just fried to death right there in the road?

"Steve, I'm sorry. You were frowning as you came over the top of the hill. It looked wrong. Can you just jog back and we'll try

1

again? You looked like you were in your own little world there buddy." The American drawl of Viv Wheatley snapped him back to reality and the intrusion irritated him.

"Does it actually make any difference if I'm frowning, laughing, or crying, Viv?"

"Sure it does. You're supposed to be our sunny little Brit, remember? Karelov is our mean and moody boy. Stick to the script."

Wheatley and his Prime Life TV crew had been following Steve O'Neill for the past three days. Within hours they would be on their way to Australia, and good riddance. They had really got under his skin. It was cold, it was wet and he had already run up that same hill five times as they filmed him from every conceivable angle. He wanted to tell Wheatley where he could stick his camera but the man from Prime Life was calling the shots, in more ways than one. Dutifully, he re-turned on his heel, fixing Wheatley with a patronising grin and trotted off back to the foot of the hill.

"Definitely the last one, OK? I've got sixteen miles to run and it's freezing."

"Last one, I promise you." Wheatley grinned back with perhaps even less sincerity.

The superb view over Edinburgh as he ran back down at least afforded some consolation. The rain and heavy cloud added to the starkness of the granite skyline. In the distance was the outline of Calton Hill and the rocky perch of Edinburgh Castle. Somewhat nearer stood Holyrood Palace and its magnificent grounds. If he felt capable of such an emotion, Steve O'Neill would say that he loved this place. He liked the people, the history, the ruggedness of the terrain. He even liked the climate for goodness sake.

There were many times when the city had a really brooding presence about it and that suited him fine. He was not without his dark moments after all. It had been seven years since he moved to the north and the bouts of depression that consumed him had become mercifully less frequent.

He had moved to Edinburgh to escape his past, and make a fresh start, but somehow it seemed inevitable that his mind would continue to punish him for the tribulations of his youth. He wanted to put it all firmly behind him but the images kept bubbling back. Up the hill for the sixth, and definitely the final time, the dark reflections were with him yet again. Why could he not blank them out? He was concentrating on his running. He was in the company of four other people. Would he be haunted by these images and this guilt forever? Damn.

"Steve, smile for goodness sake. That's it, that's much better. Boy this will look just great in slow motion with a bit of backing music. We could use that 'Chariots of Fire' music."

In spite of his mood, O'Neill laughed. This documentary would be unashamedly corny but, since he was depicted as one of the good guys, he was not about to complain further. Besides, they were finished now.

Wheatley's head popped out of the camera jeep up ahead. He was all jowls, grey whiskers and baseball cap.

"Steve, that's us almost done fella, but we'd just like to try and interview you on the run, OK? I'm going to jog alongside you with the mike. It's one take only, so if a question goes wrong, we just carry on, OK?"

"OK." O'Neill's mood was brightening at the thought of Wheatley trying to run, talk and hold a microphone all at the same time. He resolved instantly not to slow down at all.

Viv Wheatley was built for comfort rather than speed. In his pomp, thirty years previously, a quarter mile run would have represented no problem. In those days he was reserve quarter back on Indiana University's roster but the move into journalism and then broadcasting by way of SVP Television, Cougar and now Prime Life, had taken its toll. He was an international class luncher and whilst he was known to like a cheeseburger or two, the feeling was not reciprocated. Having stubbed out his cigar, his improbable girth appeared first as he emerged from the passenger door of the jeep.

He jogged towards O'Neill. The early stages of exercise always stirred long dormant feelings of wellbeing and competitiveness. Ah yes, he could have been a contender. If only he had not bust that knee ligament in college, Vivian Wheatley III would surely have gone on to win a Super Bowl ring, probably as a member of the great Miami Dolphins team of the early '70s. He had been robbed of his Hall of Fame place by that one cruel injury.

Wheatley turned and drew alongside O'Neill.

"OK, guy. Don't slow down on my account. The camera's still rolling."

Inside the back of the jeep, Melanie, the production assistant, stifled a giggle. Everyone at Prime Life liked Wheatley, even on occasions like this when he looked a complete buffoon. Clad in a bright orange Prime Life waterproof suit, with an Atlanta Falcons baseball cap wedged on and his feet splayed sideways, it was clear that this had the potential to be an extremely brief interview.

O'Neill looked ahead at the camera. He had not slowed down at all. His piercing brown eyes were half-closed in the driving rain, his dark hair plastered to his head. There was not an ounce of spare flesh on his frame and his skin was stretched like parchment across his cheek bones.

"OK, let's start."

Wheatley cleared his throat to signal the first question.

"Steve O'Neill, it's the middle of July and here we are on Arthur's Seat, the biggest hill in Edinburgh. It's freezing cold and pouring. This doesn't seem to be exactly ideal preparation for what lies ahead does it?"

There was a wheeze at the end of the question. Steve looked across and detected suppressed discomfort on Wheatley's face. He laughed. The dark thoughts from a few minutes ago had subsided once again.

"This is my home and it's by far the best place for me to pre-pare," he replied. "We have had some warm days and I have done some of my exercise bike work at the Botanical Gardens to get used to humid conditions. It's more important for me to stick to a famil-iar routine than it is to go swanning off to Florida like some of the others. I'll travel out ten days beforehand to help with publicity and acclimatise. That still leaves me three more weeks to complete my preparations right here in Scotland. I shall be ready."

"And what is your strong point?" Wheatley's questions became ever more succinct as the yards rolled by. O'Neill was ready for this and could not resist the opportunity to add to the big man's puce condition by throwing back a query.

"What do you mean by 'strong point'?"

"Best discipline." Wheatley regretted that 'discipline' was a three syllable word. He was already very close to oxygen debt.

"Running is what I do best. Swimming is worst but I think all of us will just be looking to survive the water phase and from there I shall be trying to make up lost ground or maybe even open up a lead. It's hard to predict how any part of it will pan out because we will be moving into realms of endurance where no one has ever had to compete before. The distribution of effort will be crucial."

"And the million bucks?"

O'Neill glanced across at Wheatley waiting for an elaboration on the question. None was forthcoming. Viv was trying to main-tain his warm smile for the camera. His feet were still leaving the ground alternately but his breathing pattern now sounded like a dredging machine and his eyes were glazed. He had completely gone. O'Neill thought it appropriate to give some sort of answer.

"The prize money doesn't turn me on quite as much as I'm sure it does with the others. In a way, it's a publicity stunt. I want to win this thing because it's the ultimate endurance challenge but I guess if there's four hours 'til bedtime on the road to Atlanta and the old legs and feet are crying out with tiredness, the thought of a million dollars might just take you a bit further. It's a hell of a carrot."

He looked at Wheatley, who raised a weak 'thumbs up' gesture confirming that he hadn't the breath to say 'good luck', by way of signing off the interview. Wheatley stopped immediately and put his hands on his knees. His head was spinning and he thought he was going to hurl. He spat noisily at the tarmac.

Up ahead the camera jeep stopped abruptly and Melanie ran back towards her boss. By the time she reached him, he had straightened up and was waving away O'Neill's supporting arm.

"I'm OK fella. Just hadn't got my second wind." At that precise moment he belched volubly.

"See. Just a bit of trapped wind, like I said."

His complexion suggested more than a passing digestive problem and Melanie put a steadying hand to his back as they walked very slowly to the vehicle.

In spite of his distressed condition, Wheatley could detect O'Neill jogging on the spot as he accompanied them. Jeez, was this guy some kind of exercise freak? Couldn't he even break off from his training for these few moments. He was the inventor of perpetual motion. No wonder he, the all-American boy, had been a little out of breath keeping up with him. Time to say goodbye.

"Steve, we won't keep you from your training any longer." He coughed suddenly. The full repertoire of human sound effects were at Wheatley's disposal for this, his Scottish jogging debut.

"Are you sure you're alright?"

"Of course I am. We gotta head for the airport. The next time we meet it will be warmer then this, I can tell you. Good luck, buddy."

"Thanks. Have a good trip. Bye."

O'Neill had not really stopped throughout the filming. He sped off down the road waving to the production crew in the jeep as he shot by. He glanced down at the heart monitor on his wrist. His pulse was still 90 beats per minute, so he had given his body a reasonable workout even during that nonsense when Wheatley had joined him. Ahead lay one hour and 55 minutes of sustained running and then an hour's steady swimming at the Commonwealth Pool.

His eyes focused on the far distance as his increased tempo ploughed him through the rain. It was time to work hard again. O'Neill was driven.

Back at the jeep, Wheatley was driven in a very different way. Melanie helped him into the passenger seat and the great man was most anxious to play down his discomfort.

"Fit guy, that one. It's probably as quick as I've covered a mile in the last couple of years. Old Lenny Stein back at HQ would be proud of my efforts for Prime Life today."

Melanie glanced at her colleagues but knew instantly that despite the mirth in their eyes, none of them would have the nerve to tell Vivian Wheatley III that the grand total of his Herculean exertions was actually a fraction under 300 metres.

"It was great television Boss, but we'd better get back to the hotel and change pretty quick. If we don't get the five-thirty out of Edinburgh, we'll miss that London connection to Australia."

Wheatley closed his eyes and sank back into the seat. He was starting to feel recovered. Perhaps when they got to Sydney he would try and exercise every day. He was a natural athlete after all. With a bit more preparation he could have competed in Florida himself. It was great to be fit. He hoped that Qantas would serve steak on the flight because he had certainly worked up an appetite. Australia would be a sight warmer than this monsoon trap. A better place for healthy guys. He would love it. He opened one eye. "Mel, pass me my cigar would you, honey?"

O'Neill zipped on downhill from Arthur's Seat and out past Meadowbank Stadium on the road to Portobello. Ron Hill had won a famous Commonwealth marathon victory for England along this very road in 1970.

Two hours and nine minutes in high summer. Out in front on his own. The pint-sized Steven O'Neill had been very impressed with the intensity of Hill's winning effort and had run 26 laps of his back garden circuit to celebrate.

Team sports had never impressed him. The eyesight was not great for tennis or cricket. Rugby or soccer would snap him in half but the very first time he contested his school cross-country, well that was different. No one of his age could live with him. He loved the solitude, the simplicity and the sheer joy of movement that his running brought him.

He could trace all the benchmarks in his life by reference to his running. His headmaster had called him to his study on O'Neill's last day at school. He had fidgeted nervously during the ten minute wait outside the dreaded office. His spectacles continuously misted over because he had just completed a five mile lunchtime training spin.

"O'Neill, you have made good use of some of what this school has to offer" – he could hear him now – "I have no doubts that you will enjoy your time at Oxford and that you will continue to display prowess in both academic and sporting endeavours. I am rather less certain how your curious blend of immaturity and responsibility will reconcile itself. Certain masters suggest that you still tend to 'kick over the traces' by being argumentative and playing the fool once too often. You will either be a major figure in your future career or you will end up as a hopeless drifter. I cannot decide which but I wish you well."

That was it. Thirty seconds of brutal analysis and a handshake. Fifteen years on and the jury was still out. Yes, he got a Sportsman's Second Class English degree at Oxford and an athletics blue. Yes, he lost his virginity, got drunk often and had a great time. No, he hadn't landed a job for two years after graduating, nor had he settled properly in any one place – parents in Norfolk, teaching jobs in Exeter and Durham, now working part-time as a sports science technician at the Edinburgh University fitness centre. He had experienced the thrill of international honours at cross-country running, duathlon and orienteering but, to his endless regret, there was no woman in his life and how he wished there was. This major entry in the debit column coupled with the other infamous episode completely upset the balance sheet of his life. No, he was not truly happy.

Some people were comfortable on their own. By choice, O'Neill was not one of them. He was not short of lady admirers but refused to lower his standards or expectations and Miss Right remained resolutely undiscovered.

He sometimes wondered if the reason he immersed himself so completely in his training was to prevent his brooding solitude from overwhelming him. Maybe running was his bromide fix. But it couldn't be as straightforward as that because it had absorbed him from the age of 12. It was his creative outlet, his self-expression and a way of standing out from the common herd. Through all the trials and tribulations of life he had never ever lost the discipline of daily running. The comfort blanket of routine. His relentless training regime was the mistress of his life.

The rain was still whipping into his face. His brisk pace had brought him as far as Leith. Still six more miles on the return journey to the swimming pool.

For all his training, and there had been times when he had run 130 miles in a week, he had never scaled the heights that he craved in competitive sport. Was it really worth putting his entire life on hold for the occasional international appearance? – No house, no career, no money, no family, no love interest. Where were his footprints in the sands of life?

He had resolved that the next two months would represent a crossroads in the O'Neill story. He would commit everything he had to the Florida event. Everything. This would be his Olympic Games. He was fed up with being an also-ran. 'Quite good – no cigar.' It had always been the same. He would triumph in this event and be remembered forever. He might be remembered forever just by being there because there were only four other competitors and the media hype was already building in a phenomenal way.

His invitation to take part had come right out of the blue and could only be put down to being in the right place at the right time.

He had been in Huntsville, Alabama for the World Double Ironman Championships. It had been a murderous event. Kicking off with a 4.8 mile swim down the Tennessee River followed by a 224 mile cycle and then a 52 mile run. He had finished in just under 30 hours and sneaked a place inside the top ten. The distances were mind-boggling but he had dealt with the boredom and the fatigue exceptionally well. He had never previously contested an ultra-distance Ironman triathlon event so he was operating on instincts alone. O'Neill had enjoyed the challenge.

He had walked stiffly but unaided from the finish to the medical tent clutching a cool electrolyte drink and lay down for a leg massage. As he had taken off his sunglasses, a bulky figure had filled the entrance to the tent.

"Buddy, you look in pretty good shape to me. There's been eight other guys finished already and every last one of them has had to be carried off. You look like you could do it all again. How are you feeling?"

"I don't feel too bad at all, actually. My hamstrings are a bit tight and I have this thing on my foot." O'Neill pointed to a blood blister on the tip of the second toe on his left foot, "but otherwise I feel great. I'm Steve O'Neill from England, well Scotland, actually." They shook hands.

"Hi, fella, I'm Vivian Wheatley. I work for Prime Life TV, based in Atlanta. We've had a small film crew with us for news purposes but really I'm here just to take notes. We're thinking of putting on a much longer event next year, by invitation, and we want a bunch of guys who can go the distance."

"How much further?"

"Not sure yet. Some guys can run from LA to New York if they're allowed to take their time. We want a flat-out long race with a big prize and big pressure because it'll make great TV. Reckon you might be interested?"

"Yes."

"Here's my card. Give me a call when you get back to Scotland."

The next morning, during the first breakfast sitting at the race hotel, Vivian Wheatley III had been chomping on doughnuts and coffee. He nearly swallowed the whole lot in one gulp when he saw O'Neill springing up the hotel entrance steps. The man was just returning from a training run, for crying out loud. The rest of the competitors were taking intravenous room service breakfast and shuffling to the bathroom on granite legs and here he was that little Brit acting like Jumping Jack Flash.

Wheatley knew right there that Steve O'Neill had earned a place in his starting line-up. Contracts were signed later that morning and O'Neill had been daydreaming of glory and stardom ever since.

Now he was back on Edinburgh's mean streets with only half a mile to the end of another training workout. He quickened his pace and visualised himself powering into the lead in Florida.

There would be no stopping him. He could almost taste the acclaim.

He sprinted hard as he approached the steps of the Commonwealth Pool. There was no rational reason for the flourish at the end of the run. Most runners liked to make one last effort as if to remind their bodies what it would be like in the closing stages of a race. It seemed almost inconceivable that the event for which he was preparing would come down to a sprint finish but you just never knew for sure on these things.

As he stopped, he checked the pulse monitor and stopwatch on his wrist. He had managed it in one hour and 45 minutes. His pulse registered 151 beats per minute. By the time he had got to the pay kiosk inside the building, it was down to 135 and as he changed into his swimming trunks two minutes later, it was down to 88. Good. He was within a pinch of supreme fitness and could make great use of the remaining weeks of training. It was a very satisfying feeling.

By concession, he had free use of the pool and had merely nodded to the cashier as he made his way to the lockers where he had previously changed for his run. The City Council was fully supportive of his bid for glory in Florida. It would reflect well on Edinburgh and its sporting facilities.

They knew him here at the pool, although two of the young girls working as lifeguards were relatively new on the scene and giggled to each other as he walked along the side of the near deserted pool.

Linda was perched on the lifeguard's chair at the deep end of the pool, a mop of over-permed blonde hair flopping across her eyes. Her pal Debbie was sat against the window by the children's pool, all adolescent disinterest, acne, body-piercing and aggressive wedge haircut. Linda met Debbie's gaze and discreetly raised her left hand and three fingers of her right, to indicate that S. O'Neill had just registered an 80 per cent score on her supreme ratings of the male form. They always gave the men swimmers a mark out of ten.

"Nah, seven," shouted Debbie. Such a discrepancy in the scoring system required an urgent conference and Debbie strode briskly round the edge of the pool to discuss the matter.

"No way is he an eight," she muttered.

"Ah like him. Ah've seen him before. He's got a cute wee bum and he's all muscley and taut. Definite eight," averred Linda.

Debbie looked down at the water in disgust. O'Neill was already ploughing up and down the roped-off lane in a rhythm that would sustain him for the next hour.

"Och, he's all skin and bone. Ah must be going soft to have even given that a seven. There's no meat on him at all. How comes yous know him?"

Linda winked at her. "He's been in here every day this week. He must swim two or three miles without stopping."

"Is he mental or something?"

"D' ye no recognise the wee man?"

"No. Is he famously mental?"

"Och, he's that guy on the telly. He's doing that triathlon thing in America. They've got to swim across some bloody great lake and then cycle and run for thousands of miles."

"He is mental then?"

"No, you daft cow. There's a million quid prize money and this guy could win it."

Debbie gazed back at the water as O'Neill effortlessly glided to the wall, turned and then churned his way back down the lane. A million pounds. Debbie earned a basic six pounds an hour as a pool attendant. A million pounds. Suddenly O'Neill looked much more attractive. Not skin and bones, really. Quite lithe and lovely when you really studied him. No flab at all. He was as lean as a chequebook. A million pounds.

"Linda?"

"Yes, Debs."

"Is he married?"

"No, Debs. These dedicated athletes are like monks you know."

"Do you think he's my type?"

"Nah. He probably doesn't drink, smoke, do drugs or stay out all night on Friday."

"Ah never stay out all night on a Friday. It's Saturdays."

"Ah don't think he's a party animal, Debs. He's more my type."

"Och, away with yous, you old slapper. First sign of interest from me in a fellah and Mrs Tin Knickers starts staking a claim. Yous only want him for his money."

"Who said ah want him? Ah just said he wasn't your type."

"Ah don't care what you think. Ah'm going to ask him oot."

"Tart."

"Tart yourself."

Debbie stalked off back to the children's pool, trying to work out how many centuries she would have to sit there to earn a million pounds.

O'Neill was oblivious to the employee disharmony that he had created. He had disengaged his brain completely and was not even bothering to count the lengths. At 40 minutes, he checked his wristwatch briefly before returning to his lonely furrow. God, he hated swimming. It was OK in moderation but long-distance training was a real bind.

He speeded up over the last five minutes and was conscious of the other swimmers in the fast lane moving out of his way.

He finally finished after 60 minutes and 48 seconds of swimming and hauled himself out of the pool. He sat on the side and pulled off his goggles. His heart was pounding and his upper arms were quivering from the effort of the finishing surge. He gazed around. The mop-top blonde in the lifeguard's chair was directly ahead of him. He nodded to her and she smiled back.

"You know, you are a really gud swimmer." A voice murmured close to his right ear. It was the dark haired lifeguard crouched at his side.

"Thanks," he replied, slightly taken aback by the speed with which she had materialised alongside him. Linda scowled from her vantage point. Debbie had no shame in these matters. It would only be a matter of time before she presented O'Neill with her pants.

"Are you training for anything in particular?"

"Yes, I've got a big triathlon in the States."

"Uh-huh. Reckon you might win?" She has worked out that a little over 80 years work at the Commonwealth Pool would gross her a million dollars. She smiled as winsomely as she could.

"Who knows? I'll give it my best shot."

O'Neill started to get up. He was very tired and polite conversation with the young lady was beyond him on this occasion.

Debbie could sense her grasp on the chequebook slipping. She had no record of subtlety in encounters of this kind, the majority of her romantic experiences being unmemorable fumblings behind Lasswade playing fields.

"Ah'm off duty in a few minutes. Do you fancy a coffee?"

O'Neill looked at her. She seemed about 16 years old and a bit of a hard case. Why was she coming on to him like this? He turned away and could see her pretty friend in the lifeguard's seat glaring at them. Maybe it was a bet between these two girls and Captain Ear-Rings here had drawn the forfeit. Yes that was it. He would nip this one in the bud.

"Sorry. I've got to scoot. Thanks for asking."

Already he was through the footbath and into the sanctuary of the men's changing room. His inquisitor herself got as far as the archway and then relinquished the chase. She turned to move back to her allotted post by the children's pool, carefully avoiding eye contact with Linda. To no avail. She couldn't see her but she didn't need to. All the way back to her seat she was accompanied by the uncontrolled cackling of her supposed friend.

O'Neill changed back into a clean T-shirt and sweatsuit. He did so slowly and awkwardly, for he was very fatigued and in urgent need of some carbohydrates. It was a warm sort of tiredness though. He savoured that contented glow which swept over him whenever he completed a satisfying day's training.

As he reached the foyer of the pool complex, a craving for food of any kind got the better of him. He headed for the vending machine and rummaged around in his sports bag for 30 pence in change. Mars Bar, Opal Fruits, Kit Kat – at that point anything would do. He hit the buttons for a Mars Bar.

"Was my friend Debbie bothering you just now?" It was blondie the lifeguard.

"No, no, she was just asking after my training."

"Ah was explaining to her that you're preparing for that mega-race in America. Ah saw you on the telly last week. Yous were very gud."

He blushed and glanced up at her. 'Linda' her name badge announced. She had washed out blue eyes and puffy lips. She was quite striking but probably an apprentice man-eater.

"Thanks very much. It's quite hard work but there's not long to go now." He bit off half the Mars Bar. That was a conversation killer. Linda took it as her cue to press on.

"Ah've done a bit of triathlon myself but mostly I'm a swimmer. Ah'd be glad to keep you company on some of your sessions if you think it would help. Ah do a mile or two most days. Ah could pace you if..." His hawkish gaze was unnerving her and the suggestion tailed off.

For his part, O'Neill was more convinced than ever that the two girls were making a play for him for amusement only. This was one bet that neither of them was going to win. Linda was moderately attractive and pleasant but he wasn't up for it at all.

"Sorry, I start my outdoor swimming programme this week so this might be my last visit here for a while but when I'm coming back I'll let you know in advance." It was a hopelessly vague and open-ended assurance. She knew a brush-off when she heard one.

"That'd be fine. Ah'll see you then."

"Bye."

He turned and strode out of the building back into the driving rain. 'High summer in Scotland. Welcome to Edinburgh', he chuckled to himself and trotted the 400 yards down the hill to his flat.

It was rented accommodation with mixed groups of students on the ground and first floors and his apartment on the top floor. As he reached the staircase one of the beefy medical students walked across the hallway furiously mixing an omelette in a bowl.

"Hi. Alright?"

"Not bad. How are you?"

"Fine thanks." End of exchange.

It was ever thus. Half a dozen words of greeting. He did not even know the man's name and yet they had been neighbours for seven months. Steve decided that he was at fault. He was older than these students by at least a decade. They were perfectly pleasant and the onus was on him to be sociable. He hated his lack of neighbourliness but was way too tired to do anything about it.

Into his own spartan accommodation he hit the play button on his telephone answering machine. There were messages. The first was from his mother enquiring after his health. The second was 'The Scotsman' newspaper, requesting an interview. Hadn't he already done that? One more wouldn't hurt, so they could catch him in his lunchbreak the next day.

He plucked two large baking potatoes from the sack in the kitchen, scrubbed them under the tap and shoved them in the microwave, setting the dial for 15 minutes. Just time for a bath. The simple pleasures were best.

As the bath filled, he reflected on the events of the day. He had almost forgotten about the Prime Life film crew. They would probably be in the air by now and he wondered how he would come across in the televised build-up.

He lowered himself carefully into the hot water and closed his eyes. He visualised the shaggy locks and pouting face of Lifeguard Linda. Why had he brushed her off so nastily when she was being so sweet? He hadn't trusted her motives. The old antenna hadn't let him make a fool of himself. He would know for sure when it was the real thing.

His legs ached, burned, twanged and shuddered all at the same time. They had taken a pounding but they would need a bit more conditioning yet. The body was finished for the day but the mind was still swaying. Fear and anticipation. Doubts and confidence. Melancholy and blue skies. Punishment and release. His past. His future. He was fit and very nearly ready.

He imagined himself in Florida. It was going to be glorious and it would surely give some sort of meaning and context to this sad old life of his. There were still 31 days to go but he wished it was tomorrow. Steve O'Neill just knew that he would win Sport Armageddon.

CHAPTER TWO

LENNY STEIN, inevitably, was in the chair. Wheatley, inevitably, was his right hand man in terms of status and geography. The Prime Life board was having a brainstorming session to finalise the format and line up for its 'Sport Armageddon' concept.

"No, it's not make-or-break, Joe" thundered Stein to his sales director, "You know as well as I do that if the projections come true we pay out four million and bring in six."

"But, Chief, they're just projections. The sales force are workin' hard but are barely up to a quarter of the best case figures," Joe argued.

"Look, you're either with me on this one or you're off the team completely." Joe was glad that there was a full 12 feet of board-room between him and the man with the bulging eyes. It was time to clam up. Most arguments with the Chief would plunge towards some kind of zero option denouement.

'Team' meant nothing to him. In his own mind, Stein was a lone wolf creating brilliantly innovative projects from scratch and harvesting all the benefits himself. At times like this he resented the fact that he worked in a people-intensive industry and had to surround himself with cretins like Joe.

Stein continued. "What I'm saying is, we have to think big, really big. We can't keep living off scraps that the other stations don't want or pretending that monster truck racing is classy. If we can get one event like this really hyped up then our audience profile will rise, we'll get some blue chip advertisers and some cash to spend on even better events. We have to commit to Sport Armageddon and make it work for us. So far I don't have a problem with the format. You know the logistics well enough. Lets talk about the competitors. Viv, who've we got so far?"

Wheatley cleared his throat and picked up a large sheaf of papers from the table top in front of him. Around the room three of his fellow directors exchanged knowing glances and a collective smirk. It was a common trick for old Viv to fake a dossier full of information when the true extent of his briefing notes was probably scribbled on the back of his hand. They always regarded Viv as top entertainment. In truth, he could probably run the whole shooting match far better than Mr Miseryguts in the chair and would canter home a long way clear in the popularity stakes.

"Well, strictly speaking only three of the five places are filled so far..."

"What?" Stein spluttered. "I thought we were only one short. Who hasn't signed?"

"Kogo, O'Neill and Karelov have all sent in their contracts. It's actually Gaby Vaughan who is being a little slow."

"Jeez, we have to have her on board. That's the deal with the Australian network. Is there a problem?"

"Er, well, no. Not that I know of."

Stein pressed on. "So how come we've filmed all this footage with her without having a signed contract?"

Wheatley began rummaging among his bogus notes.

"You'd better get out there to see her, Viv. Where are you at the beginning of next week?"

Wheatley continued rifling through the random paperwork. "Um, er, in Edinburgh with Steve O'Neill, I believe."

"Right, well book an onward flight to Australia and get this sorted out. If there's no signed contract by the end of next week, you needn't bother coming back. OK?"

Wheatley said nothing. He had come across a betting slip tucked in amongst the Prime Life board minutes. So that was where it was. He'd spent most of last week looking for that. He'd backed 'Silver Monkey' each way at 15-1 in Del Mar for 50 bucks. It was payday.

"Chief, I'll be on my way today or tomorrow. Leave it to me," he announced, swivelling in his chair.

The sun glinted on the huge bulk of the Qantas jumbo jet as it banked steeply to the right to begin its final approach to Sydney Airport. Contrary to visual impressions this manoeuvre was not necessitated by the huge bulk of Vivian Wheatley III positioned on the right hand side of the first class cabin.

The living legend had indeed celebrated his sporting achievement on Arthur's Seat with a large portion of rare fillet steak. Sadly this had been washed down with the better part of two bottles of red wine and that, coupled with the sleeping tablet that he had taken when they left Calcutta, had meant that he hadn't so much slept as taken a short course in death until the end of the flight.

Now he blearily peeled back his night shades and squinted through reptilian eyes at the splendours of the Opera House and the Harbour Bridge below. It was a beautiful morning, completely wasted on a man whose view was obscured by a haze of Mogadon and Burgundy. Through the fog, his bladder was sending urgent messages to the brain. It took a while but eventually the physical sensation generated a flashing red light and he shot out of his seat, intent on the bathroom. The seat belt sign was illuminated. A stewardess blocked his path. He couldn't remember her. Had she come on board in India? Well, whatever, this girl was an American, he felt sure – all henna, lip gloss, panty hose and a slightly bandy-legged stance. His head was spinning but the bladder stopwatch was demanding a touchdown within the next ten seconds. He dived to her right and she swooped to grab his shoulder.

He thought about a sidestep to her left but his stout frame had little scope for such deftness even in the broad first class aisles.

"Sir, please return to your seat, we have begun our final descent."

"Gotta pee. Let me through."

He brusquely pushed her aside and headed for the end zone. The concertina doors to the lavatories always caused him difficulties but this time it was worse than ever. He lurched into the cubicle

21

and bolted the door shut. He could scarcely contain himself. He ripped at his fly zip and grabbed. Another nanosecond and the old boy would have presented him with an embarrassing wet patch for the rest of the morning but now it was a luxurious moment of blissful relief.

His head began to clear a little, although his mouth tasted like the floor of a parrot's cage. Thank God he hadn't peed himself because the lovely Gaby Vaughan would be meeting them at the airport. He smiled at the prospect and then caught a glimpse of himself in the mirror. It had been a short course in death. He ran the cold tap and plunged his face into the basin.

There was a loud knock on the door.

"Sir, you must return to your seat immediately or we will have to unlock the door and take you back."

Could they do that? He had always assumed that the restrooms were a sort of sanctuary where no one but the smoke detectors could intrude. He grabbed a paper towel for his face and fumbled with the door.

Outside the opposition linebacker had recruited two camp male stewards to sack the quarterback if necessary. Wheatley grinned sheepishly.

"Sorry about that guys. Real emergency."

He swayed gently back down the aisle to his seat and reached into his overnight bag for some toothpaste to freshen up.

"You OK, Viv?" It was the faithful Melanie in the seat behind Wheatley. She had seen her boss's drive for the line but realised that intervention was futile.

"Sure, honey. You've done all the filming over here previously. Tell me a bit of background about our superstar."

"Gaby?"

"Uh-huh."

"She's twenty eight, five three, a hundred and twenty pounds, born in Alice Springs, lives in Sydney. Three times she's won the

Australian Triathlon Championships and she finished second in the Hawaii Ironman last year."

"Is she a hard case?"

Melanie sensed she might need to defend one of the sisters and looked at him quizzically before replying. Wheatley continued.

"You know what I mean. This is the only gal we've got in the competition and some folk think she could win it. She must be tough."

Melanie had herself aspired to a heady blend of femininity and power in the equally competitive world of TV production and felt it necessary to quash any undue stereotyping.

"Viv, she's got it all. She looks fantastic, graduated in marketing and she's a winner in sport. It is possible to be both successful and attractive you know."

"OK, OK. How come you know so much anyway?"

"I saw the promo tape that Channel 9 sent to Lenny Stein and I was in the room when he spoke to her on the phone. I think he was sweet on her."

"The Chief? It wouldn't be the first time. Is she married?"

"No."

"Boyfriend?"

"Don't think so."

Wheatley took another dab of toothpaste and reached for the comb from his overnight bag to smooth his wiry locks. It was clear that he was preening himself in anticipation but he had all the sex appeal of Oliver Hardy. Melanie chuckled. He looked like a frog no matter how minty his breath was.

The airport customs and immigration procedures dragged on for an eternity and Wheatley was not at his best especially because the clock on the wall said lunchtime but his body had lodged a counterclaim for midnight.

Beyond the customs barrier thronged the usual huddle of grandparents, sweethearts and company chauffeurs. The Prime Life crew had been told that Gaby Vaughan would meet them personally and that Channel 9 would be in attendance for a picture opportunity.

That much was expected. What completely overwhelmed them was the presence of three other film crews and around 30 reporters and photographers. It was a circus. Wheatley turned to Melanie.

"Did you know about all this?" He murmured out of the side of his mouth.

"No. I thought it was just the guys from 9 coming along. Sorry."

"Sorry be damned. This is great."

A few cameras whirred as the Prime Life crew strode forward, baggage trolleys laden with recording equipment and Vivian Wheatley's secret stash of Oreo cookies.

It was the first time any of them had been the centre of such attention. Except Wheatley. In the twinkling of a flashbulb he was transported back in time to the announcement of his football scholarship at Indiana University. The press conference called by the Department of Intercollegiate Athletics reflected their hopes for him as a starting quarterback. It hadn't materialised but, 30 years on, the cameras were still rolling for Viv Wheatley. What a guy.

The photographers jostled for position in a horseshoe configuration around the Prime Life crew eager to capture the first meeting of Gaby Vaughan and the million dollar purse string holders. An elegant dark haired young woman in a cream blouse and electric blue skirt stepped forward and extending a hand towards Wheatley.

"Welcome to Australia."

She was beautiful. Hazel eyes, natural tan, full red lips and cheek bones you could cut yourself on. Vivian was impressed. Melanie was right about Gaby Vaughan. He slowly inhaled the fragrant cocktail of glamour, fitness and success, and he gazed down at her long slender legs. Sensational. Wheatley was in love.

"You must be Mr Wheatley. I'm Karen Russell from Channel 9."

"Eh?" He was nonplussed.

"May I introduce Gabrielle Vaughan, Australia's representative at Sport Armageddon."

From Wheatley's right hand side a more petite figure stepped forward and shook his hand.

"Hi, did you have a good flight?"

She was quite diminutive but beautifully proportioned. Blonde hair tied back in a ponytail, big blue eyes, a cute little retroussÈ nose with a sprinkling of light freckles on each cheek. She was dressed in a white and pink sweatsuit with 'Zip Bar Energy' emblazoned across it. His gaze drifted down to her chest. Wheatley was in love.

"Good flight, Mr Wheatley?"

He took the second cue. "Er, yeah, great thanks. Qantas sure know how to look after us."

Even as the pink mist descended, he had instinctively remembered the corporate plug. That should ensure upgrades for everyone on the return journey. He hoped Linebacker would not be one of the first class stewardesses on that flight.

"What are your plans for this visit Mr Wheatley?" one of the local press hacks called from the back of the huddle.

"We have a reception lounge booked at the back of the terminal if you'd prefer to have a formal press conference there, Mr Wheatley," Karen Russell interjected.

"Nah, I'm ready to roll. Let's talk about things right here." Wheatley was mentally back in Bloomington and in expansive mood.

"We're here to screen a documentary on the lovely Miss Vaughan and whet the appetite of our American audiences for her role as a Sport Armageddon contender."

He beamed across patronisingly at Gaby and found his eyes drifting six inches below her neck again. There was one appetite getting well and truly whetted.

25

"Are you pleased with the pre-event publicity, Mr Wheatley?"

Hell, yes, he thought. "Well it is the greatest sports event ever," was what he actually said. "It's bound to get plenty of attention."

"Why was Gaby Vaughan selected when we have outstanding male endurance athletes who could win the event?" a voice demanded from his left.

Wheatley gave his most avuncular smile and glanced back at Gaby. Lenny Stein had not lost his touch. Even without meeting her, the Chief had come up with a rating's winner. Half the population of America would need no prompting to gaze upon her as she was jigging round Florida.

"Research has shown that, in ultra-distance events, women can operate more effectively than men. No competitive event will test that possibility more than Sport Armageddon. There was no trial for the Aussie nomination but we accepted the recommendation of Channel 9 who have some expertise in these matters."

Wheatley sounded almost plausible. He could not resist adding, "Judging by the turnout today it seems a pretty popular choice."

"It seems to me," a shrill female radio reporter called out, "that your competition is an entirely contrived event. It has no sanction from the American or International triathlon governing bodies and is being staged as a publicity stunt to suit your TV audience. It's also going to be completely unsuitable weather conditions..."

"What's your question lady?" Wheatley interrupted.

"Do you really think this is sport, Mr Wheatley?"

He tried not to falter.

"Of course, it's sport. It's the ultimate sport. No one will ever have pushed themselves like this before."

Radio lady was not giving up. "The name of the event seems to be especially crass. 'Armageddon' is the last great battle, according to the Bible. It's completely over the top. Are you expecting people to die for your TV programme?"

"No, of course not. We just wanted a title to make it clear that this is the ultimate fitness confrontation, if you will. The last word in physical challenges."

He was losing the plot slightly. This line of questioning was not to Wheatley's liking and he glanced sharply at Karen Russell. She took the hint.

"I'm sure you must be very tired, all of you. Why don't we set Gaby up for a full press conference in the lounge and our friends from Prime Life can get some rest at their hotel?"

"It might be best. We're around for four days if you need more footage."

Wheatley's enthusiasm for this press conference had well and truly waned. "See you tomorrow guys," he muttered.

Karen Russell steered Gaby towards the lounge and the media entourage trotted dutifully after her.

Wheatley walked slowly towards the exit door where a mini-van was ready to whisk them to the Inter-Continental Hotel.

As the driver carefully loaded their recording equipment in the back of the van, Wheatley slumped in the back seat. He closed his eyes. The sleeping tablets seemed to be getting their second wind and the Burgundy was still fermenting.

"Damn. I didn't like that."

"You did fine," Melanie reassured him, "and there will be plenty of time to drum up more publicity. We're all dead beat."

No response from Vivian Wheatley III but his frown remained. So far it had all been positive promotion and feedback for Sport Armageddon but Radio Lady had introduced the first major criticism. Publicly he could defend the event concept to the hilt but the question that had festered at the back of his mind had finally been articulated in a high-pitched Australian twang. "Do you really think this is sport?"

Gabrielle Vaughan relished any media opportunity. She seemed to live a substantial part of her life in the public gaze and loved it.

Ever since high school she had wanted to be famous for something. Although she was pleasant looking, her mother's stature suggested that she would be too short to be a model. She couldn't sing, act or play a musical instrument well. It had become clear that sport was to be her platform to celebrity status.

It had started unpromisingly. She was the second daughter and last child of Doctor and Mrs Alistair Vaughan, who had lived all their lives in Alice Springs. This was unfortunate, because from the moment she was born, Gabrielle Julia Vaughan appeared to be extremely allergic to a town like Alice. She was a very sickly child, suffering variously from asthma and bronchitis. A severe dose of pneumonia when she was barely six had been a worrying time for the whole family.

"Gotta get this little one somewhere on the coast, mate. This place is going to finish her off if she carries on at this rate," a GP colleague had counselled Alistair Vaughan.

She spent three months convalescing with her Auntie Glad by the surf of Collaroy, north of Sydney. Alistair Vaughan was astounded by the transformation. His pale anaemic daughter who had seemed to spend half her time confined to her bed, bereft of energy now invariably had to be dragged at dusk from the beach, where she played boisterous ball games and swam with her new found friends.

Within a year her parents had left their beloved Alice Springs and bought a house in Dee Why, a couple of miles from Collaroy. Six years on, they had a sporty little tomboy who had wasted no time in making up lost ground with her school work. By the age of 12, she had represented New South Wales at swimming in her own age group and at under 16 level. She was an outstanding freestyler and broke the National Junior record for 400 metres before she left school. In her senior year, she also began attracting serious attention from the boys. Swimming had given her a lithe figure, filled out in all the right places. Three years of orthodontic work with teeth braces had left her with a dazzling smile and the occasional overseas travel for competitive swimming had instilled an air of confidence and independence that sat well with her.

At the University of New South Wales she had enjoyed brief but intense romances with a few of her classmates and fellow swimmers. She hoped one of them would prove to be the love of her life but Gaby Vaughan was too much of a control freak to let her heart rule her head for long periods. She showed more staying power with her degree course and was rewarded with Upper Second Class Honours but her racing progress had been compromised and she struggled to qualify for the national finals. When the offer of a marketing job in Melbourne came up, she had almost no emotional ties that would made her think twice about moving away from her home state.

In her final year she had been hospitalised briefly with an irregular heartbeat condition. To enormous relief, it quickly righted itself. The problem was attributed to the stress of impending exams and her hectic lifestyle. She was prescribed a precautionary half aspirin tablet a day to help keep her blood thin and the whole family had long since forgotten the episode. Gaby hadn't. Very occasionally – two or three times a year – she would develop heart flutters. They only lasted a few minutes but worried her enough to have a private ECG check before she undertook her first Hawaii Ironman triathlon. The doctor had ruled out any link with her childhood illness and advised once a week rest days from her training workload. She was religious about her stress busting. She practised yoga daily, used a flotation tank every fortnight for relaxation, and reassured herself that for physical fitness, she was in the top one per cent of the world's population.

Gaby had pursued the triathlon when her early triumphs in swimming failed to convert to senior success. She progressed spectacularly in the new sport, winning her first Australian title at the age of 23 and remaining unbeaten domestically for two years. At world level she had always been unlucky – two bronze medals and never outside the top six but she still nurtured world title dreams.

Her obvious glamour and winning ways had brought her celebrity status in Australia and she undertook every opportunity for commercial work or to record items for 'Vaughan's View' – her weekly sports magazine programme for Channel 9. She had dated a fellow triathlete for almost two years and spent time training at the Australian Institute of Sport in Canberra and New South Wales Academy of Sport in Narrabeen, close to her home. He was not the love of her life, she had eventually decided. They broke off the relationship amidst tears and unanswered telephone messages while they were six thousand miles apart.

At Sport Armageddon's airport press conference, the questioning persisted along the familiar lines of 'what's-it-like-to-be-a-girl-in-a-man's-world?' She smiled winsomely throughout the tedium.

After half an hour, Karen Russell hustled the proceedings to a halt. This had been prompted by a stage managed episode when a seedy looking middle aged man, who had previously remained silent, enquired whether she had considered his faxed contract of the previous week.

I'm sorry, I can't place what contract you're referring to," Gaby replied.

"We sent Channel 9 details of a photographic session."

"Who's we?"

"Scorpio Publishing."

Oh no. So these were the creeps. Every six months, she received, with monotonous regularity, increased offers for her to bare all for the delectation of the readers of 'Surf Babes', 'Wet 'n' Willing' or some other noble publication.

"I believe my agent will have dealt with your enquiry."

"So, will you be getting your baps out for the guys?" Mr Sleazy was now favouring a less obtuse approach.

"No. Do you have a question about Sport Armageddon?"

Mr Sleazy was ready with his tour de force. From behind him a well muscled male model swiftly peeled off his black tracksuit and strode to the front of the hall clad only in his underpants. Incongruously, he clutched an attache case and, as he neared the table where Gaby was sat facing a bank of microphones, he spun round and faced the press corps. He held the briefcase aloft and snapped it open. It was packed with ten dollar bills.

"There's a quarter of a million dollars here, Gaby," bawled Mr Sleazy, "It's all yours and you don't have to bust a gut to earn it. Just show your body off to the young men who read Scorpio's magazine titles. How about it?"

Karen Russell had been slow to react to the sideshow but now grabbed at the briefcase. It crashed to the floor and spilled bundles of notes in a cascade.

"Whoa, baby. The offer's for Gaby only." Mr Sleazy was relishing the ad-lib opportunities. There were no security guards to assist Karen and most of the other journalists appeared too busy filming or transcribing the episode to intervene. Karen motioned her to leave and Gaby walked quickly out of the main exit. Her face was flushed and she felt angry. There was no point in her creating more of a scene. That was exactly what they wanted. Despite her best efforts over the previous 20 minutes, it was pretty obvious what the next day's headlines and photos would be. Bastards. She would show them.

Vivian Wheatley III could not sleep and was not prepared to venture any more Mogadon on the exercise. He had crashed into his king-sized pit in Sydney's Inter-Continental Hotel at seven o'clock on the evening of his arrival but by midnight he could doze no more. Damn body clock. He padded across to the window and looked down at the Kings Cross area of Sydney, twinkling 16 floors below him. What on earth was he going to do for the next eight hours? He turned towards the mini bar with the germ of a solution in his mind and noticed the red message light flashing on his room telephone.

He rang reception. Yes, there was a message. "Call Lenny." What the hell was the time in Atlanta? It didn't matter. Lenny Stein never seemed to sleep, or pause for breath, day or night. Wheatley was surprised that the Chief had not directly interrupted his slumbers because Stein was not noted for his consideration in such matters.

He dialled the hotline number in Atlanta and it was answered after two rings with a curt but customary "Yeah?" No time for pleasantries.

"Did you ring me, boss?"

"Yeah, Viv. Goddamn switchboard said you weren't answering."

"Must have been sleeping too deep boss. Been working kinda flat out lately."

"Spare me the crap. You know you've got to get to Germany quick don't you?"

"Why? What's happened?"

"That goon Karelov is in the slammer."

"What?"

"The German police have banged him up on some kind of insurance fraud rap. One of his Russian buddies has a gymnasium in Berlin and our guy has been training there for Sport Armageddon. The gym's been losing money hand over fist and Leon Karelov is suspect number one as the friendly arsonist who torched the goddamn place."

"So he's out of the contest?"

"No way. We've got six hours of documentary footage and three TV commercials in the can featuring him as our bad boy. He's gotta be here."

Wheatley knew only too well how much hype had been centred on the Russian. He had spent Boxing Day through to New Year getting snowy Red Square shots of Karelov training. It was all nonsense. The guy was an arch capitalist and bootlegger who spent most of his time in Berlin but it suited Lenny Stein to cultivate the super power connections. Ted Turner may have had his Goodwill Games but Lenny Stein would bring Karelov to the USA to chase Prime Life's million dollar carrot.

Wheatley sensed he might well be clocking up a few more air miles in the near future.

"As soon as we've got Vaughan's contract sorted, it looks like you or I will have to go to Germany to get him off the hook. Try and get her to sign up today, OK?"

"OK." The line had already gone dead.

And so it was that at eight o'clock the next morning, Gabrielle Vaughan found the Prime Life crew in a rented moke, filming her on a three hour cycle ride out towards the Blue Mountains.

She wore white cycling shoes bolted to the pedals, an all-in-one lemon leotard, dark glasses and a cycle helmet out of which bobbed a short blonde pony tail. She looked exquisite.

Wheatley, for all his jet-lagged sleep-deprived weariness was well aware of this. For the first 20 minutes, he directed the camera angles from the moke and tunelessly hummed the Rocky theme music, which he was convinced, would be dubbed over the slow motion shots. The long suffering Melanie had seen it all before and frowned as she jotted down the running order of the shots. She hated it when Wheatley turned lecherous.

His British Summer Time body clock was also perking up a little. The dormant sporting superstar in him was beginning to stir once again. Ahead he could see a straight, level stretch of road. It was time.

"Hold it there a second, Gaby. Mel, mike me up, I'm going out on the bike."

Melanie had suspected that this was in Viv's plans. A sturdy black mountain bike had been strapped to the roof rack and it was duly hauled down to convey the frame of Vivian Wheatley III, all-action cycling superstar, alongside Gaby Vaughan. Melanie deftly clipped microphones to their collars and Wheatley gave an impromptu sound check with a Richter scale burp. The fried breakfast had not been a great idea.

"OK, Gaby baby. I'll cycle alongside you for a few miles and we'll shoot the breeze about how you're doing."

He was wearing loafers, khaki Bermuda shorts, a black polo shirt that barely contained his gut; with the obligatory wrap round shades and baseball cap. He displayed all the grace and skill of a moose as he mounted up.

They pedalled off unsteadily with a queue of fans and irate drivers already forming behind them.

Wheatley said nothing for the first quarter of a mile. What was that about never forgetting how to ride a bike? He took a while to get full control of his steed as Gaby grinned at the spectacle.

"Gaby Vaughan. You're noted as a swimmer. How good would you rate your cycling ability... Oh for Christ sake!"

He wobbled dangerously as the first of the following cars shot by.

"How good is your cycling?"

"I cycle about two or three hours every day. I enjoy it more than running or swimming. I usually train with a men's team out here and I generally hold my own. Sometimes I feel like I could cycle all day. Especially when it's scenic."

Wheatley wanted desperately to maintain eye contact but the concentration required to keep himself up, his breakfast down and his pulse below 200 was as much as he could manage. He stared straight ahead. Funny, the road looked flat, possibly downhill but he was toiling hard. He could detect that Gaby was scarcely breathing.

"What will you do about eating on the move and pit stops in Florida?" The word 'Florida' was almost indecipherable as he belched again.

"I reckon I'll cycle for about fifty minutes in every hour. I can drink and eat bananas and stuff as I ride but I'll use the breaks for the bathroom to have a leg massage and cool down with ice and showers."

"The route will be dead flat," Viv observed, pausing for breath and stifling another burp. Three minutes of cycling and he was struggling. He blamed his knee injury. Loss of power on one side. Bit of jet lag. Otherwise he'd be fine. This wasn't the best day to be taking up a new sport.

"Why are you cycling in the hills?" he asked.

"The extra leg strength which uphill cycling develops is never wasted," Gaby explained. She was going to elaborate about boosted heart rates but the Prime Life viewers were to be deprived of that response because at that very moment Vivian Wheatley's mountain bike veered across her front wheel and headed for the kerb. In the moke later, he would claim that his bust knee had gone again but he barely made it to the grass verge before depositing the Sydney's Inter-Continental's cooked breakfast over his bike, the pavement and his Bermuda shorts. God, he hated Australia.

The journey back to Sydney was an unpleasant one for Melanie. She was not relishing the prospect of a long haul flight back to Europe that afternoon to bail out some goddamn Russian from jail and alongside her in the back seat, Wheatley was stinking the place out. Every window, sunroof and flap on the moke was open but the overpowering whiff of recycled breakfast was making the whole crew gag.

Gaby was with them too, her cycle strapped to the roof. She could see the funny side of it all – apart from Vivian Vomit III and his astounding aromas. She looked out of the window and the cool breeze tugged strands of her fine hair out of its ponytail. The Blue Mountains were far behind them now. She never felt more at home than when she was cycling alone there at dawn.

No relationship in her life was ever as comfortable as the one she enjoyed with the great outdoors. Why could she not make a proper loving commitment? Why did all of her love affairs end in tears eventually? She knew the true answer without any soul-searching. The only thing that mattered was Sport Armageddon.

There were thousands and thousands of training miles recorded on those roads – some had come easily, others were etched in blood and tears – all had played their part.

She had prepared well for her greatest challenge. She would make Australia so proud of her. It would be the best moment of all and the start was now just 28 days away. It had all come together so quickly but she had followed the brutal schedule she had set for herself without compromise. It would be worth it because Gaby Vaughan knew beyond a doubt that she would win Sport Armageddon.

On their arrival in Berlin, the crew had headed for their hastily arranged accommodation on the Ku'damm. Wheatley himself took a cab to the city police headquarters where Leonid Karelov's detention, for questioning without charge, had been extended for a further 72 hours.

At first, the police would not even allow him to visit the man he had travelled from Sydney to see and an early release did not look likely.

"For Chrissake, I've come straight off a plane from Australia to help this guy," he had remonstrated with the walrus-like custody sergeant.

"Sir, are you his legal adviser or a close relative?"

"I've already told you, I'm a friend and business colleague and this is gonna look real bad in the media if the German cops have screwed up. That's how it's looking to me, I can tell you."

"I'm sorry but he is being interviewed at the moment. You must wait until they take a break. I am sure we can arrange something then."

It was like talking to a block of ice but Wheatley was panicking because he could hear a clock counting down. Lenny Stein was on his way. Even as they spoke, a Concorde jet out of Philadelphia was winging its way towards London and then a couple of hours later, Stein would be in Berlin. The thought of his boss arriving at the police station made Viv shudder. Stein had never completely trusted Wheatley – or anyone else for that matter – in dealings of major significance for Prime Life. Wheatley could recruit the sportsmen, film them and set up the event as long as he reported back to the Oberfuhrer every couple of days – just to make sure everyone knew who pulled the strings. Occasionally, a Wheatley decision would be embarrassingly overruled out of sheer contrariness. It was important to everyone involved in Sport Armageddon that Karelov was quickly freed from custody. Wheatley's flight must have been no further than Bahrain before Lenny Stein was dispatching a fax to Berlin Tegel Airport saying that he would be coming to Germany to intervene personally.

Wheatley sighed. He was burnt out but he desperately needed to succeed on this particular errand and parade a few Brownie points before Lenny appeared. Progress between Wheatley and the Walrus had reached an impasse and Viv strode out to the police station car park.

Their hired Mercedes was at the back of the parking lot, and Melanie, seemingly impervious to jet lag, was lying across the back seat sipping a soda and reading 'Stern' magazine. Not for the first time, Wheatley admired her long legs and neat figure. No use though. He'd tried it on a couple of times in Atlanta and got a kick in the 'nads for his endeavours. She had opted for a blue business suit in Berlin because this was her only outfit not awaiting the laundry's attention after their hasty exit from Sydney.

"Jesus, the guy won't let me see him yet. He's just being 'ornery but what the hell can I do before Lenny gets here?" Wheatley wailed.

"It won't take long, Viv. I'm sure you'll get to see him real soon."
Melanie always tried to soothe Wheatley when he was flapping.

Wheatley kicked out at the car tyre in frustration and immediately regretted it. He was wearing open toed sandals purchased as a sad souvenir at Sydney airport. Fashion guru he was not.

Melanie returned, smiling, to her magazine, as Wheatley limped to the back window.

"What's that you're reading?"

"'Stern'. It's kinda like 'National Enquirer' only a bit classier."

"Can you read German?"

"I'm bilingual. My mom is German and I have family in Darmstadt."

Wheatley vaguely remembered that this skill appeared on her resumÈ but it was her sunny disposition that had got her the job and which continued to provide light relief on the long filming days.

The merest hint of a bad idea took shape.

"Has the jailer guy seen you yet, Mel?"

"No. I went down to the shops when you first went in."

"Could your German convince him that you're Karelov's lawyer?" There was a long pause.

"No, no. My accent's great but I don't speak like a lawyer. My uncle practises in Darmstadt though." She rummaged in her handbag and produced a business card 'Ulrich Beilschmidt', it proclaimed, an Attorney based in 'Hanau Strasse, Darmstadt'.

"Honey, you gotta get in there and make like you're Karelov's lawyer. I gotta get a break before Lenny gets here."

"Good God! I can't do that Viv."

Ten minutes later, Walrus looked up from his custody papers and smiled as the elegant lawyer strode towards him.

"Good morning. I am Ulrika Beilschmidt from 'Beilschmidt and Wolfe', representing Herr Karelov whom I believe you have in custody," announced Melanie, her knees knocking together. Her voice betrayed no trace of an American accent. All those years when Momma spoke only German at home had paid off. She proffered the business card, taking care that final syllable of 'Ulrika' was covered by her thumb. She flashed a dazzling smile at Walrus.

"I do hope my client has not been interviewed before my arrival?"

Walrus frowned. Karelov was being interviewed for the third time without any attorney present. They thought he had declined the offer of representation. He rang down to the custody suite where a detective inspector's probing interrogation was making some progress.

"Klaus, is Karelov expecting a lawyer called..." He peered either side of the thumb... "Beilschmidt?" Karelov always had one beady eye on the main chance. He had reached a rather sticky phase of the interview process. He could not afford a lawyer and mistrusted their motives but right now a time-out was vital. As the question was passed on to him, it was time to think quickly.

"Yes, it appears so. Send him down," confirmed a bemused Klaus.

"It's a lady. I'll bring her down right away."

Melanie's heels clicked loudly on the stone floor as she was led down the maze of corridors to Interview Suite number 4, where Klaus and Karelov were having their face-off. Both men's heads turned as Walrus opened the door and ushered her in. Karelov, who had always tried to be a collector of desirable women, in a small way, beamed broadly and showed off the somewhat low grade silver tooth that had replaced one of his incisors. Karelov was nearly forty years of age but he would not look a lot different when he was seventy. He was one of life's natural pirates – lank black hair, unshaven chin, heavy moustache, bulbous nose, hoody eyes and an array of shifty tics. The Russian would have been picked out in an identity parade even if he had only been included as an innocent bystander.

Through the blue haze of cigarette smoke, Melanie was surprised to see that it was Karelov who was smoking. Wheatley's description had suggested a fading Mr Universe figure and the sports jocks that she knew from her home patch of Savannah, Georgia were not often seen with a cigarette as an accessory.

Karelov was only too ready to be swept along in the little charade. He stood and greeted her like an old friend and extended a grizzled paw.

"Glad you could visit me. I am pleased to see you." His German had improved little despite the frequency of his sojourns in Berlin.

"How are you? I came as quickly as I could." Melanie found herself flushing and gushing at the same time. She glared at Klaus and pronounced, "It is obvious to me that there have been a number of interviews taking place that should have awaited the arrival of me or one of my Berlin-based colleagues." She could feel Klaus's intense gaze and was not sure how long she could keep the facade up.

"I need to spend some time alone with... my client," she faltered.

"2.55 pm – interview suspended on arrival of lawyer for Herr Karelov," Klaus recorded into the tape machine. He punched the 'off' button and strode from the room. "I will be back at 3.30 pm. My office is at the end of this corridor on the left if you are finished before then." He cursed the Walrus. He had almost trapped Karelov into some kind of admission and then the lawyer showed up. Why couldn't Walrus have stalled her for another ten minutes like he had with the TV crew?

Karelov surveyed Melanie. Honest face, officious manner. So who the hell was she? He gave her what he intended to be his macho but flirty look. She looked back at him as if he was something she had just trodden in. Her head was spinning. She had enjoyed her annual high school play in Savannah but this piece of amateur dramatics was making her feel quite ill.

"I'm not your lawyer," she hissed.

Karelov did not blink. "Who are you then – some hooker that Guido sent to bribe me into not mentioning him?" He stopped abruptly. Guido was the owner of the club and the man who had paid him to set light to it. Blunt introductions were his favourite way of trying to appear cool but, having spent three hours stonewalling Klaus, it was a mistake to have alluded to his co-conspirator's role. He didn't know who this woman was and the room might have been bugged.

Melanie also stopped abruptly. It took her a second or two to translate the colloquial German for 'hooker' but when the full rudeness of his opening gambit hit her – she hit him – a full blooded slap across his mottled cheek.

She instantly felt better and the tension drained away. Karelov stood up quickly and sat down again immediately. Neither of them said anything for a full 30 seconds.

"Sorry," said Karelov.

Melanie was in no mood to be gracious. "I'm from Prime Life TV. I work with Vivian Wheatley. He filmed you at Christmas, remember?"

Karelov did not answer. He wanted to rub his cheek but did not want this woman to know that she had hurt him. He was also sensitive about his swarthy countenance – keen at all costs to stay the right side of the thin line which separated craggy good looks from pug ugliness.

"It will do damage to Sport Armageddon if one of the competitors finds himself in prison with a couple of weeks to go to the contest. Our publicity has billed this as the ultimate sporting confrontation. You're meant to be a finely tuned dedicated super-athlete."

Much of the German phrasing passed straight over Leonid Karelov's bowed shaggy head. Over the previous days, he had thought about his appointment with one million dollars. An eight thousand dollar cut from an insurance scam did now seem to be a poor trade for the loss of a tilt at such a prize but then Karelov had spent his life chasing long shots, hopeless causes, insane dreams and a few guaranteed roubles.

If he had not had such an approach to life, he would in all probability still be gainfully employed as a coach to the Russian cycling team for the princely sum of 200 dollars a month. That would have been his meagre reward for a key role with the national squad. As a cycling competitor he had submitted to all the blood-doping, the steroid diet and the state-of-the art brainwashing techniques and the bastards still usually kept him as first reserve.

When his 'amateur' career ended he had resolved never again to allow his sporting ambitions to interfere with the pursuit of financial advancement. He had peddled a few black market Levis after every trip to the West, engaged in a bit of currency arbitrage here and there. He had seized every opportunity to race abroad and pocket the under-the-table brown envelopes that dodgy team managers bunged him. The collapse of the Iron Curtain had opened up new horizons for him and he was into Berlin in 1989 almost as quickly as the rubble from the Wall.

The triathlon concept had only slightly amused him initially but the prospect of a 300 dollar prize every weekend was a great incentive. He swam relatively weakly in those early days but he cycled and ran so powerfully that the ZDF TV coverage would keep one camera on him from the time he got out of the water and began his regular game of catch up. The crowds loved him. Karelov loved the prize money and would race all year round. For a man who had also fished for 14 hours a day out of the Black Sea ports, endurance and strength were plentiful commodities.

When he had saved 30,000 dollars, he had unwisely invested in a sports theme bar in the Ku'damm. This had crashed spectacularly following the issue of some bouncing cheques for stock purchase by his partner Ishmail. Ishmail had hastily fled to Turkey and if Leonid ever laid eyes on him again...

Karelov had not readily agreed to Guido's arson fraud but found himself with severe cash flow difficulties after the bar closure and these could not await an Atlanta payday. He would never trust anyone again.

He looked up at Melanie... even if they had blue eyes and great legs.

"So, how are you going to get me out of this one?" he demanded.

"We think they probably have enough evidence to charge you so if there's no prospect of release, we want an early court hearing, like today or tomorrow with an adjournment to September and bail with sureties so that we can take you to the States straight away. We'd also like to keep it out of the press." Melanie sounded as though she knew what she was talking about but hoped he would not ask any questions.

"I hope the Detective Inspector agrees with your plan," smirked Karelov. He was not exactly a stranger to the criminal courts – a few brawls and a couple of cheque frauds as a kid, blended with a dash of joyriding in his fishing days. How else was he supposed to travel between the bar and the boat?

"How far had the officer got with his questioning?"

This, of course, was difficult for Karelov to answer. He was not even sure how long he had been interrogated. He felt as though he had given away very little incriminating information but it was clear from some of the old-fashioned looks emanating from Klaus that the cop was playing mind games.

Klaus had opened by questioning Karelov's whereabouts on the previous Sunday night. Karelov had woven an elaborate tale about watching an NBA basketball game with a few beers at his lodgings out near the former Checkpoint Charlie site. It then became clear that he had been positively identified by some goon from his gymnasium fitness class when they were both in a convenience store just around the corner from the gym. That had been at 2.00 am on the night in question. The witness had already made a statement verifying that Klaus had purchased a Diet Sprite and a box of matches.

"Couldn't have been me then. I do not drink sugar-free drinks," he joked, cursing the ineptness that had caused him to leave home without firelighters. There's nothing so useless as an arsonist without matches.

Klaus also suggested that one of his neighbours had also heard him leave the building some time after midnight. Since the neighbour in question was a habitual gin drinker and fornicator on a Sunday night, Karelov doubted that his supposed eavesdropping would carry much weight but considered it timely to pretend that his mastery of the German language was wilting. It was at this point in the interrogation process that the foxy Melanie had smooched into the interview room.

Melanie hoped that her Prime Life colleagues had succeeded in summoning one of the Berlin-based advocates to assist in springing Karelov before Lenny Stein arrived. It would otherwise mean a further night in the cells for Karelov. She explained to the Russian that they would try to bring the matter to a head so that he could apply for bail and that at all times he was to keep his mouth shut and effect a wide-eyed look of innocence. Karelov barely had time to practice his butter-wouldn't-melt pout before Klaus returned.

Melanie felt the nerve endings jangle again but she went straight to work.

"Is my client to be charged with the offence for which he has been detained?"

"Yes."

"Is he to be released on bail?"

"The police and, more importantly the 'Staatsanwaltschaft', will seek a remand in custody. The court will have to decide that. This is a serious offence."

"When will he first come before the court?"

"Tomorrow at 10.00 am."

"Is there a court sitting at present?"

"Yes, there are two still in session."

"Then I must insist that this matter be determined today. Since there has been considerable questioning without the presence of an attorney, I think it's the very least my client deserves."

"Very well, I shall make some enquiries if you wish," sighed Klaus.

At five o'clock precisely, Karelov appeared in the dock of the last 'Amstgericht' in session.

The presiding magistrate or 'Richter Am Amtsgericht' was not best pleased to have his afternoon sitting prolonged by the extra case and peered fiercely over half-moon glasses at the defendant in the dock. Another old lag. His clerk had discussed bail terms with the attractive new defence advocate and the magistrate was assured that he would not be delayed from his tennis club by more than another 20 minutes.

His clerk set the ball rolling.

"One extra case sir, in respect of which Herr Zimmerman appears for the State and Frau Beilschmidt appears for the defence."

Zimmerman scowled. He would miss his lift home. 'Frau Beilschimdt' smiled but did not stand. Her knees were still shaking too much.

"Stand please, Herr Karelov," the magistrate requested. "Is your full name Leonid Mikhael Karelov?"

Karelov agreed that it was and also confirmed his address and date of birth. The full arson charge was put to him and he was asked if he understood. He did and was asked to sit.

Herr Zimmerman rose to address the magistrate.

"Sir, ordinarily, I would apply for a remand in custody while papers are served on the defence. In this case, it is appropriate for my friend to have sight of the transcripts of some lengthy interviews and I imagine it will be a few months before the matter can come to trial. In the circumstances I have no objections to the bail conditions on which my friend will address you."

Melanie stood up and gripped the handrail in front of her very tightly. She would normally have earned an admonishment for wearing blue instead of legal black in this particular court but this 'Verteidiger' reminded the magistrate of his youngest daughter and he gave her a warm smile.

"Sir, my client has some urgent business appointments in America during the next few weeks..." She paused while the magistrate took in the figure now slouched in the dock. Three days growth of stubble, a dodgy incisor, heavily hooded eyes and gypsy hair-do. He did not look as though his business appointments would be with the President of IBM. Karelov smiled enigmatically.

"Herr Karelov is an outstanding sportsman," Melanie continued, "he is required to attend some major sports events between now and the end of August."

She was glad the press gallery was deserted.

"Usually the court would expect the defendant to report to a police station as a condition of bail and surrender his passport. In this case I hope that an undertaking not to interfere with witnesses and a surety in the sum of two hundred thousand Deutchmarks will suffice. My colleague for the prosecution has agreed to these terms, as you have heard."

She sat down with a bump and felt a trickle of perspiration run down her neck and soak into her bra strap. Any minute now she expected to be dispatched down to the cells to commence a jail term for impersonating a lawyer. The strain of regurgitating legal terms picked up from the prosecutor and read from the draft bail form was making her head spin.

The magistrate, however, was mightily impressed. He had never taken a surety of more than 2,000 DM before. If he allowed his clerk to zip through the formalities, he would still be in time for the first mixed doubles pairing and have a record bail bond to brag about in the court assembly room.

"What steps have been taken to secure this bond?" he barked. Melanie sprang up.

"Sir, a representative from an American sports company has just lodged this sum by credit card debit with the court payment office." She looked round and pointed to Vivian Wheatley III who gave the magistrate a little wave from the back of the court.

"Has this sum been cleared in the payment office?" the magistrate asked the clerk.

The clerk picked up his red telephone and made some enquiries in a stage whisper.

"Sir, yes, funding is with the court," he announced after a few moments.

"And can you confirm how much this American representative has deposited?"

There was a pause as the door to the public gallery swung open violently and a small grey-haired man in his mid-50's strode in and took a seat in the front row. There was no gesture of apology for the loudness of his entry. Lenny Stein had arrived.

"Sir, a deposit of two hundred thousand Deutchmarks has been made by Prime Life Corporation registered in Atlanta, Georgia."

Wheatley gulped. What terrible timing. He could feel Stein's eyes drilling a hole in the back of his head as the value of the bond was announced. Oh God, why had he offered so much when it was clear that a tenth of that sum would have sufficed to spring the gook? The Chief would probably fire him again.

The magistrate was somewhat more impressed with the figure and felt that if the court office was satisfied then so was he. An hour or two later, when he had just finished a strenuous set of men's doubles, it would occur to him that he should probably have put the fat American guy on the stand to establish his bona fides and his relationship with the defendant but at the time he had just wanted to get behind the wheel of his Mercedes.

"I am happy with these arrangements," he announced.

"Sir, I have taken the liberty of preparing a bail form recording the terms," his clerk replied smugly. "The listing office has indicated available court time on 2nd September at 10 am."

"Very well. Stand please, Herr Karelov." The magistrate was scribbling a signature even as he spoke. "Do you understand what has happened?"

"Yes," lied Karelov.

"If you are not here on that date or if you make any direct or indirect approach to witnesses, you will be arrested and the sum of two hundred thousand Deutchmarks will be forfeit. You may go."

With that, Karelov was led down to the cells to collect his belongings. The magistrate strode briskly out of the side door towards the tennis club. Melanie grabbed a glass of water to prevent her from fainting and Wheatley slumped very low in his chair desperately trying to dip below the laser beam from the Chief in the public gallery.

The following morning, as the Prime Life crew, Karelov included, gathered in the lobby of the Excelsior awaiting the shuttle bus to the airport, Stein was still sniping relentlessly.

"For Chrissake man, you didn't have to bankrupt Prime Life to spring this bozo. The interest on that money will come out of your goddamned salary and we'll travel everywhere by bus. You're in economy on this flight you know."

Leonid Karvelov sat back from the fray sipping a diet Coke with rather more than a splash of vodka mixed in. He had swum four miles in the hotel pool that afternoon and was feeling very mellow.

They were clowns, these Yankees. Always throwing their money around. He had no intention of returning to Berlin in September but for now his main concern would be to milk as many dollars as possible from the event in Florida. No one would be tougher or better conditioned than him. The last man standing would be the great Karelov. He smiled and drained his glass. There were 23 days to go and he knew with certainty that he, Karelov, would win Sport Armageddon.

Melanie cradled a mineral water in the first class cabin as the Delta Airbus jet taxied before take-off from Berlin Tegel Airport. In theory, she knew she should stay sober and attentive on this latest leg of their round-the-world sprint. In practice, she knew that her body clock was in such a mess that she could have slept in the overhead luggage compartment for 36 hours without stirring. Lenny Stein squeezed her knee and she felt an instinctive re-coil of disgust.

The Great Lenny had banished Wheatley, Karelov and the rest of the Prime Life cronies to the smoking section of economy class as a punishment for their ineptness the previous day. The business class cabin was nearly empty and the spare places would have fallen within the ambit of Stein's potential gift to his colleagues but their exclusion was quite deliberate. For the most part, the Prime Life crew members were past caring about such a slight. Karelov was conducting an argument with the stewardess, pretending that his halting knowledge of German meant he did not understand that economy class passengers had to pay for their champagne.

Wheatley gazed out of the window at the light drizzle obscuring the edges of the airfield. He would retire to Kentucky and breed world class racehorses in the Fall. Lenny would sack him on their return and once the rest of the donkey work for Sport Armageddon was complete, he would claim constructive dismissal or whatever, then cash in his Prime Life stock and head for the ranch. The gee-gees were more rational than television's two-timers. His eyelids began to droop even as the engines revved for take-off. He would call his first Kentucky Derby winner 'Revenge on Lenny'. It was a long way to Hartsfield International Airport.

As the aircraft soared up into the heavy clouds, it encountered a little turbulence. It pitched slightly to starboard and Melanie spilt her drink. Stein took the opportunity for another gratuitous knee squeeze.

"You sure wouldn't prefer champagne, honey?"

Melanie was sure. Oh God, it was so difficult when your boss started hitting on you. Her mind raced back to the Prime Life staff Christmas party a couple of years previously. Stein's proffered kiss under the mistletoe turned into full-scale tonsil hockey practice. She had tried her best to rebuff him without whacking him in the groin. A couple of white wines later – bottles in Stein's case, glasses in hers, he had led her by the hand to his office on the pretext of showing her some sort of sporting highlights videotape. Well, it was certainly more plausible than showing off his 'etchings'.

It became clear after a couple of minutes what sort of highlights were on offer. As she had sat in his armchair, he began gently massaging her shoulders. A pleasant feeling indeed, which combined splendidly with the light-headedness brought on by the excess of wine. Less splendid, although athletic in its own way, was the speed with which he appeared on the arm of the chair and turned his attention to her inner thighs. She had offered firm but polite resistance but when the telephone rang barely two minutes later, her black panties were already on the floor and her blouse was finding itself undone. He ignored the ringing of his telephone but when his wife's voice boomed out of his answering machine, Lenny stiffened suddenly, and this time it was his back.

His ardour cooled very rapidly as the legendary Mrs Stein barked out a request for him to pick up cranberry sauce and chestnut stuffing on his way home. An excellent piece of 'coitus interruptus' by Mrs Stein. Melanie had said a silent prayer as Lenny's attention was momentarily elsewhere and slid swiftly from the room. She never did recover her knickers and presumed that Stein had mounted them in a trophy cabinet somewhere. It was better than the other kind of mounting which he had had in mind.

Surely he could not get too far in a Delta first class seat, however roomy the leg space? She knew for a fact that Lenny would not be supple enough for any Mile-High-Club manoeuvrings in the lavatories. She would feign sleep.

"You did real well in getting Karelov out of that damn place, Sugar," Lenny beamed. "Real well."

"Thank you."

He leant forward, for no particular reason other than to catch a glimpse of cleavage through the unbuttoned portion of her blouse. After a few moments it was evident to Melanie and a passing cabin stewardess that Stein was on a nipple-gazing expedition and he hastily reached forward to his seat-back pocket in an attempt to disguise his activities. He rummaged around and pulled out the safety card instructions. Prolonging the pantomime, he read through the procedure that would apply in the unlikely event of the aircraft making an emergency landing in water. Fascinating. Periodically, he would glance across to try to get a peripheral sighting of Melanie's bra. Before Stein had got as far as the instructions on inflatable chutes and life jackets, her breasts were beginning to rise and fall in spectacular fashion. She was fast asleep.

Stein began formulating a cunning plan to drape a blanket across her and practice some elementary fumbling techniques under cover.

He was prone to sneaky behaviour in many areas of his life. His mother, Beatrice, had become decidedly diffident towards her son, Leonard Harvey Stein Junior and would confide to fellow residents of the Maples Rest Home in Madison, Wisconsin that he was 'still a bit of a slippery little guy'. This was quite an admission on Ma Stein's part because throughout his early years, young Leonard Stein had been the apple of her eye. Maybe that was where it had all started to go wrong. Beatrice had acrimoniously divorced Lenny's father, Leonard Senior, when Junior was but four years old. The settlement bestowed upon Mrs Stein by her property tycoon ex-husband, following his dalliance with a secretary, (it was hereditary) was a record-breaker for the circles in which Beatrice moved – a million bucks plus the house. It owed as much, however, to her lawyer's insistence on a big pay-off to buy Beatrice's media silence on Leonard Senior's sexual proclivities as it did to any sense of benevolence on his behalf.

Beatrice lavished a good deal of her new found independent wealth on her only child in a forlorn attempt to buy a lifetime's allegiance. Leonard was the least popular child in their swanky neighbourhood. Other mothers came to dread the sight of his slicked-down centre-parted hair, bowtie and tailored clothes. His mother bought him a motorised pedal car at the age of six. Leonard used it to run over two little girls living a block away.

Mother bought him an air rifle at ten and one of his classmates was blinded in one eye a week later. At 16 he had a motorcycle and another school 'friend' was knocked down and seriously injured in circumstances that were not readily explained but which surprisingly brought no police action. Between times there were daily acts of spite, malevolence and generally sly behaviour but in Beatrice's eyes, Lenny could do no wrong. The knowledge of this made him very much worse.

The Jesuit College of the Nazerene in Wisconsin remembered him with no great Christian affection despite his subsequent endowment of a new annexe to the sports pavilion. His school career had survived the recorded instances of bullying and low-level extortion. It had also endured an unproven dope-peddling scandal for which a less wealthy and more servile pupil had taken the rap. In reading through Stein's school record, none of the subsequent Jesuit College principals could understand how he had escaped the rumours that prevailed over his unfeasibly high score in the Scholastic Aptitude Test. This had secured his place at the University of Florida to study business administration. The fact that most of the subsequent Jesuit College principals were reading of Lenny's appalling record from the plush comfort of The Beatrice Stein Administration Building helped preserve the conspiracy of silence, despite considerable tabloid interest in Stein's early life.

Lenny's time at Gainesville, Florida was marked by academic mediocrity. This was hardly surprising, given that the admission test that brought about his university place was actually sat by one Douglas Scadden, a classmate who had the misfortune to accompany Stein from high school right through college. Scadden should also take a bow for the B grades ultimately achieved by his bullying 'friend' because the bulk of it was earned from coursework commissioned by Stein but prepared by Scadden. Scadden's reward was the occasional cuff around the head and an invaluable contribution of $200 a month towards his tuition.

Stein had taken to golf in an enthusiastic fashion at college. His handicap never once broke 20 but he played three or four times a week, often accompanied by the hapless Scadden. Stein cheated compulsively at this noble sport and rued the lack of voluptuous women players. At that time, golf was beginning to grab increasing amounts of prime time TV coverage throughout the States.

On one occasion, Howard Westphal, a prominent golf producer at SVP television had partnered Stein in a pro-am tournament at the Torrey Cedars club in Tampa (Stein had given $800 to charity for the privilege). As they sipped gin and tonics at the 19th hole, after grinding out an honourable draw, Westphal had remarked upon the fact that his company was consistently out-bid by network rivals for the privilege of screening major golf tournaments.

"Reckon we need to start inventing a few frigging tournaments of our own just to get something on air at SVP," he said. "Our advertising boys sure love those upmarket golf audiences. Big numbers. Big spenders."

It was somewhat of a throwaway remark but four weeks later a detailed proposal for a brand-new pro-am golf format landed on Westphal's desk. He recalled his slightly dubious playing partner from Tampa. After reading the proposal he called Stein that afternoon.

"I do believe you could have something here, Leonard. I'll send a couple of our creative guys down to see you this week. You never know. We might all be hitting the big time with this one."

The 'SVP Celebrity Classic Shoot-Out' ran for six years. Stein had been very careful to ensure that he retained control of the concept and lodged an imaginative but unenforceable patent application. He also took steps to sign personal contracts on retainers of $1000 each to the participants in the pilot programme. The early lesson that in sport, money talked was a striking one, as he assembled a four-ball from the ranks of the football's Hall of Fame. The four-ball at Torrey Cedars Championship course was a huge success with a gallery of almost 3000 and an outcome that remained in doubt until the final green. Between shots the players had been interviewed with wit and insight by legendary broadcaster Arthur Jackson and the format was immediately commissioned for a series by Westphal at SVP. Nobody had needed to know that Stein had threatened 'Rocket' Ron Wood with heavy physical violence on the eve of the competition when a family illness had made his withdrawal likely. Nobody had needed to know that Stein had whispered a promise of an extra 500 bucks if Wood took two shots to get out of a bunker on the 17th hole to bring the scores level.

Stein had worked tirelessly on the success of the 'Classic' while Scadden did double time in the library. Lenny had found his niche in life. A B grade degree did not concern him. One week after graduating he joined SVP's sports division in New York.

On Day One, he spelt out his philosophy on sport to his mentor Westphal.

"We are in the entertainment business. People want excitement, risk and winners in sport. If you can give them that, they'll keep coming back for more."

It was a belief that continued to underpin his relentless rise through sports programming. He also understood that American viewers craved American winners, especially if it happened to be a Russian on the receiving end of a defeat. Failing that, 'World Series' baseball represented his idea of truly great sport – Americans only. Vivian Wheatley had been Stein's trusty sidekick throughout his time at SVP – the Shere Khan and Baloo the Bear of TV sport.

From SVP, they had moved to Cougar TV where pro-wrestling and contrived motor sport were on the menu. Giant dumper truck racing owed its origins to a Friday afternoon brainstorming session between Wheatley and Stein. Always the emphasis was on razzmatazz, packaging and hype. If it needed a few bucks here and there to ensure a hometown winner and a contented crowd, Stein was only too happy to oblige. Race fixing became a speciality of his.

The creation of Prime Life gave him the absolute power he craved. There were no owner-schedulers or institutional stakeholders to call the shots. He could buy in junk sport from around the world and create a few spectaculars of his own. As he watched Ted Turner rise through to the upper reaches of moguldom, leading to the creation of the Goodwill Games, he would sometimes feel a pang of regret that his own network represented output of the lowest quality. But did that really matter when the advertising revenue and sponsorship, notably from the tobacco and liquor industries, kept the Prime Life tills ringing contentedly? One day, he resolved, he really would blow their doors off with a massive sports event. Money didn't just talk in this game. It sang frigging arias.

Staff turnover at Prime Life was high. Few people responded well to Stein's bully boy management technique and taut purse strings. Wheatley soldiered on and Melanie had hung on in there for seven years in the hope of executive status.

Stein looked across at the sleeping figure beside him. The in-flight movie was running. He slid a hand beneath her blanket and stroked her thigh. To his horror, she screamed. He was suddenly uncomfortably aware of all eyes in the cabin looking their way.

"It's OK, honey, you were having a nightmare," he cooed, hastily attempting to play down the commotion and edging an arm protectively around her shoulder.

Too right she was having a nightmare. Melanie was desperate to sleep and knew exactly what his game was. She had been conscious of his attention from the moment he lifted the edge of the blanket. The scream may have sounded involuntary, but it was a trick she had learned in high school when a diversion was necessary. She guessed correctly that there would be no second attempts all the time she was asleep or pretending to be.

Lenny knew it too. The stiffening in his trousers had disappeared very suddenly. He picked up the in-flight magazine. 'Gold plated paperweights' caught his eye in the in-flight souvenir section. He'd never met anyone who used a paperweight but made a note to have a word with the Merchandising Director about 'Solid gold Sport Armageddon medallion paperweights'. It was amazing what sort of crap people would buy. He never over-estimated his public.

All aspects of Sport Armageddon would make money but best of all, he would become the most famous sports promoter in the world of TV. There were 12 hours of flying to Atlanta but already Lenny Stein was making plans to embellish the build-up to his great event. Twenty-two days to go. The world was about to hear from him in a big way. Sport Armageddon would be a sure-fire success but he, Leonard Harvey Stein Junior, would be the biggest winner of all.

CHAPTER THREE

STEIN could recall the precise moment that Sport Armageddon had been born. Two years previously, he had enjoyed a very sombre lunch with Vivian Wheatley at their favourite French bistro in downtown Atlanta. It was not an occasion for celebration. Over a brandy or five they had perused the viewing figures for the previous week's output at Prime Life. Their banker events were starting to wobble. Pro-Celebrity golf had lost 200,000 viewers for the third successive week in its peak-time slot up against collegiate basketball.

Their Dumper Truck Derby had slipped to fifth in its early evening face-off with the news bulletins. Both had enjoyed a good run for several years but Stein and, to a lesser extent, Wheatley, knew it was time for something new.

"Trouble is there's nothing left out there that we can buy, not even friggin' Alaskan dwarf hurling. We gotta invent somethin' new. We've got cash in the bank but our regular viewers will zap to somethin' else completely unless we keep movin'."

"What about triathlon, Chief?"

"What about it?"

"I was talking to a guy from the International Triathlon Union based in Vancouver. He reckons it's heading for the big time now that it's an Olympic event. A lot of the top competitors train in the States and we have the original Ironman Event in Hawaii each year."

"Christ, Viv. It's like watching paint dry. Swimming in a pool is boring but have you seen the pictures they get from these open water events. It's real dross. You can only screen about ten seconds of it. I'll tell you what was great TV though. A few years back when that girl in the Hawaii Ironman shat herself and crawled the last hundred yards to the line. Now that was really great."

"Jackie Ross. She's one of the world's best."

"It doesn't matter. Everyone knows her because she shat herself and finished on all fours. If we could capture that sort of desperation and competitiveness, we're on a winner. The only way I see us being able to do it is by cutting the swim down to virtually nothin', or filming it from underwater or somethin'. You gotta project these guys as characters so the viewers can relate to them. Otherwise they're just friggin' hats bobbing in the water. We gotta make it real cut-throat competition with a winner-takes-all prize."

The transition from 'You gotta' to 'We gotta' in Stein's diatribe proved to be an important step in the genesis of Sport Armageddon. For the first time he could sense the whiff of dollars and fuelled by some fine cognac, was warming to his theme.

"The other thing I don't like about triathlon is the mass participation. We gotta have just a real elite field from around the world with proper personalities and styles that people can pick out. And the American guy's gotta be there at the death."

"We're pretty good at triathlon, Chief," beamed Wheatley, basking in the glow of Martell cognac and the credit for an original idea. Only a bona fide sycophant could properly savour this feeling.

"How do we spin sixteen programmes out of this though?" Stein mused, mindful of the fact that Prime Life craved wallpaper television rather than short high-quality transmissions.

Wheatley hadn't a clue but he knitted his brow, trying to feign deep thought. After 30 seconds deliberation, he ventured a suggestion.

"Maybe a knockout competition with a Grand Final."

"Nah. This thing has to unfold like a story. We don't want too much repetition. I wanna build-up some more cred in this business so that we can nick viewers away from the big guys."

"What about if we stage a real big triathlon right here in Atlanta?" Wheatley was to reflect later that he had never before put together three original ideas in a month but this particular lunchtime was to be the high water mark of his creative input at Prime Life.

"Yeah." Stein's eyes blazed. "A million bucks prize money and a massive point-to-point Ironman event that finishes in Atlanta right outside our office building. Yeah."

They both leant back in their chairs. Stein ordered another round of brandies and two huge Cuban cigars. For the next 20 minutes they tried to think of pitfalls that could undermine this bold event. There were none. The brandy compounded the effect. It was perfect.

That night Stein had his recurrent dream about being the world's biggest TV mogul. And he already knew who he wanted as his main event sponsor. It was Zing Cola who would surely kill to steal some of Coke's home town thunder. He already knew the event's name. It would be 'Sport Armageddon' – the ultimate contest. He was a genius.

Wheatley, meanwhile, was having a recurrent nightmare about missing transatlantic flight connections. He knew the donkey work in assembling the Chief's latest toy would fall to him. He was a big mouth.

It was to be several months before the logistics of Sport Armageddon came together. Stein remained adamant that the swim should be as short as possible, but in keeping with the 'ultimate challenge' hype, he realised that the distance had to be a fraction longer than anything previously contested in a triathlon. He was therefore extremely angry when the swim at a newly launched event in Mexico, the 'Decatriathlon' was set at 38 kilometres.

He called a press conference to confirm that, all along, Sport Armageddon's swim distance in Lake Okeechobee was to have been 40 kilometres. Stein learned a lesson from this experience about being too specific on the race details. Sure, the swim would be 40 kilometres and the cycle and run would be in excess of the

Decatriathalon distances of 1800 kilometres and 422 kilometres but full details would only be released, for maximum publicity, in the fortnight before the start. There were other good reasons for this. If Stein wanted to, he could route the whole shooting match through every one-horse town in Florida State. Logically, however, he could see that it ought to run south to north up the east coast. He still planned provisional detours to Orlando and Tallahassee, but their city councils were not being as accommodating as he would have liked towards his brainchild. Lenny made flamboyant promises about the impact on tourism and the exposure that the event would bring to locations en route.

"The Tour de France has got nothing on this," he declared grandly to the Chamber of Commerce in Daytona Beach.

"We reckon we could be looking at more than one hundred million viewers worldwide daily." He was trying to drum up additional TV advertising placement from them and could substantiate his claims with some very impressive graphs, charts and projections, created as a work of pure fiction by Prime Life's marketing department.

He was like an old style Wild West huckster trying to sell his elixirs to bewildered locals – long on hype, short on truth. The route was sketchy but the provisional event logistics had actually been worked out in military detail by Stein and Wheatley.

The swim would traverse the eastern edge of Lake Okeechobee between Taylor Creek and Pahokee.

Lake Okeechobee was a controversial choice but despite all the reasoned objections, Stein could think only in terms of superlatives. It was claimed to be the largest freshwater lake in the USA. Of course the race had to start there. Lenny was also very taken by the fact that the Lake was only 14 feet deep all the way across – perfect for underwater shots of the swimmers filmed from the bed of the Lake.

"But Chief, it's polluted with pesticides and burnt sugar cane."

"It's not that bad. I've checked the water quality figures with Environmental Services. It's legal."

"It's got alligators and cottonmouth water moccasin snakes."

Lenny said nothing but Wheatley could have sworn that the Chief's eyes twinkled at that point. Was he considering sacrificing one of the competitors to an alligator attack live on Prime Life?

"I've thought about that. There hasn't been a bite from either of those critters for about six years but here's what we're going to do. Each of the participants will be swimming in a special wetsuit, which will protect everything except their hands, feet and face against goddamn snakebite. Each swimmer will be accompanied by two boats. On one, there will be cameraman and a doctor as well as the guy's trainer and supporters. On the other we'll have a race referee and a warden armed with a high velocity rifle looking out for 'gators. It'll look great, huh?"

It was Wheatley's turn to sit in silence.

"It'll look great," Stein continued, "I can see it now. Safari hat colour co-ordinated with the athlete's colours. It'll be really great. Also, I've been looking into what happens on some of these ultra swims. They do them in pools and the swimmers get out for a rest and food every once in a while. We're going to have the support boat towing a little covered floating pontoon with shade, food and water. Every time the guy gets out for a break, the referee halts the boats and the pontoon.

"If they wear hooded tops or high collars, there shouldn't be too much problem with sunstroke. If we get especially made wetsuits, we can also have them insulated, so they don't get cold in the water after twelve hours. And here's a trivia question for you, dude. What other two essential items will need to be on the pontoon?"

Wheatley hated it when Lenny gave him quiz questions. He always had to have a guess.

"Flippers, Boss."

"Very funny. No. They'll suffer skin maceration on their hands.

61

You know, when your skin gets all wrinkly after it's been in water a real long time. It can be treated using a hairdryer. And Vaseline because they'll chafe like sonsofbitches. That reminds me. Call Vaseline about some advertising."

Stein's grasp of detail was extraordinary. If only his moral values were as impressive, thought Wheatley.

"From Okeechobee, they'll head out on the cycle ride. The supporters will need to transfer to the recreational vehicles and motorhomes and we've paid for two cops to ride out with each competitor. They could be six hours apart comin' out of that swim so we'll need two helicopters to film overhead. The gaps between them are important, so we need a graphic on screen showin' the gap from first to second to third. Doesn't matter if it's accurate. If in doubt, make it up and make it look like the guy in second is always catching up. What have you got as fillers during the swim?"

During the preceding months, Stein had taken the dramatic decision to show Sport Armageddon on-screen round the clock. It was a bold move, requiring careful formatting, massive pre-event publicity and hours of spin-off footage to pep up the live action."

"Chief, I reckon I'll have about eighteen hours of edited footage for each of the competitors by the time we start. We'll also have two hours footage on each of the cities and tourist resorts they pass through. We've bought in Hawaii Ironman historical tape..." Stein looked up "...We've set the sequence where Jackie Ross crawled to the line to music." Stein beamed. Wheatley had learned a few tricks over the decades after all. "Let me guess, the Rocky theme?"

"Not exactly. It's 'Start Me Up' by the Rolling Stones."

Stein beamed again. Twice in one day – a new personal record. He pressed on.

"Cycle heads west one hundred and ten miles to Fort Myers then Highway 41 to Miami – distance of...?"

"One hundred and fifty miles, Chief." Wheatley had, only the previous week traversed that particular route. Slightly more stylishly than the Sport Armageddon cyclist. He was in a chauffeur-driven BMW but he still felt like a gladiator.

"Miami. Jeez! The audience figures will be great round there. Can't we get a Hispanic taking part in this thing?"

"There aren't any good Hispanic triathletes," Wheatley lied. In fact he had not a clue.

Stein was already off up the road

"Too bad about the Keys. We go from Miami to Fort Lauderdale..."

"By the scenic route, Chief."

"...By the scenic route – thirty six miles."

"To West Palm Beach – forty five miles. Then the boring section... you need to work on this, Viv, try to get them cycling through the night on this bit."

As if the competitor's progress through Florida could be regulated to suit Prime Life's output, thought Wheatley. Actually, it could.

"West Palm Beach to Cocoa Beach – one hundred and fifty miles then, hurrying along with our lucrative little detours via Orlando, Gainesville and Ocala missin' out the tight-assed city councillors of Tampa and then back to Daytona."

"How far from Cocoa Beach to Daytona on our route?"

"One hundred and eighty miles." Easy in a car, especially when you are asleep.

"Bike ten laps round Daytona Circuit. They've paid ten thousand bucks for that little PR stunt."

"Yeah, great touch that."

"Run through St Augustine – second oldest city settlement in the Continental US – got the footage?"

"Got it, Chief."

"How far to Jacksonville?"

"Ninety two. A hundred if we go out to the Beach."

"A hundred it is. Bike-to-run transition in Jacksonville then Brunswick – Savannah – Milledgeville – Eatonton – Atlanta."

"Three hundred and thirty miles, Chief."

"I absolutely love it." Stein had worked up quite a perspiration just thinking his way round the route of Sport Armageddon.

"It's beautiful. A twenty five mile swim, a twelve hundred mile cycle and then a three hundred and thirty mile run. The ultimate contest."

The cycle ride was only a few miles longer than the Decatriathalon distance held in Mexico – but the run was 70 miles further. He was proud.

Stein's face clouded over momentarily. "We've got to make sure some of these suckers race close together. We gotta have a goddamn race not a procession."

"We will, Chief." Wheatley wasn't sure exactly how this would be achieved but the Chief would no doubt have ways of keeping it exciting.

"It's a killer event, Viv. Prime Life has got itself a winner, here."

At the Prime Life board meeting, Wheatley continued to fidget. He was anxious to be away down to the bookies to claim his $750 from 'Silver Monkey' and gently caressed the winning ticket beneath the table.

"Let's assume that Viv gets Gaby Vaughan signed up this week. You guys all know that I have some doubt about the choice of PJ Kogo. We've agreed that we need someone to represent African-Americans but right now I would be concerned to have a Hispanic, given that Miami is a major venue en route."

Wheatley was on the point of making his most inspired contribution to the day's proceedings.

"Chief. You have said many times that we need to think big on this project. If we are serious about syndication our pictures worldwide then the African market may be a better bet than the Spanish-Cuban connection. And we've all agreed previously that we like the 'Olympic rings' feel of one-competitor-per-continent...or almost."

'Son of a gun,' thought Lenny Stein. Every once in a while his feckless deputy would get a sudden rush of intelligence that was a credit to his training. He paused.

"You're absolutely right, Viv. But if that is the case, are we absolutely certain that Kogo is the right man to sustain that interest? He's your sole choice. We have relied on your judgement so far."

All eyes were on Vivian. Beneath the table, he began twisting the 'Silver Monkey' ticket uneasily.

"Sure. Sure. He's absolutely the best there is. I'd stake my life on it."

A life that would not be worth too much, if PJ bombed out in Sport Armageddon.

CHAPTER FOUR

NO ONE messed PJ about. He was the sixth son of a leading Kenyan industrialist who had claims on one of the Nandi tribal leaderships. PJ's father had no urge to pursue his chiefdom birthright. He was too busy generating money from coffee beans at the company premises in downtown Nairobi. His youngest child, Philemon Joseph Kogo, 'PJ' to anyone outside his family, had enjoyed the best education available from Nairobi Academy and had followed all his brothers as captain of the soccer team. It ran-kled with him that it was so much a matter of routine and general expectation that he would captain the side from central midfield. True, he had earned his place on merit with his fierce tackling, slick passing and inspirational leadership but as the sixth son of John Kogo, he needed to make his mark in a different way.

"Father, all of us have captained the Academy soccer team. It's like we are a production line. Some of the teachers even call me 'Ben' because my brother was doing exactly the same thing two years ago," he complained.

"There is nothing wrong with being the last of a great era, Phil-emon," his father chided. "When you graduate they will realise what a contribution the Kogos have made to football at the school."

"They probably said the same thing about Benjamin. Do you know I even have the identical exam grades in the same subjects that he achieved? I need to find a way to be myself without being compared to all my brothers."

John looked at his 16 year old son over the top of his glasses. "What exactly did you have in mind, Philemon? I hope you are not planning to burn the school down." Despite his flippancy, he had some sympathy for PJ's search for an identity. This was the young man who had received some of his school shirts as hand-me-downs five times over. Perhaps he should not have sent all of them to the Academy.

"I would like to study in America, father."

"And what would you like to study in America, Philemon?"

"I would like to go to California and study politics. It is something that we can learn from the Americans that can benefit our own systems of government."

"An American college education is very, very expensive Philemon. If you are successful in pursuing this new ambition, I could help you a little but I cannot see how it could all be paid for. Had you thought about that?" He guessed rightly that PJ would indeed have thought about that. His youngest son was noted for being meticulous in his planning and much more considered than his classmates or his brothers at the same age.

"Father, I believe I could study for a scholarship and this would pay for my tuition and my housing. Benjamin's friend Joseph Kang had such a scholarship to study mathematics in America."

"Joseph won a scholarship put up by the Commonwealth Institute to help international relations. He was also one of the brightest pupils the Academy ever produced. I don't wish to dampen your enthusiasm my son, but these are difficult ambitions to chase."

"I can get such a scholarship," PJ insisted, "I will study hard and when I am in America, I will work to make extra money to pay my way."

"It is good that you have such a dream, Philemon. We will just have to see if it comes true."

Over the next 12 months, PJ applied himself whole-heartedly to his attempts to win an academic scholarship to study in the USA. He sat the Scholarship Aptitude Test required by the American Schools and reached scores in the 88th percentile. These proved good enough to earn him an interview with the Nairobi branch of the Rotary International organisation, which had an endowment for just one boy to study for a degree overseas.

PJ could not sleep on the eve of his interview with the bursary adjudication panel. As he paced the house late at night, his father offered encouragement and words of wisdom.

"Philemon, there is nothing that you can do except rest and relax."

"But what sort of questions will they ask? I wish to prepare."

"They will ask you about your reasons for wanting to go to America and why you wish to study politics. These are matters that you have answered in your own mind many times. You can only be yourself. Now you must try to sleep."

John Kogo knew how much the scholarship would mean to PJ and wished there was more that he could do to help a youngster trying to make his way in the world. The fact was that although his coffee business was flourishing, it was now supporting four of PJ's brothers. His enquiries at the bank had suggested that he could only set aside enough ready cash to support PJ through just 12 months in the USA. His son was on his own on this one but John knew that he would pursue it until the very last door slammed in his face.

PJ had presented well at his interview. His bright-eyed enthusiasm and future plans had impressed them all. It would therefore have been no consolation at all to PJ to know that on a split decision, the bursary had been awarded to an equally driven young man from Nairobi to help him study engineering at Cambridge University in England.

PJ was desolate but not in the least bit shaken from his master plan. If he had to toil for ten years he would eventually pay his way to America.

He pitched into his studies and his soccer, fuelled by the frustration of his lack of progress towards America. He was the outstanding all-round sportsman of his year and when the Academy asked him to make up the team for the Nairobi Cross-Country Championships in February, he was happy to step in at the last minute.

The team was limbering up for the race when he noticed two well-built middle-aged white men standing near the start. His schoolmaster did not know who they were but spoke briefly to a colleague from a rival school.

"PJ, I have good news," his teacher announced as the team moved towards the start line.

"Those men are from America. They are looking for great Kenyan runners to go to school on running scholarships."

PJ could not believe his ears.

It was an Act of God, he decided, to have these important men here to give out free tickets to America on the very day that he had come to race. His imagination ran riot as he envisaged himself winning the race by five minutes and being presented there and then with an air ticket to the West Coast and a suitcase full of money. The fact that he was the novice runner on the Academy team was of purely academic concern at this stage.

His trance-like state continued as the teams lined up for the start. PJ's gaze never left the two stout Americans. When the gun went, he shot into the lead and for the first mile of the race, he looked superb – head high, eyes blazing and legs floating, at one point, he was 50 metres clear of the boy in second. His teacher's entreaties to slow down fell on profoundly deaf ears. PJ was heading for Hollywood.

In the second mile, PJ's dream burst. Tears welled up in his eyes as first one, then two, then eight runners sped by. His legs filled with lactic acid and his early extravagances were fully repaid. The leading boys had trained and prepared themselves for these Championships and the difference in conditioning showed. By the third mile, PJ was in twentieth place but in the final agonising 800 yards, he dug deep into his reserves and, punching his arms wildly, he clawed his way back to ninth place at the finish. He was the first home for Nairobi Academy and earned the praise of his teacher as he was helped from the finishing funnel. He lay on his back on the hot, parched ground. He felt sick, dizzy and bitterly disappointed.

"They will not want me for America after that run will they?" he asked his teacher.

"Perhaps not, Philemon, but you ran really well for a first race. It is five years since we had anyone in the top ten here."

"It is no good if I cannot go to America."

"Would you like me to speak to the American college gentlemen for you?" PJ sat bolt upright.

"Yes please, sir. Tell them I can become a great runner if I train in America."

"I will see what I can do."

The two talent scouts had ambled across to talk to the race winner but 20 minutes later, PJ's teacher saw his opportunity.

"Excuse me, gentlemen. I have a very disappointed boy on my team. He wants to come to America to run on a scholarship. He is the boy who led early on but finished ninth. He is a soccer player and this was his first race."

"I saw that guy. He battled back pretty well at the end – he's a real fighter. My name's Ian Driscoll, University of Oregon."

"And I'm Dave Smith from Arkansas." His colleague also proffered a hand. "Most folk here think we've got a whole bunch of free rides to give out but the fact is that Ian and I probably only have three full track scholarship each to play with and there's always problems getting SAT scores and academic transcripts from Kenyan schools. We probably can't help anyone here today. The Military Championships last Saturday were a better bet."

"Is there any possibility of help for PJ? He dreams of studying in America?"

"Well, if he's a soccer player normally, that was a promising run." Driscoll replied. He may be of interest to some of the Junior Colleges. Give me your address and I'll let you know in a couple of weeks if there's anything we can do."

And so it was, two months later, that Philemon Kogo enjoyed

what he believed was the happiest day of his life, when his teacher, who had taken three or four calls from the States, presented his father with a formal written offer of a track scholarship to Riverside Junior College, south of Los Angeles.

"It says James Kariuki and Nourredine Morceli the Olympic Champions studied there," said his father when he read the letter some time later.

"It is a good place, father. I can go, can't I?"

"I will look into it Philemon, but I do believe it could be a great opportunity for you."

"It will, father. And now I must go for a training run because I am to become a great runner."

The fact was that PJ had hardly run at all since his suicidal bid for glory at the Championships but he immediately set about cultivating his new status as an American collegiate runner. He ran for an hour from his house to tell his friend Desmond the good news.

When PJ finally arrived in Los Angeles, he truly believed he was Master of the Universe.

His first semester was as disorientating as it could possibly be. PJ struggled with just about every aspect of his Great American Dream – the traffic, the food, the local accent, the money, the class timetable. He also had problems with living in a runner's dorm that was 12 miles from the campus. It was no bother for his flatmates, all of whom had cars but, on the occasions when he could hitch a ride from them to school, it was not always easy to synchronise transport back home. His choice of study courses involved two nights a week when he had lectures from nine until ten-thirty at night. On a couple of occasions the police were called when he was spotted trying to walk alongside the freeway to get home. There was no bus or train that could assist. America was a car and plane kingdom. When the gasoline ran out, the USA would probably have to close down, PJ believed.

Matters came to a head one afternoon seven weeks into his stay at Riverside. Coach McGuire beckoned him into his small office alongside the back straight of the track.

"Sit down, son. We need to talk about a few things. How would you say things are goin' along?"

"It is all very confusing still, Coach. So much is very different to Kenya."

"Your class grades are OK though. Half B's and half C's right?"

"Yes Coach, but I am having to work very, very hard in preparing for my class tests. Everyone else seems to find it much easier than me."

"And are you homesick?" McGuire was in his late forties but the loneliness he had felt during his first months at University of Tennessee was still a vivid memory.

"Sometimes I miss home but it is not too bad. I write to my parents once a week and telephone every Sunday."

"What I need to know, son, is how come you're missing about half the practice runs we put on?"

"I have an afternoon class on a Tuesday and I am afraid I have had a lot of tests for which I have had to study hard."

McGuire could not afford to be unduly sympathetic. As he had explained to a colleague that lunchtime, it was McGuire's ass that would be on the line if their only Kenyan import of the year blew out by the time the Conference Championships began in November.

"The thing is, fellah, we've invested a lot of money in bringin' you here and right now there's not much evidence of a return. Then I get a note this mornin' from the Dean of Social Sciences tellin' me you nearly picked a police rap for walkin' on the freeway at midnight. What's it all about?"

"If I run home, Coach I can take one and a half hours. If I walk it can take two and a half."

"Jeez, you walk all the way back to Loma Heights? Doesn't one

73

of the guys give you a lift?"

"Sometimes, but my evening classes finish too late."

"I guess I should have given you some help settin' your schedule."

McGuire was becoming uncomfortably aware that he had been remiss in not offering the naive Kenyan better guidance. He cursed himself for trading his natural Kentucky concern for Californian indifference when he had moved to LA ten years before. Perhaps it was not too late.

"I think, PJ, that we need to get you in a dorm on campus. At the moment running seems to be way down on your list of priorities."

Four days later PJ had moved all his worldly goods into a fraternity house barely 400 yards from the Social Science teaching block and within half a mile of the athletics track.

In many ways, that was the start of his problems. He did sufficient training to ensure that he made the Riverside scoring team in all of the cross-country meetings but it was all too obvious to the coaching staff and his teammates that he was seriously underachieving. Forty miles a week was barely enabling him to scratch the surface of a prodigious talent. The fraternity boys, meanwhile, quickly tried to acquaint him with the traditional extra-curricular activities of wine, women and song. On more than one occasion PJ raced with a hangover caused by a Budweiser or six too many. When Jennifer Ellis finally appeared on the scene, PJ had almost gone off the rails completely. Jennifer was a slightly built sophomore whose family had worked their way out from the mean streets of Watts, Los Angeles to the tranquility of Marina del Rey. Her father had a stake in a small real estate business and Jennifer had shown great promise as a half-miler. In her first year at Riverside she had dabbled with triathlon and despite a weak swimming phase, was beginning to make a name for herself on the circuit in Southern California.

Her first words to PJ were at the gym, where he was mooching his way through the compulsory session of upper body weightlifting, which followed each Wednesday's long run.

"You'll hurt yourself if you do it like that" – PJ was trying to bench press a modest weight from a position where the multi-gym weights were just above his forehead instead of his chest.

From such unpromising opening gambits are great romances forged and many conversations and several weeks later, PJ began to accompany Jennifer on her long cycle rides, perched awkwardly on her house-mate's bike.

She taught him how to get organised, how to study, how to train and how to moderate his alcohol consumption. The housemate whose bike he borrowed was Leanne Wheatley, daughter of the great Vivian Wheatley III, professional fat man and casting controller for Sport Armageddon.

Two years after graduation, when PJ had settled in Los Angeles, working for Jennifer's father's business, the happy couple got married. The fat guest who was also the father of the chief bridesmaid looked on from the back pew of Marina del Rey Baptist Church and knew at once that his quest for a credible black athlete to take part in Sport Armageddon was over.

In the preceding four years, PJ had embraced Bacchus and the American lifestyle with a passion. His running had not reached the heights that had been hoped. He finished runner-up in the Conference Championships but the team had won, so McGuire was delirious. The University of Nevada at Las Vegas had offered him a track scholarship, which he immediately declined. The things that were really important to him had been accomplished. He had a B+ average grade, he was engaged to be married and, unbeknown to McGuire, he had travelled secretly with Jennifer to participate in the Hawaii Ironman Triathlon, where he had finished in the top 50 competitors. McGuire did not know but Viv Wheatley did and discussed the situation at some length with Stein.

"It's just perfect, Chief. The guy's virtually an African tribesman and there aren't many of those doing the triathlon."

"But he's no friggin' good is he? He'll disintegrate during the swim."

"Leanne says he'll be OK. He swam two miles in the Ironman without any trouble and he hardly did any training. He'll handle the Lake as well as any black guy could."

"If you're wrong on this, you'll be out of a job," Lenny spat, not for the first time. "We can't afford to lose our black viewers just 'cos this guy can't float."

"Trust me, boss."

Stein gave a withering look.

"Just get some proper African shots in the preview. Really hype up the Rift Valley roots OK? If he can't swim we may as well get some kind of mileage out of the black contender angle."

Wheatley sighed, foreseeing, as ever, that he would be clocking up a few more unwanted air miles in pursuit of the right 'image' for Sport Armageddon.

The schedule was getting very tight for splicing in the 'PJ at home' stuff. They had already used generic backdrops from the desert south east of LA to give an illusion of Africa. He would delegate this mission.

Melanie was dispatched, with full executive responsibility for the first time, to shoot the footage in Kenya. Wheatley claimed that high blood pressure and a pulled muscle from his Australian cycling adventure made him a no-show for this trip. The fact that the Prime Life team were booked on a return flight from Nairobi precisely 20 hours after their arrival may also have had something to do with his reluctance. On the outskirts of the city they filmed some highly implausible action of PJ running 'barefoot in the bush'. It caused blisters to his Americanised soft feet and he insisted on wearing sunglasses and shorts, fearing that Melanie's mission was to have him so typecast that he could end up brandishing a spear.

Melanie was not exactly sure what she was supposed to accentuate but knew from her work with Wheatley in Moscow, Edinburgh and Sydney that the global combat elements of Armageddon were symbolised by clichÈ's – Red Square in snow, Castle in rain, Opera House in sunshine. They used up most of their remaining filming time trying to get some zebras in the background.

In no time at all, the camera was bundled away with assurances that the remaining interview footage would be overdubbed in the States.

PJ, who was staying on for a week to visit his family, watched from his father's jeep as the Prime Life team reversed their hire car back to the main road and sped off towards the airport.

The preliminaries to Sport Armageddon had been very undignified. He was not so gullible as to not realise that his recruitment was as the nominal minority group interest but he did not care. It shamed him that he had begun to lose touch with his African roots. He would atone for that and he would make Jennifer, his family and his country proud of him. He would conquer the challenge of the swim and beat them all. PJ had prepared thoroughly. Whenever he had really wanted anything in his life, he had achieved it. PJ Kogo already knew beyond any doubt, that he would be the winner of Sport Armageddon.

CHAPTER FIVE

"THE most important decision that we have to make," continued Stein to his boardroom colleagues in Atlanta, "is who will be the US representative in Sport Armageddon. We simply cannot afford to get this wrong. Whatever the overseas syndication figures may be, our audience is still likely to be around eighty per cent home market. We need those people to stay tuned in throughout the contest. Our major advertisers and sponsors, especially Zing Cola have made that point real clear. That is why we have risked the sliding payment scale for our advertisers. Even Superbowl doesn't do that. Our standard tariff is halved if viewing figures drop below two and a half million during peak viewing periods and doubled if we beat fifteen million."

A series of unsmiling glances were exchanged around the table. Fifteen million people tuning in to Prime Life seemed like complete pie-in-the-sky but the Chief had an unerring habit of homing in very close to his financial targets, however implausible.

Vivian Wheatley looked down at the twisted betting slip in his hands. Perhaps he would use the winnings to buy a stake in another thoroughbred racehorse. True, his ambitions were as a breeder rather than as a trainer, but he could not resist the lure of the turf on race-day. He actually owned one fetlock of 'Silver Monkey' as part of a media syndicate and he would travel to see it race as often as his schedule permitted. On those adrenalin-packed days at the track, he felt more involved and a greater sense of belonging than he ever experienced on Prime Life duty. It was probably time to do something about the imbalance between the work and pleasure elements in his life.

"Can't we still hold some kind of trial to get the top American?" It was Joe, the Finance Director.

"Nope." Stein replied.

"Why not?"

"Because it's hard to find any trial event friggin' long enough especially at this stage. Sport Armageddon is twelve back-to-back Hawaii Ironman events for goodness sake. Besides, the last thing we want is some kind of robot. These endurance athletes can be a boring bunch you know. Eat-sleep-train-eat-sleep-train. We need someone a bit spunky. Mr Wheatley here has presented us with a shortlist of his customary length. At the moment, we have just one athlete under consideration. His name is Brent Ryan."

Brent Ryan himself was not aware of such shortlists and accordingly shouldered this burden very lightly. As a rule, he did not allow many things in life to get him down for any length of time but that evening he had plans for a certain young lady getting down with him for quite a while.

"Sure, Dad. Anyway, I gotta go because I've got an open water swim tomorrow so I need some sleep."

"Have a good one, son. 'Night."

"'Night."

Brent put down the receiver and leant back on the pillows. Outside, the Denver party animals were just making their way to the fast food joints, prior to hitting the bars and clubs for a wild Friday night. In his third floor room at the Best Western, Ryan was not part of that scene at all. He clenched his fist and felt the tension of a rock solid bicep. He was tanned from the recent Colorado heat wave and after a couple of days of light training, he felt strong, fit and at the peak of his powers. At 28 years of age, he knew there would not be many times in his life when he would feel this well-conditioned again. He had built up relentlessly and purposefully towards Sport Armageddon for more than four months, even though his nomination had yet to be formally confirmed. It had been a punishing physical schedule. His family back in Columbus, Ohio would be so proud of him. They were in awe of his monastic dedication to training – the way he had taken himself off to the high altitude of the Flatirons, at Boulder, to hone himself without any distractions. The man was clearly something special, the Irish ancestry had imbued a fighting spirit, his father concluded, but the fanatical commitment was unique to his youngest son. Such determination deserved to be rewarded with success.

The bathroom door swung open.

"You got mah Spritzer there, honey?"

Ryan reached for the side table where he had poured a generous measure of dry white wine. He handed her the glass. She swigged half the contents and giggled.

"We need some music, baby. I'm ready to dance."

Brent grinned. He knew what was coming next, in a manner of speaking. He picked up the remote control and tuned the TV to an easy listening local radio channel.

The opening chords of Shania Twain's 'Man! I Feel Like A Woman' belted out. These were the recumbent one's sentiments exactly. He turned the sound down seductively low. His guest's name was Sharon. He thought her surname was O'Malley. He had met her at a gym in town three weeks previously and the sum total of their relationship was a Nuggets basketball game and a night at the Best Western the previous weekend. If this was to be a repeat performance of that burlesque show, he was all in favour.

Sharon was a willowy, elegant girl. Some of her friends described her as 'stunning'. Most independent observers would regard this as an understatement. Sharon was like a raven-haired Grace Kelly with ice blue eyes, fine bone structure, dazzling smile and long lustrous wavy hair. Her short black cocktail dress showed off a flawless figure.

Sharon began to sashay across the room keeping her eyes firmly fixed on Brent, reclining on the bed. The girl had natural rhythm he thought to himself, not for the first time.

In the background, Ms. Twain indicated that she too was ready to go really wild and let it all hang out – yeah.

A slower seductress, closer to home, smiled winsomely at Brent as she dipped her left shoulder. She continued to dance and reached behind her back, smoothly unzipping her dress.

Brent felt a shudder of anticipation as she gently slid the shoulder straps of the dress to one side and let it swoosh to the floor.

Underneath she wore a black silk slip, which barely came to the top of her sleek caramel thighs. For the first time she broke eye contact with him as she turned away and eased the slip over her head, dropping it sensuously on the counterpane as she re-connected with a smouldering gaze.

Brent didn't even know how old she was as she shimmered barely four feet in the front of him wearing nothing more than black high-heels, hold-up stockings, black G-string and matching pop-up bra. Pop-up bras were well named...

Shania Twain was really going for it now. Never mind about men's shirts or short skirts ... He was way, way beyond third base.

She leant towards him, her pert breasts almost in kissing range. He could see her nipples bursting forward like bullets. She turned and invited him to unclip her bra. Suddenly his quivering hands had turned into two left feet as he fumbled anxiously. The strap came free and she turned allowing it to fall forward and revealing the most fabulous breasts he could ever recall.

"Come on baby. I feel like a woman." The room had suddenly acquired an echo.

He could scarcely contain himself but Sharon knew the most rewarding strip was strong on tease. For Brent it seemed like forever before she began to play slowly with the waistband of her skimpy panties. Her eyes never left his but she knew her routine was working well. As her final item of underwear dropped to the floor, but still wearing her high-heels and stockings, she stepped towards the bed and kissed him passionately.

Ryan was three hours late for his lake swim the next morning.

He covered six miles in open water in just over three and a half hours – his best ever – and that was the enigma of Ryan. He was a closet playboy with a liking for high dosages of Coors Light and curvy women, but when he did train it was with a fiercesome intensity. It was the kind of competitive streak that had created problems for him in all the regular school sports. He had shown promise as a quarterback with his high school team in the leafy Columbus, Ohio suburb of Arlington. His prospects had not flourished in the wake of broken ribs sustained by a hostile opposition nose tackle who had the temerity to sack him twice in one game. At the age of 16, with a similarly explosive career in basketball, his despairing father decided to direct him to the less contact-based individual sports of running and swimming.

As a medley specialist, his swimming was on course for a scholarship with one of the sunbelt university schools, probably Miami or UCLA. However, all that early morning pool training had a very limited appeal for Brent Oliver Ryan and his dabbling in running became slightly more regular, not least because several of Arlington High School's premier league babes were on the running team. Ryan's interest in both flourished.

"Son, you're quite good at a few sports. Why the hell don't you knuckle down and get real good at just one of them?" His father despaired. "You could still be on the Olympic team at the medley, you know. Coach reckons in three years you'd be right on schedule."

Ryan did not welcome criticism from his father and, in truth, rarely incurred any. It was just that he really did not feel ready to be typecast as a sports jock. So he did apply himself – to his studies – and instead of picking up a sports scholarship, got a place on academic merit at the University of Florida. His father, somewhat taken aback by this new string to his son's bow, agreed to underwrite the four year English Literature major.

Ryan found that a sustained effort in the first trimester was rewarded with a B+ grade point average and, having shrewdly calculated that even if he studied every waking hour, his lack of creativity and flair would prevent him from being top of the class, he looked for other distractions.

For five months, he sought Baccanalean excess – slow horses, fast women, marijuana joints and endless parties. Over the Spring Break weekend he boozed for 48 hours straight and consumed a surprisingly high proportion of the ales brewed between Cape Cod and Portland.

His end of year GPA dipped to B-, but he gained not an ounce in weight and realised that sport was truly what he craved. It was more extreme.

He signed up with the university cycling team at the start of his second year and within a few weeks was holding his own in time trials with any of his elite colleagues.

Ryan preferred the open road to the velodrome and with his thirst for new challenges, it was only a matter of time before he was drawn to the triathlon.

In this, too, he sampled early success. He also sampled a brush with the collegiate disciplinary panel when a $1000 prize from an event in Tallahassee had to be hastily returned in order to preserve his NCAA amateur status.

The sporting press was not slow to latch onto his tanned good looks – dark hair and piercing blue eyes – coupled with a regular winning habit. He could also handle the media with consummate ease. A quick joke at his own expense to set the tone, a few more self-effacing comments sprinkled in, but all done with a ready smile and a happy-go-lucky charm. They fell for it every time and, if it was a lady interviewer, the serial flirt in him would inevitably resurface.

After sustaining B- grades through to graduation, he decided to stay on in Gainesville and try to make a living from his triathlon endeavours. A nutrition bar and aspirin endorsement helped bankroll him through year one.

Back in Tallahassee for the first time as a professional, he was asked about rumours of a romantic attachment with visiting Australian triathlete, Gaby Vaughan.

"There's really nothing goin' on between me and Gaby. We had dinner last night and that was all. I'm sure her boyfriend would be horrified at the suggestion of anything more than that," he twinkled to the guy from the cable station. Like hell. He had tried every trick in the book to bed her and could still feel the throb of frustration. He was a man completely unused to rejection.

"You'd make a glamourous couple." The cable station man was not giving up.

"Gaby is a beautiful lady. She would make any couple look glamorous." Good line, Brent boy. Use that one again.

"How do you fancy your chances tomorrow?" Did he mean for getting laid or the Tallahassee triathlon?

"Well, I've prepared real well. My running's not as strong as it could be but there's seven or eight of us in with a chance. Depends on the second half of the bike ride, which is my weakest event. Look out for me, I'll be the one on the three-wheeler with a basket of cookies on the front."

Cute, thought the interviewer, especially since Ahoy! cookies were one of the event sponsors. The interviewer was Vivian Wheatley III from Prime Life. Ryan won the Tallahassee event and a few more besides. When the time came, Wheatley had no doubt who should have the coveted American berth for Sport Armageddon.

"He'd better be friggin' good. We need an American winner, Viv. I don't see much ultra-distance background."

"He'll be fine, Chief. I've made an appointment for him to see you next Friday."

You only get one chance to make a first impression. As Brent Ryan was ushered in to Stein's inner sanctum at Prime Life in Atlanta, his appearance had been the subject of careful planning. The mild autumn weather in Gainesville, for that was where he based himself for his full-time triathlon career, had faded his golden boy tan, so two sunbed sessions were booked and his hair was lightened a shade. The earring had gone. He wore a tweed jacket with Levi 501s. The image which he sought was 'All-American preppy sports jock'. The transformation was complete and Stein bought the whole package.

In his mind's eye, Stein knew exactly what he was looking for in America's lone Sport Armageddon competitor. It would be Steve McQueen meets Mark Spitz – someone who could put a few extra noughts on the viewing figures and the advertiser's pay cheques as the contest unfolded. Someone who could withstand all the TV hype and tabloid scrutiny that would come his way. Above all, someone whose strength of personality and winning ways would suck the American viewing public's attention relentlessly towards Sport Armageddon.

Lenny had no qualms about putting his product to the test with some direct tactics. He was on the telephone as Melanie brought Brent Ryan into his office and motioned him to sit down. Actually, he was pretending to be on the 'phone so that he could scrutinise Ryan at first hand without the need for conversation. Wheatley had prepared a comprehensive video tape and written dossier on Ryan but this was Stein's first face-to-face encounter.

"What about the drugs testing results?" Stein enquired into the receiver, his eyes never leaving Ryan's.

"Stanazolol? Who's he?" Ryan looked bemused.

"Hold on. I've got a guy here who might know something about it." Stein held his hand over the receiver and asked again.

"What's Stanazolol?"

"It's the drug Ben Johnson tested positive for in Seoul – part anabolic steroid, part stimulant."

"Oh right...You seem to know a lot about it. Know where we could get some at short notice?"

"At a weights gymnasium or a pharmacist near here, I should think." If anyone within earshot had had any appreciation of cricket's noble technique, they would have applauded the straight bat with which Ryan had opened his innings.

"You ever taken any?" Stein persisted with his bodyline bowling attack, palm clamped across the mouthpiece of the telephone receiver.

"No."

"Would you tell me if you had?"

"No."

Lenny took his hand away from the receiver. "Listen. I'll have to call you back this afternoon. Bye."

He stood up and extended a hand across the desk.

"Hi, I'm Leonard Stein."

"Brent Ryan." The man of the same name beamed.

"What can I get you to drink?"

"A diet soda, if you have one, please."

"Won't you join me in a Jack Daniels or a glass of Krug. We may have something to celebrate here?"

"No, a Zing Cola will be fine."

"Don't tell me you're one of these puritanical super-athletes – vegetarian, early nights and you never touch alcohol."

"Oh, I do occasionally," Ryan replied, relieved that he had munched a few mints on the way down to alleviate the alcohol-induced dog breath sustained the previous night.

"Melanie, a Zing Lite and a Jack Daniels please, Honey."

"If Jack Daniels comes on board as a minor sponsor of our little event, would you drink it then?" Lenny had few qualms about linking sport with alcohol and tobacco, within Federal regulations of course, and had no truck with anyone at Prime Life who demurred.

"If they paid me enough, I'd swim in it." Ryan replied deadpan.

Lenny smiled. He could get to like this boy.

"So tell me a bit about yourself, Brent. Are you married?" Lenny knew the answer but sought more.

"No."

"Engaged?"

"No."

"Dating?"

Brent's eyebrows furrowed. They'd only been introduced two minutes previously and the guy was already checking out whether he was a druggie, an alcoholic or a fag.

Fortunately, Lenny's briefing pack contained enough press cuttings of Ryan with beautiful women for the third prong of his attack to be surplus to requirements.

"How much do you know about Sport Armageddon?"

"Well, I know its going to be at least ten times the Ironman triathlon distance and I know its going point-to-point across Florida."

"Let me stop you there a moment," Stein interjected. "It will be more than ten times the Ironman distance. That was the original plan but we hear the jokers in Monterrey, Mexico have beaten us to the punch. They've got an event in the pipeline, which is ten times the Ironman distance so we'll definitely go further than that. How would you feel about it?"

"It's a massive distance, especially in summer in open water and on open roads. You couldn't really go much further, especially on the swim, otherwise you'd have a death on your hands."

Stein's eyes lit up. The possibility of someone dying live on Prime Life TV in pursuit of his million dollar carrot. Hell, that really would upstage the friggin' networks.

"I thought you were a strong swimmer son?"

"I am but this is a contest of survival not just speed swimming. Anything could happen."

Stein scribbled furiously on the yellow legal pad in front of him. 'This is a contest of survival', he wrote. Great, it would make a perfect slogan for a trailer. He looked up. This boy would be the one. There was no point in prolonging the meeting unnecessarily. He was a busy man.

"Brent, let me explain something to you. I'm not in the business of sport, even though most of Prime Life's output is sport of one kind or another. At present, our viewers tune in for an average of eleven minutes at a time. We are the zap channel and they want immediate entertainment. I'll do whatever it takes to attract viewers and advertisers and get this station to number one. More than anything else our viewers want to see Uncle Sam as biggest and best. Reckon you could handle that?"

"Sure."

"OK. I hope that in August you'll be a million bucks better off for that one reply."

"A million bucks?"

"Sure. That's the first prize. It's the only prize. Winner takes all. Didn't you know that?"

"No." Ryan was stunned.

"Well keep it to yourself for now. Any leaks and you're out. We haven't announced it on TV yet. If you stay smart, you will be America's man in Sports Armageddon. Melanie will see you out. Bye."

"Bye. Thanks." They shook hands. Ryan's usual composure had deserted him. His head was spinning. Melanie escorted him to the lift. He hit the ground floor button, leant back as the doors closed, and exhaled slowly.

A million bucks. Jeez. He closed his eyes. A million dollars. He had thought about this event quite a lot in the past fortnight, as

Wheatley had gradually filled in more information about the contest. He had never mentioned prize money and Ryan had never asked, the assumption on his part being that it would be around a 10,000 dollar purse. He had wanted to win it for its own sake, and because that little tease Gaby Vaughan needed a good whipping, but now....well there could only be one winner. Brent Ryan knew that he would win Sport Armageddon.

CHAPTER SIX

LEONID KARELOV had been in the USA continuously since his remand on bail by the court in Germany but Stein had made sure that he was well used in PR and media opportunities throughout America. It suited Karelov fine because he was paid at least 100 dollars for each of them and his training regime was variable, to say the least. It suited Prime Life as well because, apart from the publicity spin-offs, it meant that through their press officer, they could keep an eye on Karelov and bump him back onto the straight and narrow where necessary.

Melanie had warned all of her colleagues that he was not a man to be trusted and she spoke from personal experience. Soon after arriving from Germany, he had tried his sleazy best to woo her and when subtlety had drawn a blank, tried a more direct approach by squeezing her buttocks sharply one morning in the lift. His first prize in the build-up to Sport Armageddon was another one of her power-packed slaps. It was his second blow from Melanie, the previous one having been administered in the police cells. She made it clear, in no uncertain terms, that three strikes and he was out.

So, on a day when Karelov was selecting his favourite records on radio station B100 in San Diego and then being interviewed by the LA Times, the second Sport Armageddon contestant checked into Atlanta.

Vivian Wheatley III had technicolour memories of his last brief encounter with Gaby Vaughan when he had deposited his breakfast at the roadside in the Blue Mountains. Even for a man whose life was a smooth continuum of faux pas and gaffes, it was an embarrassing episode. His subsequent travels for Prime Life had presented difficulties for him in trying to follow a fitness regime but he was proud of the fact that by sheer willpower, he had shed seven pounds from his oversize frame. He believed this would make him look rather like Arnold Schwarzenegger because surely anything left would be solid muscle.

Accordingly, he presented himself at the head of the welcoming committee for Gaby Vaughan at Hartsfield-Atlanta Airport, suitably attired to show off his newly re-excavated physique. An extra-large flamingo pink Sport Armageddon 'I'm for Gaby, Baby' T-shirt was stretched to its limits but offset by a large St Christopher medallion. He cared nothing for impartiality where testosterone was concerned. At the last minute, he had decided against the lycra cycling shorts, mainly because they split as he put them on, and instead wore a marquee proportioned pair of khaki Bermuda shorts. This natty ensemble was set off by a lime green Prime Life baseball cap clamped firmly over his wayward grey locks. He looked a fine specimen. Melanie usually offered gentle guidance if his wardrobe selections were too extreme but he was flying solo this time.

"Gaby! How are you, Sugar?"

Vaughan stepped into the VIP lounge and the waiting Prime Life film crew together with a gaggle of journalists stepped neatly into position.

Gaby was wearing a pink sweatsuit, and as Wheatley stepped forwards to hug her, it looked for a moment as if the clash of his pink torso and hers would send the TV pictures into a strobing neon confusion. Her Prime Life contract for participation in Sport Armaggedon required her to wear the appropriate shade of pink for all her media appearances. This was to be her racing colour and the livery for all of her support vehicles, crew and equipment. Prime Life merchandising had sold a great many fuchsia leotards to the matrons of South Georgia who felt as if they knew her, even before she had set foot in the State.

"Good to see you again, Viv." Vaughan flashed her irresistible pearly smile. Wheatley was in love again.

"My dear, may I be the first to welcome you to the USA for Prime Life's million dollar ultimate challenge. Are you in shape?"

Was she in shape? Jeez, of course, she was in shape. Hadn't he just hugged her for a few seconds longer than decorum permitted just to feel that firm bust pressed against his own southbound flesh?

"I have trained really hard for this. It's just a question of resting up now."

"Will you win?" Wheatley's eyes widened as his microphone headed towards her nostrils.

"Reckon I'll be hard to beat, mate."

It's a weird accent, thought Wheatley but the natives are going to love her. What an inspired piece of casting Gaby Vaughan had been – the Aussie superbabe, cheered on by both men and women – for entirely different reasons.

"Let me escort you to your hotel. You must be exhausted after the flight from Australia."

"Thank you, that'd be most welcome, Viv."

The jetlag was a bogus image. She had spent the previous two nights in New York and was beautifully rested but, compared to the other strokes that Prime Life had already pulled, it was an innocent enough hoax.

Wheatley offered his arm. Gaby took it and they strolled across the concourse to the accompaniment of popping flashbulbs – a veritable Eliza Doolittle with her Henry Higgins. Viv dispensed his most beatific smile. What a guy. Centre of world attention yet again. The Prime Life cameraman grinned. Wheatley was completely predictable but given the choice he'd rather spend a week with him than an hour with Lenny Stein.

Steve O'Neill arrived that evening. No fanfares. No bugles. He had been portrayed as the brooding and moody Celt in all the pre-event hype and had no fan base to match Gaby's. More pertinently, he landed just after the main TV news bulletins and his arrival could be re-staged the following morning if Stein deemed it necessary. It was not necessary because the local media just could not get enough of Gaby Baby.

'It's Gaby Mania' announced the following day's Atlanta Constitution and Journal.

O'Neill saw the headlines on the newsstand across the lobby as he checked into the Hyatt Hotel in Atlanta, the race headquarters for the duration of the event. Stein had persuaded the hotel to erect a neon sign across the main entrance, which pronounced the Hyatt to be 'Prime Life Sport Armageddon Mission Control'. It was visible from every floor of the Prime Life office just 200 yards down the road. Stein had transferred some of Prime Life's studio and editing facilities from the main building to the Hyatt and a satellite dish receiver stood conspicuously on the hotel roof to receive direct feed from the event. He had succeeded in getting Zing Cola to become principal event sponsor and the company had paid for the installation of the dish in return for it being painted corporate 'Zing Green' with the Zing name in two foot high letters. Lenny remained master of the 'contra' deal despite anything that Oliver North's investigators might contend.

While the receptionist processed his registration, O'Neill took stock of his surroundings. Lenny's idea of pre-event hype and publicity made Las Vegas look upmarket. Every square foot of the ground floor atrium seemed to be a shrine to Sport Armageddon. A giant video screen played a continuous loop of event trailers, location previews and competitor profiles. There were concession stands selling 'Sport Armageddon' official merchandise. The stands had been colour co-coordinated with a selection of products devoted to each individual competitor. The Zing green stand with Brent Ryan goodies such as 'frogskin reflective shades', 'racing line' swimwear and 'Go USA' flags was doing a roaring trade. The neon pink booth had also drawn a small crowd, many of whom had wandered down from the hotel restaurant, slightly tipsy on the 'Gaby Baby' pink gin cocktails to make matching purchases of baggy sweatshirts, energy bars and car stickers.

The red 'Karelov' stand had just two browsers, looking at the proof content of the range of 'Karelov cocktail' drinks. Vodka appeared to be the main ingredient.

Reggae music blasted out of the 'Kogo' stand. Okay, so it wasn't exactly an authentic African sound, Lenny had mused when the Kogo CD first appeared on the merchandising shortlist but it sold well enough and the bottom line was what mattered.

Tucked away in one corner, O'Neill caught a glimpse of an A2 sized poster of him running up Arthur's Seat with a murky looking Edinburgh in the background. He looked ghastly. The poster was framed with tartan. God, didn't they realise he wasn't Scottish? It didn't matter. The stand in garish yellow (or 'Burnished Gold', as Stein would have the punters believe) had no browsers. The plump matron working on the stand recognised Steve and waved a half-eaten 'genuine Highland shortbread' biscuit at him. He nodded but then looked away.

"A little quiet on your stand right now," observed the courtesy car girl who had brought him to the Hyatt.

"Uh-huh." He was in no mood for small talk.

"Suite 1503, Mr O'Neill. Welcome to the Hyatt. Take the elevator to the fifteenth floor and turn right. Would you like a hand with your bags...." the receptionist stopped. O'Neill was already beetling across the lobby towards the lifts.

As the doors closed behind him, O'Neill cursed himself for his rudeness. "Politeness costs nothing," his mother had always reminded him. O'Neill was fitter than he had ever dreamt possible but he was not well.

The dark clouds that had been hanging over him for the past few weeks in Scotland had begun to envelope him completely on the flight to the States. He had experienced bad weeks previously but nothing like this. He feared he was drifting towards clinical depression but he would fight it. O'Neill would work it out for himself without any outside interference. He did not need help from anyone.

PJ Kogo was next to arrive in Atlanta, on an internal flight from Los Angeles, at noon the following day. He had spent so much time swimming vast distances in open water that he thought he must have developed gills. The furthest single swim had been ten miles in Lake Tahoe the previous month. It had left him bedridden for 72 hours. He feared the water quality of Lake Okeechobee. He feared the snakes but above all he feared his own lack of buoyancy and swimming technique and that he would bring shame on Kenya by not completing the opening phase of Sport Armageddon. He had not run for a couple of weeks because what was the point in practising a discipline not required until at least a week after the start of the race? He might be back home by then.

His wife had been concerned at the intensity of his recent efforts and fretted. On two occasions he had retched all night long as the stagnant lake water swims had made him ill.

Jennifer accompanied him to Atlanta. Mrs Kogo was looking forward to crossing swords with Lenny Stein for the first time. She had made her point in typically uncompromising fashion to Vivian Wheatley on one of his many visits to their home.

"I won't allow you to keep on stereotyping PJ as the event's token African American, Viv. You know that don't you?"

"Sure we do, honey. But actually he's very much African for the purposes of Sport Armageddon. Lenny Stein's original idea was based on one representative from each of the five continents. All five Olympic rings."

"He has his dignity though. He's a proud man. Some of those tribal costume pictures that Prime Life have tried to pull have been ridiculous."

Wheatley did his best to look contrite. He liked the Kogos, but how could he be too apologetic when Prime Life's share of the black viewing public was at an all-time high. They had played the ethnic card well but, on reflection, there was no doubt that with the cycle route looping through Miami they should definitely have had a Hispanic competitor. It would have enabled the Prime Life advertising sales team to generate some extra revenue to target that key market. Too late for all that now, though. PJ would have to do.

PJ was determined to leave nothing to chance on the dreaded swim phase. After a brief press conference that evening, he would be taking a flight down to West Palm Beach and spend the remainder of the week hacking up and down Lake Okeechobee. At least then he would know exactly what to expect.

The press conference was designed to coincide with the arrival of the last, but by no means least, Sport Armageddon competitor in Atlanta. Brent Ryan would be arriving from Denver mid-afternoon (to go live on early evening news bulletins). Zing Cola was sponsoring the whole event but also had a link-up with Ryan personally. To extract maximum publicity from this, a green liveried jet, would be chartered for the flight from Denver to Atlanta.

A press contingent of 20 newspaper reporters and TV film crews would make the flight with him.

In his race HQ office at the top of The Hyatt, Lenny Stein watched a bank of TV monitors showing the broadcast output of all of the national stations and the top six regionals for Georgia and Florida. One national and four local stations had live coverage and were screening interviews and pictures of Ryan on board the plane. It didn't matter to Lenny that there had been a substantial payola diversion of event sponsorship proceeds to buy off many of these stations. The depth of exposure and pre-event hype was a personal triumph for him. He smiled contentedly and leant back in his chair.

"What time's Ryan due here, Melanie?"

"He'll be less than an hour now. They'll whisk him from the runway to here in under twenty minutes." Melanie replied.

"Press conference ready to go in the ballroom?"

"Yes, Chief. We think there's about a hundred press guys,

already there."

"A hundred? That's great. The eyes of the world are turning our way at last."

He believed it. Melanie was not sure just yet.

"Reckon I'll make my way down to the press conference in half an hour," he announced.

"Don't cross the lobby, Chief. You're meant to be introduced with a fanfare. Take the back route through the kitchen."

Stein never liked to be observed taking the back route to anywhere but if it meant a fanfare for him, he'd make an exception.

When Lenny finally arrived at the ballroom, he peeked from behind the curtain into a darkened auditorium packed with media representatives. On the stage was a lectern picked out by a single spotlight and a long trestle table covered with a Sport Armageddon tablecloth. There were seven empty seats each picked out by an individual spotlight. The back drape bore the logos of the seven 'Gold Medal' sponsors of Sport Armageddon. To the side of the stage, two video screens were running promotional footage of the event.

"...Daytona Beach will indeed be a spectacular and crucial venue for the Sport Armageddon Cycle phase..." intoned the narrator.

After a few minutes, from behind the curtain, Vivian Wheatley gestured to a technician to stop the tape.

He stepped forward into the lectern spotlight. As he did so, the auditorium fell silent.

"Ladies and gentlemen," Viv began, "the ultimate sporting contest is now just six days away. Welcome to Atlanta. Welcome to Prime Life Race HQ. Welcome to Sport Armageddon."

He stepped back. The spotlights disappeared. The room was in total darkness. From the Dolby sound system that had been especially installed came the pre-recorded voice of Lenny Stein.

"My friends, this was always destined to be an event of superlatives. The mother of all triathlons. The biggest prize purse. The largest distance. The toughest challenge. Now there is no turning back…"

The video screens sprang to life as the opening strains of the Rocky film theme music blasted through the wrap-around sound speakers. Fast moving imagery kept pace with the beat. First there was Steve O'Neill driving through the rain in Edinburgh, then Gaby Vaughan powering her bike through Sydney's Blue Mountains, Karelov in Moscow, then PJ Kogo running across the fields on the outskirts of Nairobi and finally Brent Ryan gliding through the waters of Lake Tahoe. Stein peeked through a gap in the curtain. He could see the front row of the press contingent. These were seasoned, cynical hacks but they were transfixed. One had his mouth agape. Yes! It was working. They were buying into the whole friggin' deal. He felt like Barnum and Bailey rolled into one. This was going to be his greatest triumph.

The competitors were then introduced. The taped voice-over was in the style of a Las Vegas heavyweight boxing bout.

"Five feet nine and weighing one hundred and forty pounds, from Edinburgh, Scotland…" Bagpipes struck up 'Scotland the Brave'. The auditorium filled with warm applause and Steve O'Neill slipped into the spotlight and self-consciously took his seat. He was still on a real emotional downer and felt powerless to deal with it. Best to soldier on through the evening's circus and then try to get some more sleep.

There was the expected rapturous reception for Vaughan and Ryan. Lenny had told Viv to place Prime Life staff throughout the invited audience to keep the enthusiasm high and to initiate some bogus questions if the interview session showed signs of flagging.

Each of the contestants wore their race colour sweatsuits with the logos of Prime Life and their individual sponsors. If they did but know it, the revenue from just four corporate sponsors who bought a Prime Life advertising deal covered the million dollar prize purse with something to spare. Lenny would be in profit even if they failed to sell another flagon of Karelov vodka. Profit was great – Mammon of course, where Stein's worship was concerned but what he really craved for from this project was to be the top player in US cable broadcasting, and hence the world. He believed he had got his ingredients completely right.

The first question was scripted from one of the tame newspaper feature writers.

"Doug Alred, Jacksonville Bugle," he introduced himself. "Mr Stein, has the build-up to Sport Armageddon fulfilled your personal expectations?"

Lenny gave an expansive grin.

"Certainly it has. When I look out into this room, I see a large deputation from the finest newsgathering services in the world. In every newspaper, magazine and on all the TV stations that matter, there is nothing but positive expectation about Sport Armageddon. Rightly so. This is the greatest sports event of all time."

It was hyperbole day in Georgia, although the press conference went on to draw decidedly mixed performances from the competitors.

O'Neill's black mood made his answers even more taciturn than usual. Vivian Wheatley was riled by this. He could brood as much as he wanted back home, but this was a goddamn press conference to promote the event. Viv's sense of compassion did not extend to compromising the hype to accommodate O'Neill's mood. Karelov's English was laughable in places and several TV researchers went off to source tapes of his interviews from LA the previous week, purely for entertainment purposes.

PJ Kogo was also brimming with serious intent and spoke endlessly about the swimming phase and his wish 'not to let my people down'. Stein had briefed him with that particular phrase and it was used several times. Ryan spoke in platitudes, saying exactly the right thing for sponsors, PR and TV soundbite purposes. As Lenny listened to his American protege, he knew immediately that Brent's media persona would not need pepping up in the remaining days. The last thing he needed was for the USA to be represented by a cardboard cut-out. Ryan had to become more conspicuously flamboyant. The viewing public would tune in more for an Agassi than a Sampras.

Gaby Vaughan alone shone in this environment and time after time questions came back to her. She even managed to get in a few wisecracks about 'women on top'. Stein wrote himself a memo about T-shirt slogans in the final merchandising run. The whole thing took just over an hour with a further hour spent in small groups. Vaughan was avalanched, with more than half the room paying court at her table. O'Neill had just two Japanese TV crews as company for his session.

Lenny reviewed the following morning's papers earnestly. It had not been a sparkling press conference but never mind the quality, the column inches were great.

"120 hours to Showdown in the Sun" wrote Doug Alred in the Jacksonville Bugle. "The most extraordinary sports event of all time will commence at 4 pm on Thursday on the edge of Lake Okeechobee. Ahead of the five brave competitors lies a swim, a cycle and a run of gargantuan proportions, for this is Satan's own triathlon. It is expected to last ten days and will finish in downtown Atlanta."

"City councillors are known to be ambivalent towards the event which has no permit from the triathlon federation but they have only limited powers to prevent its progress. Prime Life's legal advisers confirmed yesterday that with only five competitors and a restricted number of support vehicles, the possibility of a technical public order offence was negligible and an attempted injunction to prevent the race entering South Georgia highways was swiftly dismissed a month ago. The public appetite for the event is soaring. The only prize is a cool million bucks for the winner but at what cost to their health?"

Stein frowned. The front page report continued.

"Medical experts at North Florida University believe that the risk of heat exhaustion caused by over-exertion is very high and have written to the Prime Life TV organising team suggesting that the race be suspended between 10 am and 6 pm each day. There has been no official response to this."

Stein remembered the letter from the university bozos. Viv had shown it to him. As if they would take the race off-air during peak viewing hours. Who did they think was calling the shots? As far as he was concerned the mid-day Florida sun would just spice up the contest. There would be no concessions on that. This needed to be a pure, start-to-finish goddamn race.

PJ Kogo also read the report that afternoon. More accurately, he had the report read to him in its syndicated version, as he lay in a darkened hotel room in Belle Glade, Central Florida. He had been sick, very sick. His belly ached from retching and Jennifer had got some tablets from the pharmacist to try to quell his biliousness. This was the worst he had ever been and he was frightened. The swim had not been a success. He had entered the water at half past six and by mid-morning, he could go no further.

Jennifer tried to tell him that it was enough. That he should not exert himself unduly with the race five days away but PJ was a man fraught with self-doubt.

"Jennifer, I can run, I can cycle but I have tried hard and I cannot swim for so many hours at a time. I am just not built for it."

"Honey, you must just take it in small stages. You know you can rest as much as you need to. Maybe we should look at doing an hour of swimming followed by half an hour's rest."

PJ looked at her through half-closed eyes.

"Maybe, but at the moment, it looks like one hour of swimming followed by half an hour of puking." He felt terrible.

"Tomorrow morning, we'll just try that, three lots of one hour in the water with long breaks in between. See if that's any better."

PJ rolled over in bed and belched as he did so.

"Maybe," he whispered. He closed his eyes and wondered if he would ever wake up again.

Wheatley and Stein looked at each other.

"She means it. I'm sure, Chief. This is no hoax." Wheatley murmured. "What the hell should we do? Do we tell the competitors?"

"Christ, no. We can't afford any kind of boycott or withdrawal. We have to defuse this ourselves. You can't give in to every crank who tries to sabotage a public event. We have a right to proceed. This is the USA."

It was Stein himself who had taken the second call. The first had been traced to Tuscaloosa, Alabama and had been fielded by Wheatley at the Hyatt. In a 60 second diatribe, the woman caller had spoken of 'traitors in the midst' of Sport Armageddon, of betrayal, revenge and an eye for an eye. Wheatley tried unsuccessfully to interrupt her but in the end had put the phone down. He had met women like that over the years and learned that once they were rolling you could not get a word in edgeways. Retreat was the only defence. He found it chilling though, because she was not ranting. It was more like she was reciting a mantra to some undetectable drumbeat.

Stein had been dismissive of this first encounter with Zelda.

"Just some nutter trying to get a piece of the action. I'm sure we'll get plenty of them."

It was an assessment that he was to revise dramatically when an ashen-faced Wheatley handed the receiver to him in the control room early the next morning.

"It's her," he mouthed.

"This is Stein."

"This is your worst nightmare, Mr Stein."

"Who's calling?" The voice sounded vaguely familiar.

"I already told you. Listen to me, Stein. Your circus will end in blood before it reaches Atlanta. There is nothing you can do. There is nowhere you can hide. I have waited too long. All traitors must die. I know the route that will be taken by Sport Armageddon. The lakes and roads are always open, Lenny. It's out there in the open that I will close down the circus. One of the clowns will die. Bye, bye."

The line went dead. Stein rang the switchboard and asked for the call to be traced. When the number was finally tracked down at mid-day, it sent a shiver down his spine. "This can't be right." Wheatley spluttered, "Are you sure this is the same voice as the one that called last night?"

"Definitely, Chief. She did all that stuff about killing the clown."

"Christ. We gotta do something about this."

They both knew that there was, at the very least, a measure of crazed intent behind the woman's threats. How else could they explain the fact that her first contact had come from a phone in a street in Tuscaloosa at eight o'clock the previous night and by nine that morning she had made the follow-up threat from a payphone in the lobby of the Atlanta Hyatt Hotel? She had only been 12 floors beneath them at that time.

"Viv, we gotta get to this woman before she harms our race. We need to find out who she is in the next twenty-four hours. Imagine if she starts repeating these threats to the press. See if you can come up with anything before we get the police involved."

Wheatley looked blankly at the Chief. He didn't mind recruiting elite athletes from around the globe and putting together a 1300 mile race for a million bucks. But, just at that moment, he was not sure he had the wherewithal or indeed the appetite to track down Mr Stein's worst nightmare.

CHAPTER SEVEN

NOT everyone was in love with Sport Armageddon. Zelda could remember the first time the event was brought to her attention. It was Lenny Stein's spectacular press launch at Amelia Island. Fireworks, laser show, rock and roll music and a cast of thousands. All of the competitors were introduced to a crescendo of noise and disco lights. It was completely over the top.

Zelda had known true love once. Just once but it was meant to be. She should still have been with Loverboy now but Loverboy had destroyed her. When she caught her first glimpse of Loverboy at the Sport Armageddon press launch, Zelda's blood chilled. Not a day, not a night, not an hour had passed since their split when her thoughts had not been on vengeance. Now she knew that it was time to exact retribution. An eye for an eye, a tooth for a tooth. They could not live together and they could not live apart. Everything was pre-ordained. Loverboy would have to die so that Zelda might live again.

Zelda's neighbours knew her as Sonia Harper. The Federal Government and Social Security people did not know her at all. As far as official records were concerned, she did not exist. No social security number, no bank account, several forged passports and driving licences. She lived in a run-down trailer park south of Jacksonville, where her neighbours were an anti-social blend of itinerant workers, problem families, recluses and alcoholics. None of them could claim they knew Zelda well but newcomers to the site would invariably be appraised of the Zelda myth within their first few weeks, usually embellished by Will, the site warden.

"Good looking girl, that one who lives in the big green trailer by the woods," an earnest hick would pronounce.

"Stay away from her, she ain't nuthin' but trouble," would be Will's customary caution.

"Hell, I've been with some feisty women in my time. Reckon I could handle her just fine."

"Son, take my advice and keep right out of her way. You'll end up hurt."

If the young hick raised an eyebrow old Will would beckon them closer and in a conspiratorial whisper perpetuate the legend of Zelda.

"Couple of years back a guy about your age started hittin' on her and eventually she invited him to her trailer for a drink. He hadn't been in there more than fifteen minutes when he came runnin' out screamin' blue murder, blood pourin' from his groin. It sure looked like he'd been stabbed but he took off and no one ever saw him agin."

Young hick would cross his legs at this point.

"The other thing is," Will continued, "No one knows what goes on in that trailer of hers. The windows are blacked out, there's alarms and the damn dog. One time the Austin boys thought they'd try busting into it while she was out. The eldest one took a jemmy to the window and damn near electrocuted himself – burns right down one side of his body. She's got the whole trailer wired up. I should go and check it out for myself but she always pays her rent up front with a tip, so most folk just leave her alone. You'd be wise to do the same."

Zelda was always impeccably dressed, although her outward appearance would vary dramatically. She possessed an array of wigs and hair extensions, spectacles and jewellery. On consecutive days, she might be a nubile young blonde teenager, the next she was like her own mother with tightly permed grey hair, horn-rimmed glasses and a much older complexion. The trailer park folk paid no heed. She no doubt had her reasons.

She was a woman of independent means. Her parents had both died in the past six years and Will presumed that she lived off her inheritance. Certainly there was no evidence that she worked for a living, although she would leave the trailer park for weeks at a time. Sometimes the dog went with her; sometimes she left it at kennels nearby. He believed there had been a spell when she stayed inside her caravan for seven straight days without surfacing, even for a moment. Yes, she was truly a dang weirdo, Will reflected.

Zelda had been an attractive and sporty young woman. That, no doubt was what had attracted Loverboy to her, even if it was a decade ago. Ten years of bitterness and simmering resentment had left their mark.

Now though, as Loverboy appeared on screen again at Amelia Island, she knew that better days lay ahead. Amelia Island? Her Loverboy was now less than an hour away for the first time in all those years. A quick cab ride and Zelda could exorcise her ghost tonight. The thought brought a grim smile to her lips.

No, she reflected, Zelda would have some sport with Sport Armageddon. Loverboy would know despair just as she had. She had endured ten years of darkness. That would be a fair trade for ten days of fear. Already she was thinking ahead and just knew that she, Zelda, would be the curse of Loverboy and Sport Armageddon. She would be all their worst nightmares at once.

CHAPTER EIGHT

THAT evening at the Hyatt, Gaby Vaughan was helping herself to pasta and fruit in the competitor's hospitality room. During the day it served as a private room for individual media interviews. At night it doubled as a mini restaurant. She looked around for somewhere to sit. There was only one seat available and that was directly opposite the quiet British guy. Maybe he wanted to be on his own. Steve O'Neill had prised himself away from three consecutive room service meals in an attempt to be sociable but now he sat alone, head bowed, avoiding eye contact, as he sipped mineral water and picked at his lasagne.

"Mind if I join you?" Gaby smiled.

O'Neill looked up.

"Err, no. Be my guest." He braced himself for the inevitable session of small talk.

"Did you train today?" she asked as she sat down facing him.

"Uh huh."

"What did you do?"

"I swam six miles in the hotel pool and ran twenty miles."

"Where did you run?"

"A guy from the hotel showed me the Peachtree road race loop and I did that three times."

"Oh, I did that loop this morning. What time were you out there?"

"'Bout three o'clock this afternoon." O'Neill was not in the best frame of mind for validating happy coincidences.

"Are you biking tomorrow?" Vaughan could keep the questions coming all day long.

"Yup, a hundred miler. Want to join me?" Where the hell did that come from?

"Sure, I might only manage about seventy though. I have a run afterwards. I'm practisin' the transition."

"You can owe me the extra thirty then." She giggled. He looked up for the first time. She was quite beautiful. Massive blue eyes and glowing tan, with her hair damp and scraped back after a shower, a swim or something. He smiled and looked away. It was the first time in five days that he had smiled.

"What time are you setting off?" She peered at him quizzically.

"Ten o'clock from outside the front entrance."

"Great."

He wasn't conventionally handsome but there was something about him that reminded her of a certain other triathlete with whom she had once been close. The strong silent type with a hint of hidden depths and a faint twinkle in those sad old eyes. He looked tired though, very tired in a world-weary way rather than just training fatigue. His features were sharp but he had a warm, albeit rare smile. She would have to get to know him better before she could judge him properly. A 70 mile bike ride would be a very good start.

Leonid Karelov was not indoors. He was heading north out of town past the Woodruff Memorial Arts Centre. It was fast approaching ten o'clock but Karelov rode with a smirk on his face. Beside him was his friend Nemo, a Chicago-based Pole who described himself as Karelov's mentor. Despite the traditional enmity between Poles and Russians, Nemo had appeared at his side in Europe and the US during some of Karelov's greatest triumphs. He was a diminuitive grey haired, flinty-eyed individual in his fifties. He was as lean as a whippet and whilst he was undeniably fit – capable of matching Karelov on the bike and in the water, but not on the run because of an arthritic knee – his reputation was dubious.

Many eastern Europeans seeking fame and fortune on the American road running circuit had consulted him and all had shown dramatic improvement during a few weeks residence in the Nemo household.

"I am a motivator of men. They train like dogs when they are with me," he would assert when questioned about his coaching prowess. Dark mutterings remained, though. None of his charges had ever failed a drugs test but his despised reputation as a 'medicine man' endured.

Karelov's smirk remained. He believed he had already put one over on his more sophisticated opponents. Why on earth did they believe they should restrict their training to daylight hours when the important battles of Sport Armageddon would be won in the night? Only Karelov's body clock would be ready. He might have trained sparingly for two weeks while he pursued the Yankee dollars on the media circus but Karelov knew how to train smart as well as hard. Besides, he had his friend Nemo to help him. No man could stop him.

Karelov was actually wrong in assuming that he was the only nocturnal trainer, for Brent Ryan was going very strong on the mattress miles. In his suite at the Hyatt, Ryan lay back on the aforementioned mattress and stared at the ceiling lampshade. His mind drifted ahead to Thursday afternoon when at last he could fulfill his dreams. He pictured himself with an unassailable lead, cruising majestically through downtown Atlanta, the streets thronging with fellow Americans, all chanting his name. He pictured himself coming out of Lake Okeechobee in last place and then, one by one, picking off his opponents on the cycling and running phases. He pictured himself leading the whole way from the first stroke of the swim. Sometimes he would suffer unbearable fatigue and pain, sometimes he would perform like a machine but always, always, always, he would win.

And a million bucks...plus the publicity and endorsement spin-offs. He would be made for life. He would buy a ranch in Montana and take helicopter flying lessons so that he would be able to visit Los Angeles regularly. And the babes...how they would flock to him.

He felt a warm sensation by his ear lobe. One of the interim babes was having a nibble, perhaps eager for some more mattress mileage despite the intensity of their recent session. She had neatly styled blonde hair and a lithe figure but he was miles away and couldn't even remember her name. He reached out and stroked her thigh instinctively. She rolled towards him and began to kiss his other ear. Christine? Sharon? Tracey? Linda? Anne? Anne, that was it. She was the Prime Life girl who had been manning the Brent Ryan souvenir stand all week and now she was manning Brent Ryan himself.

He had scored her seven out of ten for the previous session but she went on to achieve an eight and an unprecedented nine before midnight. The following day, however, she came unstuck when she sought to cash in her scores with a tabloid newspaper. Her mistake was to approach Doug Alred of the Jacksonville Bugle first. He listened carefully to her story, making copious notes of all the salacious detail, promising to 'get back to her once he had spoken to his editor'.

Alred immediately reported the matter to Stein and later that same day, after an eyeball session from Stein, Annie left Prime Life's employment with 2000 dollars. Alred's reputation as a tame reporter endured and the matter was regarded as 'closed'. Brent Ryan was given a stern warning about his future conduct and he assured Prime Life that he would be celibate for the next three weeks. There were just three days to Sport Armageddon. It was all getting pretty serious.

Vivian Wheatley III had not wet himself since he was five years old as far as he could recall. The following morning however, he very nearly broke the habits of half a century. He leant against the windowsill and struggled to control his breathing. The room was spinning around him and he could only see it in black-and-white. Vivian Wheatley was scared.

He grabbed for the bedside telephone and frantically marshalled his thoughts.

"Yeah," said Stein tersely on the other end of the line.

"Chief, she's been in my room."

"Who has?"

"The mad woman that's being making the telephone threats."

"What?...When?"

"Just now. I've been in the shower for five minutes. I've come out and there's, there's a note on the bedspread and..."

"What does the note say?"

Wheatley did not have to look again at the note. In fact he found himself instinctively shying away from the bed towards the far corner of the room.

"It says 'the circus is closing down. Loverboy dies soon'. It's signed with a 'Z' and there's something else, something else..."

"What else?"

"She's left...She's left a dead rat with its eyes gouged out or somethin'. Oh, dear God. It's horrible."

"OK, OK. So it's not a prank. We gotta act fast. I'll ring down to reception and get the main exits sealed. I'll see you down there in two minutes."

The line went dead. Wheatley buried his face in his hands. He had always had a morbid fear of rats and this incident had chilled him to the marrow. She was in his room like some kind of ghost. How did she know it was his room? How did she know she would not disturb him? How did she get in? Most disturbingly of all, was it him she was planning to kill? As he muddled his way into his clothes, his mind was still in a whirl. What on earth could there be lurking in his past that could have so enraged this witch?

The hotel had co-operated with Stein's request to try and trap 'someone who had just stolen a valuable watch from his colleagues room'. The security staff made a thorough search of the premises in an attempt to uncover any unauthorised thirty-something lone female, possibly disguised as a chambermaid. At Lenny's express insistence, the police had not been called.

An hour later they had to conclude that the intruder had either made good her escape or was still in the hotel as a guest.

There had been dozens of single women checking in during the previous 24 hours. Many were no longer in residence. There were no new chambermaids. The hotel management would not release the names of the female guests without a police request to do so. Lenny did not push the point. Hell, it was the easiest thing in the world to give a bogus name and address and pay cash. He had himself, played 'Mr Smith' to a succession of southern belles at hotels throughout Georgia.

The forlorn Wheatley had the distasteful task of carefully disposing of the rodent evidence. He took the opportunity to check into another suite of rooms.

"We gotta tell the competitors," Wheatley insisted to his boss the next time they had the opportunity to discuss the incident in private.

"Why? It may just be you that she's after?"

Wheatley looked his boss in the eye. Stein returned the stare, unblinking.

"Well then, I'm going to go to the police. I don't know any women whose name begins with 'Z' and I haven't broken any hearts since I was in high school. She's a nutcase. I'm callin' the cops."

"Not until after the event finishes."

"But she's said she'll kill me before then."

"She hasn't. She's said she'll kill 'Loverboy'. It just happens that she left the advice note in your room."

"For God's sake, it still means trouble. She's after Ryan or some-

114

one. It could even be you that gets murdered."

Stein did not flinch.

"I have taken extra security measures. There is an Israeli-trained private security team that will cover the key players at Prime Life and all the competitors. They will shadow them round the clock starting from tomorrow morning and will ride with the contestants during the race. We will announce it to them at a briefing tonight. Then we must forget about this goddamn woman. She's a distraction. We need to stay focused on getting this event completely right, OK?"

Aside from the turbulence created by the 'Z' woman, Stein had decided to crank up the publicity machine.

The Sport Armageddon competitors and their coaches claimed that his most recent proposal was madness but Lenny merely reminded them of their contractual obligations to publicise the event.

"There's not even an argument about this," he argued at the briefing. "Its not like I'm asking you to travel great distances across the US. We just need to boost the race coverage in a couple of areas in Florida. Its been very mixed this past week."

"Your back-up team bikes and equipment will travel to Okeechobee by road. You'll meet up with them on Tuesday after we've flown via Tallahassee and Key Largo. I'm not asking you to fly long-haul."

He knew nothing about the final detail of elite pre-race preparations but he knew quite a lot about money and if Tallahassee and the Keys were now stumping up $10,000 for a last-minute road show appearance, he wasn't about to turn prissy on them. The competitors didn't need to know about the financial agenda. Their irritation was tempered with relief that he had decided not to try and lengthen the event by weaving the panhandle and southern extremities of Florida into the race route itself.

It was, however, news that added another layer of grey to Steve O'Neill's mood. He could not shake it off and complained bitterly about the change of plan to Gaby as they completed their final training run in Atlanta.

"I reckon it's because he wants to see how many media boys he can drag that far south. Just to test his popularity."

"I've noticed that it's the news hacks who attend our press conferences, not the sports correspondents. It's not being presented as a sports event. Looks to me like he's pitched us somewhere between the truck racing, 'Gladiators' and 'Baywatch' viewers."

Baywatch, yes, thought O'Neill. The bouncy Gabrielle Vaughan had at least brought more spring to his stride as they had regularly shared their training load for the past few days. It was not sufficient to raise his melancholy mood completely. Gaby felt she was getting to know him well but not well enough to ask him what it was that was keeping him so subdued. She liked him though and he appeared to enjoy her company. It was, she decided, by far the best option compared to the lecherous Karelov, the introspective PJ Kogo and the unbearably flash Brent Ryan.

Ryan had attempted to revive their former acquaintance during a brief interlude at the Hyatt weight training room. In normal times the room was a rather antiseptic and low-impact 'gymnasium' but Karelov and Ryan in particular had imbued it with the musk of human sweat.

Ryan had just completed a 30 minute upper body workout when the fuchsia clad Vaughan breezed in. They nodded to each other. They had not seen eye to eye in meetings at a number of triathlons around the world, mainly because Ryan's first point of reference was her chest. They did see eye to bust, as it were, and that was the main problem. She could read him like a book.

As he dabbed at perspiration on his neck with a towel, he gazed upon her taut body. It all came back to him. She straddled the bench press support. She could feel his eyes drilling through her as she began a set of fast repetitions.

As she finished, he was standing over her.

"All set for the trip to Tallahassee then?"

Opening chat-up lines remained a problem for him. He practised them just as assiduously as he practised removing a bra with one hand but it was a very haphazard business.

"Uh-huh."

"I've just done an upper body circuit. Is that what you're goin' for."

"Uh-huh."

"I reckon the cycle and swim are going to be as hard on the shoulders as the swim. Mine were killing me after Hawaii."

"Uh-huh."

"Don't reckon there's anything else I can do for my heart, lungs and legs."

He looked down. There was something he thought he could do for her but she was not a woman who responded well to unsubtle manoeuvres.

He took a step back.

"How long will you be working out?"

"About twenty minutes."

"Well, have a good one. Are you eating afterwards?"

"Yep, its a great pasta bake in the hotel restaurant."

"Would you care to join me?" Ryan was trying to sound casual.

"Well, actually I've already arranged to have dinner with Steve but do join us. We said we'd be there for eight o'clock." He could have sworn she was patronising him.

"Sure, might just do that. See you."

He strode from the room and felt the anger welling up. Damn. Steve O'Neill? That skeletal creep who doesn't even look at you when you talk to him? The finest babe in world sport was blowing him out in favour of that jerk. No way. And he didn't play gooseberry for anyone. It was room service pizza and beer for him that night.

He'd show those two colonial chums who was boss when the real action started on the Lake.

Then maybe 'Miss High and Mighty' would work out the pecking order for herself. With barely two days to the start of Sport Armageddon and Brent Ryan didn't just plan to win. He would whup their sorry-assed hides.

Stein might have been disappointed by the quality of the media turnout in Tallahassee but he knew of no such emotion. Instead, it was an obvious cue for blame and post-rationalisation.

"Come here, Viv," he hissed as they left the stage. Wheatley knew what was coming.

"I looked out into that audience and I saw nothing but hick reporters from crappy newspapers. Where were the national press and overseas TV guys?"

"A lot of them couldn't get flights to Tallahassee and a lot of them are seeing us down in Key Largo or West Palm Beach," Wheatley replied hastily, knowing from experience with Stein that anything said with conviction had at least half a chance of being believed.

"How many is 'a lot'?"

"'Bout thirty or forty guys, Chief," Wheatley lied at speed again.

Stein's eyes narrowed. Wheatley didn't like the look of it. He could feel a 'plan' coming.

"We need a stunt in Key Largo. We need something to get us on the front and back pages. I've invested too much in this baby to lose momentum less than two days before the start."

"Do you have any suggestions, Chief?"

Stein peered hard at his henchman. He almost sounded sarcastic but surely he wasn't deft enough to manage that?

"I'll tell you exactly what we need. We need some damn hatred between these competitors. They're acting like friggin' brothers-in-arms. Get one of them to attack one of the others and make it spectacular."

The Chief was probably right, Wheatley mused. A further level of hype was required, just to be certain. He would leak possible friction in the camp to some of his media buddies. A chartered plane and some fancy hotel suites in Key Largo for at least 20 of them should do the trick. The 'Z' woman was out of sight and out of mind. The Sport Armageddon rollercoaster was absorbing him fully once more.

The following evening's press briefing in Key Largo was sensational.

"Sport Armageddon will pass within fifty miles of here," Stein pronounced solemnly as if referring to a coronation procession. "I would expect the turn north to Miami and Fort Lauderdale to be the most crucial section of the whole event."

He had said exactly the same thing in Tallahassee the previous evening with reference to the bike-run transition at Jacksonville Beach. Truly, he was Billy Bullshit.

"With the start only hours away, I'm going to ask our competitors in turn, how they believe the race will develop at that point. Starting with our African star Philemon Kogo..."

PJ mumbled a few non sequiturs about taking his time on the swim, resting up and then playing catch-up. He glanced anxiously to O'Neill on his left by way of passing on the soul-searching baton.

O'Neill did not look up. "I would say that once the cycle stage comes out of the Everglades, the possibility of a slight breeze from the Atlantic will be most welcome. I gather we are also expecting very large numbers of roadside spectators through Miami so, if there is a clear leader, he or she will be able to draw on good support at that point."

Some of the press contingent appeared to be nodding off. Gaby Vaughan was due to speak after O'Neill. A case of the bland leading the blonde, if ever there was one. Stein seized the opportunity to pass the question on to Brent who was seated nearest the podium.

"Brent, would it be a sound tactic for one of the strong swimmers and bikers to have gotten a big lead at the Miami turn?"

"Sure, but don't forget, it could be real quiet between Fort Lauderdale and West Palm Beach on Highway A1A."

"Would you prefer to be well in command by that stage?"

"Definitely, and I think that's possible. I have prepared for it."

There was a loud snort from his right hand side. Ryan glared at Karelov who was sniggering.

"You got a problem, bud?"

"I have prepared for it," mimicked Karelov. "You are arrogant son-of-a-bitch," he continued in surprisingly smooth English. "Don't you realise this is a man's event and you are just a small stupid boy."

Vaughan and Ryan both stared at him.

"Typical American," Karelov continued, under his breath.

"What was that?" Ryan knew what he heard.

"You are a vain little boy. Like many Americans you become soft. When this event gets tough, you will go crying back to daddy."

Ryan was on his feet, alarmed at Karelov's dramatic embellishment of Wheatley's script. This was only partly choreographed. There was complete silence from the stunned media representatives.

The next phase, which Wheatley had indicated should be 'a scuffle with perhaps a shirt being ripped', went distinctly ad lib. The latent actor in Leonid Karelov sprang to life as he grabbed the mike stand from the table in front of him and swung it viciously at Ryan. Unfortunately, Ryan was just ducking his head to manhandle Karelov and the mike stand caught him a sharp blow across the temple. He slumped to the floor as the room's entire sound system crackled, fizzed and then shut down.

"It was an incident," wrote Dong Alred in the following day's front page lead in the Jacksonville Bugle "of startling savagery".

"No staged fight this. Ryan was detained in hospital overnight with suspected concussion and Karelov shouted insults at him as he was carried from the room. Police are looking into the episode, which appears to be a throwback to Karelov's tough adolescence. It is thought that Brent Ryan's injuries are not serious enough to delay the start of Sport Armageddon which is scheduled for 4 o'clock Eastern on Thursday.

The American public will no doubt side more strongly than ever with their own Brent Ryan. Extra security has been called in to protect the most reviled man in America, Leonid Karelov."

"Dumbass friggin' Commie," said Wheatley as he scoured the newspapers. "He nearly blew the whole thing."

"Dumbass nothing" replied Stein. "This is the finest publicity money can buy. We were even on CNN. Everyone knows about Sport Armageddon now."

Ryan's injuries were not serious. He was discharged from the hospital in Key Largo in time to catch the charter flight to Palm Beach International Airport. He asked the nurse to increase the size of the gauze on his lightly grazed forehead before facing the media throng at the hospital entrance.

Zing's marketing men were also pleased with the carefully contrived publicity machine that Prime Life had rolled out. Initially they had kept a slight distance from Sport Armageddon in case the brand was tainted with the whiff of made-for-TV junk sport. Now they took the opportunity to run a series of TV commercials based around their golden boy Brent Ryan. He was perceived as the glorious American under-dog who had been viciously undermined by a damn Ruskie. You could take the man out of the communist system but you couldn't take the communist system out of the man.

For the remainder of the contest, Karelov would be a man apart, his black-hatted isolation spotlighted by Stein's decision to surround him with a permanent posse of bodyguards. Indeed, as the other competitors arrived at West Palm Beach, Karelov was not with them. He would arrive later, courtesy of a helicopter chartered by National Enquirer who had pumped thirty thousand dollars into Prime Life's coffers for the exclusive on 'Karelov's rage at US golden boy.'

As Kogo stepped onto the tarmac at the airport, he reached out instinctively for Jennifer's hand. As she took it, she could feel that he was shaking. This swim, this wretched swim was driving her beloved husband to despair. She had told him over and over that it didn't matter if it took him a week to conquer the Lake. He was putting unnecessary pressure on himself. They talked about it again that night.

"It's not worth busting a gut over. Nothing is worth risking your health," Jennifer pleaded.

"Of course I must bust a gut. This is a race. I am a racer and I am the only representative for Africa. I must let nobody down. We have spoken of my pride, Jennifer."

His eyes were aflame. It wasn't a swim. It was a rite of passage. There did not seem to be anything she could say to soothe him.

"Look, just have a final chat with Coach Bell from the swim team at Riverside. You've listened to his advice up until now. I know the long practice swims haven't gone to plan but Coach will at least help get you in the right frame of mind."

She was already thumbing through her Filofax. If she couldn't get through to her husband, she knew a man that could.

Coach Bell had just finished the afternoon workout with the College team and was in a mellow mood. He had a lot of time for PJ and Jennifer and was glad to offer a last minute pep talk.

He and PJ talked, or rather Coach Bell talked and PJ listened for the best part of an hour. When it was over, PJ replaced the receiver and smiled.

"Perhaps I am wrong to be afraid. I have some tactics that will help me now. All will be well."

He took Jennifer's hand and they sauntered down to the bar, where some of his fiercesome opponents were enjoying a late supper.

Gaby Vaughan did not look especially fiercesome in her non-regulation white cheesecloth blouse and tailored jeans. O'Neill, was sprawled opposite her on the leather upholstery.

Gaby was becoming quite fond of him. Steve was very fond of her but neither wanted to be the first to betray their true emotions so the cosy meal-times and intense training sessions had continued with only minimal movement in the position of their respective trenches.

It was an implausible match. She was dribbled over by most sports jocks and fans in North America and she had spurned them all. She was drawn to the one man who showed minimal interest in her but who had a soul, like hers, that craved the challenge of endurance sport. She was physical perfection, vivacious and extrovert. He was skeletal, sullen and pensive. But in time honoured fashion, the mating game was working... slowly.

She felt emboldened to ask what it was that was troubling him.

He paused. "There is something," he said quietly. "I will tell you about it sometime."

And that was about as expansive as he was to be all evening. Gaby wished she had not asked but at least it appeared that he might trust her enough to confide his innermost fears. All in good time. She had a few secrets of her own that she might need to tell him.

Karelov had just finished his final cycle ride. He was ready to gorge himself on pasta and then rest right through to the race start.

He came out of the shower in his room and lay down on a couple of towels draped across the bed. Nemo set to work, pummelling lactic acid out of aching muscles and kneading life back in. He was a skilled masseur and Karelov trusted him implicitly. Karelov started to doze off as Nemo worked relentlessly on his tight shoulders and lower back. He lost all track of time but was brought back to life around 30 minutes later as a needle was jabbed into his buttock.

"Careful, you bastard," he muttered. "What's in it?"

"Why, vitamin B and iron, of course," Nemo laughed as he pumped the milky white fluid steadily into Karelov's bloodstream.

"Why do I have so much vitamin B?" Karelov was laughing as well.

"Because it makes you strong and helps you beat those goddamn Yankee soft boys."

They both continued their cackling and were still grinning as they made their way out into the warm Florida air, trailed discretely by bodyguards, in pursuit of West Palm Beach's finest lasagne, a short while later.

Brent Ryan was jabbing away too, but the target of his injection was Sharon, his love interest from the Best Western, Denver who had paid a surprise flying visit, believing she was his girlfriend. She had rung up to his hotel room on arrival, which gave him the five minutes that he needed to dispatch Anne of Prime Life, who was free to visit him at leisure now that she was off the organiser's payroll. As Anne's elevator descended to the lobby, Sharon's arrived at level 15 and two minutes later, she found herself sprawled on Ryan's floor, legs akimbo, underwear askew as they vented pent-up sexual energy. In Sharon's case it had been stored up for fully ten days. In Brent Ryan's case, it had been fully ten minutes since he had pleasured Anne, but what the hell. It was definitely his final mattress mileage before the race began.

Stein was making his way back by chauffeur-driven car to West Palm Beach from the final Prime Life technical meeting at Belle Glade. He was pleased that public interest was building dramatically during the final countdown.

As the meeting had closed, he and Wheatley had talked through the last-minute PR opportunities.

"'Zing' are really happy about the way things are going. I know it's meant to be a rest day for the competitors tomorrow but we need to get some more hype. Let's milk it for all we've got tomorrow. Have them meet the journos in small groups. Spread a few rumours about Ryan suing Karelov for two hundred thousand bucks. Say they've been fighting in the hotel. Tell 'em Kogo's descended from a tribal chief who's put a curse on the other guys. Tell 'em Gaby's had silicone implants."

Viv knew exactly what he had to do. He had come up with a photo opportunity of his own. A team of armed security officers would stand guard over a stack of a million one dollar bucks with the competitors lined up in front. The Prime Life lackies were already working ahead on all the towns that the cycle and run would pass through, but for now most eyes were on a still, calm section of water.

The Chief was not calm or still. He was in overdrive, bursting with ideas, hustling until the last advertiser's cheque was cashed.

Stein replaced the carphone receiver.

"How far from here?" he asked Eddie, the Prime Life limousine chauffeur.

"Should be back at the airport in around twenty minutes, Mr Stein," Eddie declared.

Lenny checked his watch. It was ten to eleven. Jack Daniels time. He reached forward and opened the walnut fronted drinks cabinet. He sprang back almost immediately as a dead rat dropped from the cabinet door to the car floor.

"Jesus Christ. What the..."

Eddie stopped the car immediately, leapt round and opened the rear passenger door. He stared at the floor.

"You OK, Mr Stein? Where the hell did that come from?"

Stein was staring too. His heart was racing. "The drinks cabinet. Eddie have you had the car all day?"

"Er, yeah, Mr Stein since I took you to Belle Glade at breakfast time."

"Where was it parked overnight?"

"The Airport car park."

"And have you been in it all day?"

"No, I had lunch at Domino's but it was locked outside."

Stein noticed a cassette tape in the drinks cabinet. He looked at it for a moment. He was fighting to get his head straight. He had forgotten all about the mad woman but now she had penetrated the heart of the organisation again. Like a ghost.

She was playing games with them – and Stein was on the losing side. He didn't like it. He was starting to think rationally again. What if the cassette was an explosive device? If she had wanted to, maybe she could have killed him already. Who was this woman? What did she want?

"Eddie could you give me a few moments, please. I'll call you once I've played this cassette." His composure was returning.

Eddie had seen the tape too. He flicked on the hazard lights and strolled back down the highway verge to light a cigarette.

Stein slipped into the driving seat, put the tape in the deck and hit the play button. He fancied he could hear some 'New Age' music in the background. It sounded like wind chimes.

"You know who this is, don't you Leonard? It's 'Z'. Just little old me, Lenny, your worst nightmare. Hi. You know we're not just counting down to the circus. We're counting down to checkout time. I could have taken out Loverboy anytime, anywhere but I want the big stage. I want to tease and torment you. It's coming to Loverboy. It's coming soon and you'll do me such a big favour by having the world's media there. It's coming soon. Bye, Bye Lenny."

There was no more. Stein hit the stop button.

Was it him she was after? Was this the warped revenge of one of his long-forgotten conquests? Was it for one of the competitors? Was it one of the Prime Life staff? He suddenly felt vulnerable and alone.

"Let's go, Eddie," he shouted and slipped across to the passenger seat.

Sport Armageddon was ready to roll. Lenny switched on the car air vent to help wick away the sweat that was beading on his forehead and neck. He was running scared but there could be no turning back. Stein had come too far. He just needed time to think.

CHAPTER NINE

THE morning of the Race from Hell was spent in a variety of ways by the million dollar aspirants of Sport Armageddon. They were based at the Hilton Hotel next to Palm Beach International Airport.

Leonid Karelov believed he was the smartest operator of them all. Over the previous few weeks, he had been gradually adjusting his body clock, getting used to less and less sleep. Where possible, he had scheduled 5 am to 11 am as his range for sleep and on race start day, he had refined this further by taking to his bed at 6 am to sleep to beyond noon and awake refreshed for the final count-down.

PJ Kogo had hardly slept a wink all night despite his new 'plan'. The Lake Okeechobee swim would be a defining moment for him but he also feared Prime Life's reaction to his tactics, and Lenny Stein's wrath in particular. He lay on the bed in his hotel room, watching the event previews on TV, trying to convince himself that he was a legitimate contender. He dozed, he visited the bathroom endlessly, he sipped electrolyte drinks and munched energy bars. He talked through all the permutations with Jennifer.

"The fact is that I do not feel very well at all. I don't know if I have fully recovered from some of those hard training swims. I think I am coming down with something. I am not sure I should be doing this."

They were the usual pre-event doubts of an athlete but PJ, who had no qualms at all about soccer or running, always had them in abundance before the swimming phase of a triathlon.

Jennifer had seen it all before and offered words of reassurance. She was quite certain that, as soon as he was underway, all his phantom ailments would miraculously fade. That was if Lenny Stein, the old African stereotyper, had not bludgeoned PJ to death over Coach Bell's secret racing plan. Now that did worry her.

Steve O'Neill had enjoyed a fitful night's sleep. His mind was still troubled and he resolved to do something about it on his return to Scotland. He hoped this contest would purge him of his worries and that a shrink would not need to get involved. Maybe he could make a fresh start. Maybe his friendship with Gaby would survive the event. Maybe the dark skies would lift. Maybe...

He had a large bowl of porridge with brown sugar and sliced banana for breakfast and sipped diluted orange juice. There were six hours to go. The waiting time was the hardest time of all.

Gabrielle Vaughan was busy fussing over the logistical operation that would follow for the next ten days or so. She went over it for the third time with Jane and Patsy who had been assigned to her all-women back-up team by Prime Life.

"Two spare wetsuits, goggles, Vaseline, drinks, food hamper, first aid kit, hair dryer and thermal blankets for the support boats. Clothing, spare bikes, ultrasound machine, massage table and oils for the support bus in readiness for the cycle."

"Correct," said Jane and Patsy in unison.

"Support services – laundry, accommodation list, medical back up all been checked?"

"Check," they chorused.

"I reckon we're about ready, don't you?" said Patsy to Gaby.

"Yes. Ready as I'll ever be."

Brent Ryan had enlisted the help of a sports psychologist as a member of 'Zing Team Ryan', his back-up crew. He had insisted on taking Brent by helicopter to the shores of Lake Okeechobee at dawn the day before the race.

They had stood on top of the levee and gazed out over the Lake's 730 square miles. The opposite shore was invisible. It lay more than 30 miles away. He had deliberately chosen a section of the Lake away from where the Sport Armageddon route would pass.

They lay against the grassy bank. The sun was already deadly.

"What do you see, Brent?" the good doctor enquired. He had been much impressed in his youth by the old boy who posed the tricky, mystical questions to the hapless 'Grasshopper', his Kung-Fu TV protÈgÈ.

Brent looked at Dr Psychobabble. He was not in the mood for mind-games but he was shelling out 400 bucks a day for this guy's services so he ought to play along.

"A huge expanse of water."

"Close your eyes."

Brent did as he was told again.

"Breathe slowly and deeply in through your nose and exhale to the count of three."

Brent did as he was told.

"As you breath out, listen for the sounds of Okeechobee."

For two or three minutes, he listened, and picked up the distant sounds of the Lake's bird population and the gentle lapping of the water on the shore.

He felt warm and pleasantly relaxed. They had practised this technique.

"It's not a huge expanse of water," the doctor whispered in his ear. "It's not even a lake." He paused.

Ryan continued to breathe deeply and evenly with his eyes shut.

"It's a pathway. It's a channel."

A longer pause.

"It's a pathway to the stars and it will admit only one person. The eyes of the whole sporting world are upon you. The hopes of the whole of the USA rest with you."

Ryan was breathing more quickly.

"But it's not a burden, it's an honour. An honour that only you can carry off. An opportunity of a lifetime and you are ready for it. You are supremely fit. You could not possibly be better prepared. All of your life has led to this point. Now you are ready to seize your destiny. You are relaxed. You are ready. You are a winner." A smile was playing at the edge of Ryan's lips.

"Keep breathing slowly and deeply. Picture the moment when you step on to the pathway. Imagine the first strokes of this unique journey. Imagine the last few yards. There will be no fatigue. Nothing can stop you know. You are too many training miles ahead of all the others. You are a winner. Your time is now. Open your eyes. Let's go."

As they headed back to the helicopter, Ryan felt light and exhilarated but strangely the image he could not eliminate was of Gaby Vaughan struggling just behind him. She would not last long. He knew he would win Sport Armageddon.

Lenny Stein had decided to call the final meeting of all the competitors at one o'clock on race day, just before they were transported to the start. He wanted to keep the announcement low-key and informal, so he briefed Melanie to convey the necessary information.

"I'll sit in at the back of the room honey, but you let them know real casually about this little problem. Play it right down."

The meeting was attended by all of the competitors and their support crews. They sat in separate groups and most of the contenders avoided eye contact with each other. There was, after all, barely three hours to the witching hour.

Vivian Wheatley outlined the procedure that would be followed. The support crews would travel ahead by road to the Lake with the competitors following later by helicopter – mostly for dramatic effect. When he had completed the formalities, he shuffled his sheaf of briefing notes.

"OK guys, listen up. Melanie's gonna talk you through some extra security measures that we are going to introduce once the race is under way."

Melanie stood up and walked to the centre of the room.

"One of the problems with holding a high profile event in public areas," she began, "is that you cannot control a determined nutcase trying to spoil the event. All of you are experienced triathletes; you know how you can be inconvenienced by wayward vehicles or ill-disciplined spectators once you are out of the water.

"Since we launched Sport Armageddon earlier this year and began publicising the event, there was always the chance that someone could try to hijack it or try to manipulate it for publicity of their own.

"It has been a long time coming but in the last week or so, we have received two messages from a woman threatening to kill someone during the event. We do not take her particularly seriously. It's only been a couple of ranting telephone calls so far..."

She glanced at Lenny. He could not look at her. Melanie was sure there must be more to it than that, otherwise the Chief would not even have put it on the agenda. Still, those were her instructions.

"She has raged about someone that she calls 'Loverboy'. The phone calls have been brief. We have no extra information at present. As a precaution, Prime Life is assigning an extra security guard who will travel with your support vehicles once the swim is completed. We can do no more than that. In your contracts, you have acknowledged that your personal safety is ultimately your own responsibility.

"We would like to trace this woman and if she is known to any of you then please notify us immediately.

"She sounds as though she is in her twenties or thirties. She speaks with an educated American accent, possibly local. She may have the initial letter 'Z' in her first name. We don't know too much else."

There was no outward reaction to any of this news from the individuals assembled within the room but three hearts beat slightly quicker and the tiny hairs on the backs of three necks stood on end.

The realisation suddenly hit them and the same thought flashed. 'Z' was coming for them after all these years.

At two o'clock precisely, the helicopter took off from Palm Beach Airport. On board were just the five competitors and Vivian Wheatley. It would be a 20 minute flight.

While Stein was keen for maximum publicity and competitor access for the media, he had directed that the competitors be left to themselves for the final hour before the start.

He hoped to generate some sort of mystique and tension by keeping them removed from the press during the final countdown. Once the event was underway, there would be a strict protocol permitting only Prime Life to conduct TV interviews with competitors.

On the helicopter, the competitors were clad in tracksuits styled in their designated racing colours. No one spoke. Kogo, sipping water, appeared terrified, O'Neill sullen, Vaughan serene, Karelov jut-jaw determined and Ryan confident. They were about to find out which was justified.

Beneath them, a stream of support vehicles and media cars was threading its way north on Highway 98. Prime Life's television output for the day had reached almost fever pitch, albeit with frequent commercial breaks. Okeechobee had never known anything like it. The Grove Beach area had been popular for days. The Blue Cypress Golf and RV Resort was at maximum occupancy. Even Mrs Davis's Palm Reading service was doing record business, although she claimed to have seen it coming. Okeeburgers were the haute cuisine dish of the day.

The helicopter touched down on private land just outside the Rim Canal near Taylor's Creek.

As the door of the helicopter swung open, a Prime Life lens poked in. The scene that greeted the competitors was pandemonium. There must have been a few hundred media personnel from around the world and several thousand spectators swarming on the levee and the narrow foreshore. They walked smartly to the large marquee just back from the water's edge. This would now be the final holding zone in the 30 minutes to the start.

Wheatley and two security guards quickly hustled them into the sanctuary of the tent.

Outside, the local radio station was booming out Del Amitri's 'Kiss this Thing Goodbye', as the road show disc jockey did his best to whip the crowd to even greater enthusiasm. Brent Ryan's name was mentioned frequently and more than half the crowd seemed to be wearing their green 'GO USA' T-shirts and singlets.

The temperature was 91 degrees.

A large video screen was positioned at the top of the levee, showing Prime Life's live transmission. There was a buzz of expectancy about the place as the clock in the corner of the screen ticked down to 15 minutes to go.

It was cramped inside the tent. Few words were exchanged. Karelov had changed into his racing wetsuit in full view of everyone. He had his eyes closed while Nemo administered a final shoulder massage.

Gaby Vaughan had slipped into her racing costume rather more discreetly behind a partition and was applying sunscreen to her face. She remained pert and poised even in an outfit that made her look like a pink penguin.

O'Neill was in one corner on an upright chair. His head was bowed. Music played on his personal stereo but it could not dissipate his melancholy. He swigged from a bottle of mineral water and prayed for release when the gun sounded.

Ryan was busying himself in the centre of the tent with an elaborate set of callisthenics. These, he had been told, would optimise blood flow to the muscles most prone to fatigue around the shoulders and neck. Nemo eyed him suspiciously. Dr Psyche returned the stare on behalf of the USA and the free world.

PJ Kogo was struggling to maintain his composure. Jennifer had scrutinised the rule book, such as it was, for Sport Armageddon. There was nothing to prevent him taking his planned course of action, but he feared the Prime Life response. He must do what he had to do.

A smartly dressed waitress from the catering company was discreetly serving black coffee, bananas and chocolate to the competitors.

"OK guys, quiet please." Wheatley was shouting to a silent tent. The hubbub was all outside.

"There's just over ten minutes to go. I'd like all of the friends and supporters to move outside right now. Then Lenny Stein is goin' to take up the microphone and introduce you one by one. Please wait inside until you hear your name and then come out waving. There will then be just a couple of minutes when you must stand still behind the start line. The cannon will start you at four o'clock precisely. Everybody got that? Good luck to all of you. Let's make it a good one, OK?"

As the hangers-on slid out of the tent one by one, Wheatley moved round the contestants. A silent handshake to PJ and Steve O'Neill. An unacknowledged 'good luck' to Karelov. An unrequited kiss on the cheek for Gaby Vaughan and a hearty hug and whispered 'Go USA' to Brent Ryan that might as well have been delivered to a block of ice. These were highly tuned athletes standing at the edge. They were in their own little worlds and his presence was an intrusion. The blend of fear and anticipation was palpable.

Wheatley strode out of the tent and gave a thumbs-up signal. Stein took his cue.

"Ladies and gentlemen," he boomed into the roving microphone. "History is about to be made. Five of the most gifted endurance athletes in the world will pit themselves against the ultimate challenge and swim, cycle and run from here to Atlanta, Georgia. The prize is the ultimate – one million dollars – winner takes all. For months we have awaited this moment and now it is upon us. Let Sport Armageddon begin."

There was a crescendo of applause and chants of 'U-S-A, U-S-A'.

"First will you welcome, the challenger from Africa. An endurance athlete in the finest traditions ... From Kenya ... P ... J ... Ko ... go."

PJ stepped out, blinking into the sunlight, gave a nervous wave and moved to the left hand side of the start line, beneath a gantry smothered in sponsor's logos and housing TV cameras. A digital clock recorded five and a half minutes to go.

"From the east of Europe, one of the toughest warriors in world sport..." The booing had already begun. "Please welcome Leonid Karelov of Russia." Karelov grinned and gave a double handed wave in response to the jeers and cheers.

"The only female competitor in Sport Armageddon is from Sydney, Australia. She's here to prove a point... Gaby Vaughan."

There were a couple of wolf whistles from the crowd as she twinkled to the start line, her blonde locks tucked inside the wetsuit hood. Karelov towered above her on the start line.

"Great Britain has a fine heritage in endurance events and the old country has sent its very best challenger to fight for one million dollars... Steve O'Neill."

A cursory wave, generous applause and O'Neill strode briskly to the line.

"Last and by no means least, you will have read of the difficulties faced by the American challenger but he's here and ready to do battle. I'm sure you'll want to give a great welcome to the USA's contender... Brent Ryan!"

There was a deafening roar as Ryan, wearing his sponsor's wrap-round shades, took centre stage both arms aloft, waving to his massed supporters on all sides. He grinned broadly. They loved him.

A throng of accredited photographers was admitted to the front of the start line to take the last pictures on dry land for the following morning's newspapers. Vivian Wheatley noted with relief that there was not a deranged looking woman among them. They had been briefed that they would be allowed precisely one minute to complete this task as the competitors fidgeted nervously and gazed out across the Lake. Inevitably, the photographers craved more time and Wheatley had to help the security staff hustle then back behind the barriers with less than 90 seconds to go.

"Good luck to you all. May the best fighter win," Stein boomed, "I would ask for silence for the final minute before the start and then we will count you down over the last twenty seconds. Quiet please for the start of Sport Armageddon."

Miraculously, the whole foreshore fell instantly silent. It was a curious, pregnant lull, punctuated only by the helicopter high above, the whir of photographers' camera drives and the engines of the support craft putt-putting out on the Lake.

O'Neill stared at the horizon. Kogo gulped nervously. Vaughan took a final swig of energy drink. Ryan flexed his shoulders one more time. Karelov grinned.

"Twenty..." the silence was broken by Stein, "...nineteen, eighteen..." Gradually more of the crowd joined in and a cheer begun to rise as they kept time with the countdown clock on the giant screen and the start gantry.

"Nine, eight, seven, six, five, four, three, two, one..."

The four o'clock time signal sounded and a fraction of a second later, the ornamental cannon detonated dramatically from the top of the levee.

"Sport Armageddon has begun," yelled Lenny Stein. The crowd roared.

Four contestants surged across to the water's edge. Karelov, sprinting, hit the water first just ahead of Ryan. O'Neill and Vaughan followed a short distance behind. Kogo stood motionless behind the start line.

Geoff Wightman

CHAPTER TEN

NOT all of the whooping crowd realised that PJ had failed to start. Many had an obscured view. Many were cheering for the sheer hell of it, without properly appreciating what had happened.

As Karelov headed out with a powerful front crawl action between the buoys marking the swim route, some people were in no doubt. Hal 'The Mouth' Morris, the lead commentator for Prime Life's event coverage spluttered into the microphone.

"From my position on the start gantry, I can hardly believe my eyes. The rest of the field is just one hundred yards across the Lake and we appear to have lost twenty per cent of our starters already! Kogo is walking slowly back to the tent. I think he has pulled out of the race altogether. He had serious doubts about the swim and his ability to go the distance but this will be a devastating blow to his supporters if he fails to mount any challenge at all. What an extraordinary start to this extraordinary event."

By the time PJ had reached the tent, Jennifer was back at his side and gently took his hand. They disappeared inside, moments ahead of Stein and Wheatley who had dashed across the shore spectacularly. Stein shot into the tent. Wheatley paused at the entrance and bent double. Damn! He had popped his knee. Why did these setbacks always befall ex-athletes? What a thin red line it was between supreme fitness and the injury scrap heap. He cursed. Stein stuck his head through the awning.

"Viv, watch the door and don't let any press boys in until I've sorted this out," he ordered.

Mr and Mrs Kogo were seated at the far side of the tent and Jennifer was rummaging through her husband's sports bag for a couple of energy bars.

"What the hell do you think you're doin' son?" The veins on Stein's temples were bulging as he stalked across the marquee.

Kogo looked up but said nothing.

"I can't believe you've done this. In full view of ten thousand people here and millions around the world – you've wimped out. What's the matter with you?"

Kogo continued looking but still said nothing.

"I guess I had you all wrong, son. I thought you were a friggin' winner but you're not. You're a chicken. I'll sue your ass for this." Stein was breathing hard from the dash to the tent and the anger he felt. PJ was completely calm.

"What's the matter with you? Are you sick or just plain yellow?"

Kogo maintained his gaze.

"I go at eight o'clock," he said quietly.

"What?"

"I go at eight o'clock."

"What? What do you mean?"

"The temperature will be much cooler then. My plan is to swim as much as possible in the night air." Stein paused to allow the apoplexy to subside slightly.

"For Chrissake. Why didn't you tell me that?"

"Would you have agreed anyway? It would have spoiled the symmetry of the start."

He had a point but Stein's mind was racing ahead. Damage limitation was not really the objective. It was more a question of trying to turn a negative into a positive.

"Are you gonna stay here in the tent until eight o'clock."

"Certainly."

"You'd better. You owe us one."

Lenny paced up and down the middle of the tent. The other TV stations would have a field day with this development unless it was pitched the right way. His media rivals had already opened a book quoting even-money odds on none of the competitors making it as far as Atlanta.

He sat down on one of the flimsy canvas chairs. To one side was the remainder of the coffee in a glass jug. It would take him a few minutes to come up with plan B and he reached across to pour himself a coffee. His arm froze in mid-air before he could even pick up the jug. He stared in horror at the half-empty phial of clear liquid propped up against the coffee. Beneath it was a scrap of paper with a scribbled message:

'Yes, it's poison. The circus has begun. Z.'

Stein felt sick and faint. The waitress. It must have been the goddamn waitress. She was the Z woman. Almost all of the competitors would have taken a last drink of coffee. Z had been right there in their midst and had administered poison ten minutes before the start. He buried his head in his hands but almost immediately stood bolt upright. The Kogos must not know of this latest development. PJ and Jennifer were at the far corner talking quietly to each other. They were not looking his way. He turned his back on them, wrapped the phial in a napkin and walked towards the marquee awning.

At the entrance, the ample frame of Vivian Wheately III threw a large shadow across the width of the canvas and a large barrier to the thronging masses of the Fourth Estate.

"Step inside a moment, Viv."

Wheatley edged inside the tent keeping the flap firmly shut.

"Kogo's going to start late but there's worse news," Lenny whispered in his ear. "The mad woman has been here. She must have got in disguised as a waitress. It looks like she may have poisoned the coffee."

Wheatley's face drained. He had drunk two cups himself.

"Get this liquid analysed and find out if Kogo took any. We can get his stomach pumped but if she really did it then the other swimmers will be dead in the water before we can get to them. I have a hunch she's bluffing. She's only after one person."

Wheatley was speechless as the napkin was pressed into his hand.

In spite of everything, Stein affected a nonchalant air as he strode out towards the press. Microphones homed in on him from all directions.

"I am afraid fellas, this will be the first of our Prime Life exclusive bulletins. You'll have to watch the Diamond Vision screen if you want to know what's happenin'."

He beckoned to the shore-based Prime Life crew to accompany him back to the tent. Wheatley had not moved from the awning. He was staring down at the napkin, his other hand pressed against his stomach.

Stein ignored Wheatley and the Kogos as he swept back in with the cameraman and sound boom operator.

It would also be the first unscheduled test of Prime Life's massive outside broadcast system, which was intended to move seamlessly between their land, water, air, studio and roving cameras. Hal the Mouth made the transition for the benefit of Prime Life viewers including those watching on the giant screen...

"Well, as Leonid Karelov of Russia maintains his thirty second advantage over the chasing pack, we cut back to the start to find out about the story of the race so far, namely the Kenyan, Kogo's failure to even enter the water. With him in the competitor's assembly tent is the Sport Armageddon President and Prime Life CEO, Leonard Stein. Can you hear me, Mr Stein?"

"Yes, loud and clear."

"Can you tell us the reason for PJ Kogo's no-show?"

"Yes, I can Hal. We have always billed Sport Armageddon as the ultimate battle of hearts and minds. You need to be brave but you also need to be clever to win a million dollars. Kogo has decided that his chances are hugely improved if he undertakes the first phase of this marathon swim closer to dusk. He will begin at 7.45 precisely. I believe it is an intelligent decision but one that requires a steely nerve. He is effectively giving away up to ten miles to all of his rivals in the hope of conserving his energy for later stages. It might work well for him. Certainly we will keep a camera here to see him on his way at 7.45 just before the main evening news bulletin on Prime Life." And before the newspaper deadlines, he thought, publicity instincts still intact despite the fear factor.

"So you have known of his intention for some while."

"Of course. But in the interests of fairness and impartiality, it would not have been right to let any of his opponents know of his plan. I am glad it is now out in the open. Would you like to speak to Kogo?"

"Yes, is he there?" Asked Hal the Mouth.

Stein dug an elbow into PJ's ribs just to the right of the camera. There was a huge cheer as his sombre features were nudged into frame on the Diamond Vision screen.

"PJ, you must be feeling very confident about your swimming ability to let everyone else have this sort of head start," said Hal.

"No, I am not a strong swimmer. I will be treating this one long distance as a series of shorter distances and taking a good rest between each phase. Once I have overcome the swim, I believe I have the endurance to do well on the cycle and run."

"But just how big a lead do you think you can give someone like Leonid Karelov and still be competitive?"

"Four hours is nothing compared to the many days of Sport Armageddon. It will be playing 'catch-up' after the swim. It will make it interesting."

It friggin' well will, thought Stein and if there was any more nonsense of this kind from PJ Kogo, he would see how interesting a double dose of arsenic and a prize money retention would be.

PJ emerged again from the tent at 7.44 pm. He would like to have waited those few extra minutes but he recognised a slap when it was on its way. He pulled up the hood of his wetsuit and adjusted his goggles. There was a great reception from almost all of the large crowd who had waited on, fuelled by pizza and beer. He gave a thumbs up to his support crew out on the Lake, waved and grinned to the crowd as he sprinted for the water. The light was still good and the air temperature a little lower as he glided out. He planned to alternate front crawl and breaststroke once he was out of sight – Stein's sight in particular – but for now he felt strong. As Jennifer urged him on from of the support boat, he thought of the massive physical challenge that lay ahead. PJ's Sport Armageddon was now truly underway and on his own terms.

It was not the sort of start which Lenny Stein had intended but with no adverse effects reported in the first four hours of swimming, he breathed a sigh of relief that Z's latest stunt was no more that that. Preliminary analysis by one of the medical support teams had shown that Z's phial contained nothing more poisonous than sugared water. His enquiries of the Catering Company revealed that there was not meant to be any waitress service provided with the refreshments. Nobody had really noticed what she looked like – blonde, bespectacled and unremarkable was the consensus. She had disappeared like a ghost again; Stein hated her and resolved to destroy her.

Up ahead, Karelov was still churning through the water. He was around seven minutes clear of Ryan in second. Vaughan was a further two minutes behind but taking a break. O'Neill brought up the rear five minutes back.

Gaby Vaughan lay on the floating pontoon. All of her support craft were anchored up at the direction of the race referee. Her alligator-shooting outrider, with the incongruous pink headband on his big game hunter's hat, switched his gaze from the smooth surface of the water to the smooth surface of her wetsuit. With her blonde hair tucked out of sight she was more pink shrimp than mermaid. Her shoulders ached and Patsy ministered to them. She had only planned a three minute break to take on board some liquid carbohydrate but the neck massage felt so good that she decided to wait on for Steve to catch up. Perhaps they could swim an hour or two together and lend each other some moral support through the graveyard shift.

O'Neill was having a terrible time. Although no one on his support boat was a friend or acquaintance, they could sense that all was not well. His technique would alternate between an exaggeratedly slow front crawl to sudden wild thrashes for 30 seconds at a time. His mind was playing tricks on him.

On several occasions he caught a fleeting glimpse of a giant bass, or 'lunker' as the angling community referred to them. Every single time he was convinced it was an alligator heading for him and immediately panicked. When the underwater cameraman from Prime Life passed beneath him on the lake bed 14 feet below, he thought he would have a heart attack.

With the sheer monotony of the opening hours of the swim, his depressed frame of mind threatened to overwhelm him. Time and again, his thoughts flashed back to the days that had first brought on the darkness. He had been responsible for the death of a child. There was not a single day or night of his life that went by when that thought did not come back to haunt him. And always he could see the eyes of the child's mother as she left the courtroom. The father was ranting and raving from the public gallery: "You're nothing but scum. We face a life sentence and you just walk away scot free from here."

The mother had said nothing. Her eyes and her tears said it all. There were days when he wished himself dead in return for the child. There were days when he trained so hard he nearly collapsed in his attempt to outrun the anguish but it was always, always there.

It had been ten years and two months ago. Shortly after eight o'clock in the evening. Marie Bowen, aged five had been playing with friends near her home in Guildford, Surrey.

She stepped between two parked cars to retrieve a frisbee from the road. A gust of wind blew it a couple of yards further into the carriageway and she dashed forward to retrieve it. She was killed instantly as a VW Beetle driven by Steve O'Neill caught her with its nearside wing.

He was breathalysed at the scene and tested positive, right on the legal limit of 35 micrograms of alcohol per 100 millilitres of blood. By the time he got to the police station, it showed negative by breath test and blood analysis. It was the considered view of the Crown Prosecution Service that he should face no charges for a potential drink-drive offence but he was tried for driving without due care and attention. He was acquitted, with the magistrates deciding that although the consequences of his driving were horrific, his handling of the vehicle was within reasonable objective standards.

The Bench Chairman, sensing distress in the dock as well as the public gallery, said that it was a ghastly accident that could not have been avoided in the circumstances. His remarks set off uproar from the family of Marie Bowen. The local newspaper and radio reported the proceedings in full and made great play of the 'marginally legal' breath test that they had discovered.

O'Neill's recollections of that period were a haze of tears, despair and guilt. He was still alone and the blackness of it all never seemed to take a break. He had lost all contact with the other school friends with whom he had enjoyed a couple of drinks on an empty stomach that lunchtime. He had completely reinvented himself in the intervening years and not necessarily for the better. If only he could turn back the clock or snap out of the never-ending trough.

It had taken him under yet again when he arrived in Florida and yet the worst news of all had hit him earlier that very day. At the final briefing meeting, his had been one of the racing heartbeats when the 'Z' woman's death threats were revealed. Marie Bowen's mother was American and her name was Zoe.

O'Neill felt the clunk of heavy-duty plastic against his forehead. Despite frantic shouts from his and her crews, O'Neill had very skillfully swum right into the back of Gaby Vaughan's floating pontoon.

It was approaching 10 o'clock on Day One. Sport Armageddon was six hours old and he had never felt more in need of companionship.

The impact had not hurt but Gaby leant from the side of the pontoon and kissed his forehead. This was progress indeed.

"How are you, buddy?" She grinned. The girl was 100 kilowatts of pure energy.

"Fine, thank you," he lied.

He began to hoist himself inelegantly onto her pontoon but the commotion that broke out from the Prime Life officials on both support boats reminded him that he could only take a break on his own platform. O'Neill slid sheepishly back into the water and re-emerged on his own float which was positioned diagonally behind Gaby's.

He reached for a chocolate bar and carton of milk from the support boat. This, he felt, would be the best for his grumbling guts.

"Actually, I don't feel that great. Apart from everything else, I've got stomach cramps. I don't think the water here is too pure. How far have we got?"

They checked with the marshals and learned that they were almost exactly at 13 kilometres. They were less than one third of the way through the swim distance. It was a very daunting prospect. Karelov, they heard, was swimming like a machine way up ahead. The Prime Life helicopter hovered directly above them and sent urgent ripples across the surface as it used its night-vision facility to record the happy couple and update its leaderboard caption.

"C'mon mate," said Gaby. "Let's swim side by side for a couple of hours. Do you think you can go right through to twelve o'clock without stopping? We can take a break then. I just feel we really need to get over the halfway point. This is bloody hard."

"Let's go," said O'Neill and they were away, preceded by their respective posses of support crew, sharpshooters, security guards and marshals – a small flotilla of environmentally-friendly boats towing their mobile homes. Behind them the lady in pink and the man in gold swam in perfect synchronisation. It soothed O'Neill's troubled mind slightly to share the workload as they pressed on towards the midnight hour.

Lenny Stein slept fitfully that night. After the nonsense with Kogo, he had followed the race from a motor launch for an hour, before joining the Prime Life helicopter on a couple of sorties. Then he had taken to his bed at Pahokee. It might, he decided, prove to be his last night's sleep in a proper bed because he planned to spend most of the race in the outside broadcast bus. It would link with Atlanta HQ to control the Prime Life output. The huge vehicle contained a couple of camp beds that would be used in rotation. Apart from the cramped nature of the accommodation, the main disadvantage was that it was shared by Hal 'The Mouth', who seemed to reach decibel peaks of excitement approximately every ten minutes – in an event that was likely to last more than a week. Before he retired, he received confirmation of three more private detectives joining the payroll. They would work round the clock and were already mingling with the crowds at Pahokee. Lenny could not altogether eliminate the possibility that her target was him. Whoever she was stalking, it could ruin his event. This was one deadly game that Stein could not afford to lose.

He was soaked in sweat when he awoke. As a man without a conscience, sleep usually came very readily. On this occasion, he had experienced a vivid nightmare in which none of the positions in the race changed from Day One to the finish. It would be a procession that would turn off the viewers and his beloved advertisers in droves. He had a vision of Karelov's ugly face thrusting further and further ahead of his American golden boy. It could not be allowed to happen. He switched on the TV. Hal 'The Mouth' was jolting the six o'clock Prime Life viewers wide awake.

"...Now Brent Ryan is forced to take a break at last as his bid to close the gap on Karelov runs out of steam. I think Ryan's back-up team was assuming that the Russian would be out of the water for longer than the six minute break he took at 4 am. So, as we watch Ryan taking a well deserved pit stop, Karelov has the chance to extend his lead of almost three quarters of a mile. He looks fantastic. This man who took a slug at Ryan last week is powering away from the field and heading for the final few hours of this mammoth swim phase."

Stein scowled and picked up the phone to his henchman Wheatley, in a room just down the corridor, who was in a very deep slumber. He could not operate at his sleek and sparkliest best without at least seven hours of night-time sleep. It was some while before he remembered who he was and that the ringing noise was not just in his head.

Stein was talking before he could even get the receiver to his ear.

"You won't have seen it but Karelov is friggin' fifteen minutes clear of Ryan. We need to do something. Get the helicopter to pick us up outside the hotel at seven. We need to have something developing in time for the breakfast show audience."

By the time the helicopter took to the air, Stein had hatched at least three bad ideas and two good ones. He was going to pep up Day Two of Sport Armageddon.

At precisely 8.10 am, the sharpshooter on Karelov's red liveried lead boat sprang to his feet and dispatched four rounds from his high-velocity rifle into the water just behind Karelov. The last one missed the swimmer by inches.

Simultaneously, there were shouts from the referee's craft, which backed towards him at speed. Nemo, who knew nothing of any pre-arranged stunt, leapt into the water to rescue his charge. It was pandemonium and all of it was captured live on camera by the heli-telly and Prime Life boat that just happened to be nearby.

"Sensation!" bawled Hal 'The Mouth', voice husky as he neared the end of his second commentary stint. "It looked to me as if a 'gator was closing in on Karelov from behind and it has just been shot by his eagle-eyed marksman. Boy did that look close. Let's check the slow motion of that dramatic incident."

The action replay was inconclusive on the reptile's approach, but Hal 'The Mouth' was at great pains to draw the viewers attention to a slight break in the surface which could just as easily have been caused by Karelov's leg kick. The incident was replayed 30 times during the remainder of Prime Life's output that day.

Karelov had dived onto the pontoon in a split second. The helicopter swooped lower to try and capture close-up shots. The Prime Life boat officials were still shouting across to the rifleman who pointed to where he believed the deceased beast had sunk. Order was finally restored and Hal 'The Mouth' was able to pick up the threads for the peak-time audience.

"Well this incident seems certain to allow America's Brent Ryan to close the gap on the Russian. I can see Karelov now and he does look very badly shaken by the whole episode."

Karelov was scowling and chewing his way through the second of two energy bars. A Sport Armageddon official had an arm over his shoulder. It looked like a consoling gesture but the whispered conversation belied the body language.

"But I am ready to go again," said Karelov.

"What, are you stupid or somethin'? What if the thing wasn't killed outright? It'll be mad as hell at the next thing that goes in that water. Let's at least give it a minute or two and see if it surfaces again?"

"You saw it the first time?"

"Sure. Another second and it would have bitten you in half."

Karelov looked at Nemo.

"I give shoulder massage," said Nemo, seeking to make the best of the enforced pit stop. As he ministered to his reluctant protÈgÈ, the Prime Life graphics team worked overtime to give the viewers a striking indication of how America's finest was closing the gap with every second, as they gawped across their waffles.

"Serves the bastard right for taking a swing at our guy," was the response from more than one household as the two most violent incidents of Sport Armageddon were juxtaposed on screen.

Melanie was riding in Brent Ryan's boat. She could hear the Prime Life output through headphones and gazed back wistfully at the Adonis in green. She had fallen for Brent Ryan soon after she first met him on a filming assignment in Colorado. Of course she knew he was arrogant and selfish and that he played the field but she found the twinkle in his eye irresistible. He just exuded sex appeal. Melanie was not some doe-eyed teenager, about to make a fool of herself in pursuit of an unattainable man, and that was exactly what drew Brent Ryan to her. In the run-up to Sport Armageddon, they had spent considerable time in each other's company, although never alone. As a matter of reflex, Ryan had tried to flirt with her and was surprised to find that, although she was good conversation, she did not automatically respond to his cornball chat-up lines. This marked her out as an A1 challenge for him and they had enjoyed a couple of discreet dinner dates in Atlanta and Key Largo. To his frustration, he had yet to accommodate her in his busy mattress mileage schedule.

Ryan looked up from the water and swam a few moments of breaststroke to get a position briefing. Melanie hastily scribbled on the whiteboard, 'Karelov +12; Vaughan and O'Neill -22.' She gave a thumbs up sign and yelled, "You've gained three minutes."

Ryan grinned and blew a kiss towards her. He plunged back into his relentless front crawl. That girl had great legs, showcased on this occasion by some khaki shorts, white sneakers and team green top, with sunglasses propped on top of her tousled hair. Brent Ryan never fell in love but in her case he might be prepared to make an exception. She was a honey. How much he wanted to be intimate with her and how galling that the best he had managed was a chaste kiss after each of their evening dates. She wanted him, he could tell. He could see it in her eyes.

Melanie sat back in the support craft and kept her eyes peeled for venomous water snakes. No one at Prime Life should have been able to guess their feelings for each other. She was petrified of Lenny finding out. She would have to speak to Brent about blowing kisses. That sort of monkey business could easily be caught on camera.

She had managed to persuade Vivian Wheatley a couple of days before the start that someone key to Prime Life should ride with the Team Ryan support crew because Brent was vital to the success of the event. To her surprise, they readily agreed and she was released from her general administrative duties. Lenny had no qualms about suggestions of bias or favouritism. He had heard them all countless times before. He had also figured that it would do Ryan's glamourous image no harm to have the company's top babe in his pit team but the boy had better not try and get her into his personal pit first. Lenny had known her longer.

"He's going real well. Karelov's still recovering in his boat, you know," she remarked.

"I know, sweetheart. Reckon our boy's form and timing looks pretty good right now." Ryan's father was also in the support boat and was feverishly punching in the distances from the latest TV updates into a laptop computer. The return data included average speeds and projected times to catch the Russian swimmer. He smiled as the machine indicated that Karelov would be caught in under an hour, even if he immediately resumed swimming at his previous pace. At Zing Cola's hotel the company marketing team was cheering. Dr Psyche also allowed himself a flicker of a smile. 'Pathway to greatness', he recalled.

Some way back down the same pathway, PJ and Jennifer Kogo were not smiling.

This was proving to be hell in water for the African. He was managing to stick resolutely to his regime of an hour's swimming followed by a rest of up to half an hour. It was torrid stuff. His guts twitched from the water he had swallowed. His shoulders and neck felt as rigid as concrete and ached painfully. Every few strokes, he fancied he could see a cottonmouth water moccasin snake. When he learned of the reported alligator attack on Leonid Karelov, he was close to quitting. It was only pride that kept him going back into the water.

"This is terrible," he sobbed to Jennifer as they approached ten o'clock, 14 hours after his own designated start time. "How on earth can I continue?" As if to illustrate the point, he hung his head over the side of the pontoon and vomited into the water.

He lay back under the shade of a canopy at one end of the float and closed his eyes. His wetsuit top was rolled down as Jennifer tried to stimulate life into his shoulders with a vibrating massage pad. She was worried for her man.

"I need to get the race doctor to you, babe."

"No," replied PJ firmly. "I can deal with this." With the hottest part of the day approaching, he would have dearly loved to have rested in the shade of the pontoon for a few hours but he knew it would be twice as bad if he tried to resume after that. He must press on.

"Looks like Kogo's in real trouble," pronounced Hal 'The Mouth's' stand-in commentator. "You will have just seen him being sick. Sorry about that viewers but this is sport in the raw. It's not for the faint hearted. Kogo is now losing ground, or should I say,

Geoff Wightman

'water' to every one of his opponents. Apart from the four hour head start that he gave them, he is swimming considerably slower than anyone else and taking five times as long with his rest periods. It's clear from his original game plan he will not enjoy swimming in the heat of the day, but as I speak he is getting back into the water. He does seem a pretty determined character."

PJ tried to let his thinking drift away from the horrendous task in hand. For a while, he thought about the previous day's meeting and in particular the woman who had issued the death threats to Prime Life. He considered that he had led a largely blameless existence since he arrived in the US but there was one episode that he had replayed over and over again.

When he had moved into the fraternity dorm at Riverside College, his housemates had seen it as their mission to lead him astray. They had partied relentlessly and drawn PJ into the mandatory beer drinking contests. After one night of notable excess, PJ awoke to find one of the girl partygoers in his bed bedside him. Neither had any recollection of the conclusion of the night before. It was out of character for both of them.

She had hurriedly gathered her things together before dawn, to leave the house as quickly as possible. In the kitchen, one of PJ's supposed fraternity buddies who was still partying had mocked her embarrassment.

"God, I hope you didn't have unprotected sex with PJ. The guy's HIV positive."

"What?"

"Didn't he tell you? He should have done but you guys should have been careful anyway. AIDS started in Africa."

The girl had fled from the house in hysterics. PJ did not see the funny side and tried in vain to track her down to explain. Not long afterwards she left Riverside. She was a 'very stressed out' case, according to the few students on her course who claimed to know her. Extremely traumatised. Extraordinarily angry.

PJ did not have Aids. The girl did not contract Aids but he had never had a chance to make his peace with her. A mutual acquaintance had heard that she was taking Aids tests every month for a long time afterwards...

She was clearly disturbed but surely to God, not mad enough to come hunting for him all these years later? He was not a man who cultivated enemies and the prospect of this being his lone avenging angel made him shudder. He wanted to rationalise himself out of the target zone. His woman was indeed from Florida, he recalled disconcertingly, but maybe the 'Z' name let him off the hook? His one-night stand was called Sonia.

As the swim dragged on endlessly, PJ did not know which was worse – the rests on the pontoon, where he felt bilious all the time or the swim phases where he felt exhausted, sore and scared. He flinched as he saw something moving in the water beneath him and then breathed a bubbly sigh of relief as he realised it was the underwater cameraman.

The bastards appeared to be revelling in his discomfort. Well, never mind what the contract said about co-operating with the TV coverage. He would not let his feelings show any more than he had to. With that thought firmly in his mind, he rolled over onto his back and reverted to a sedate paddling action. His shoulders and neck felt immediately relief at the change of stroke. He allowed himself a smile, which ironically for him, was caught on the motor launch camera. He could certainly keep this stroke going for more than an hour. The race did not always go to the swiftest.

A pair of hawk eyes hovered overhead. They belonged to Leonard Stein. He peered down at his creation. From the height at which the Prime Life helicopter was hovering, he could see Karelov, Ryan, Vaughan and O'Neill. Or at least, he could see all of their little flotillas. He would need more than binoculars to see Kogo but he was, at this point, indifferent to PJ's plight.

Having closed to within four minutes of Karelov, Team Ryan members were reluctant to tell their boy that the Russian was back in the water and swimming as if he had an outboard motor. The gap was now back to seven minutes, with Ryan aching for a rest.

Nemo had pushed Karelov back into the water the moment he had seen the American's boats approaching. To hell with the alligator, if there was one. The little Pole did not want to award the damn Yankee the psychological edge of being able to see his man. It was time to go again. Karelov was rejuvenated.

Stein watched on the monitor as the close-up zoomed in on Karelov's effortless stroke.

"Cut to Ryan," he barked to Wheatley.

"Cut to Ryan," Wheatley yelled into his headset.

The camera cut to Ryan. The comparison was an unfortunate one because he was progressing at a visibly slower stroke rate. Even Hal 'The Mouth's' stand-in struggled to accentuate the positive in the pictures of the American.

"Cut to a commercial break," Wheatley yelled into his headset.

"...We're going to a commercial break. Right after that, you can see the Gaby Baby tape from Bondi Beach – we've had a lot of requests for that – and a preview of the swim-bike transition at Pahokee. Within a couple of hours Sport Armageddon will be back on dry land. It's still the USA and Russia heading the race. Join us right after this..."

The Sport Armageddon fanfare heralded the break, followed immediately by the Zing 'Gold Medal Sponsor' logo – and a punchy commercial for Solaire Tan – the official sunscreen protection cream of Sport Armageddon, tastefully illustrated by Gaby Vaughan.

Stein, as always, felt a throb of satisfaction as another 30 seconds and 9000 bucks worth of advertising revenue nestled sweetly in the bag.

He would not meddle any further in Karelov's lead, he decided.

At least, not for the rest of the daytime session. The commentary team would just need to hype the classic 'hare and tortoise' elements of the swim phase.

The sun was fiercesome. Ninety-four degrees Fahrenheit and 90 per cent humidity. But in Steve O'Neill's private world, it remained dark and cold.

Every six strokes on his right hand side, he caught a glimpse of Gaby moving gracefully through the water. He drew some comfort from her closeness and their shared endeavour. It was certainly establishing a relentless rhythm to their swimming and helping conserve energy. He was unconcerned by the massive lead built up by Karelov and Ryan.

Stroke – exhale – stroke – breathe – stroke – exhale – stroke – glimpse – stroke – breathe. He was not a killer. But the girl had not taken her own life had she? Who else had killed her if he hadn't? He was a drunken, murdering, losing waster. He should have been the one to die. Not the kid. She had never done anything to harm anyone. But was he the one being hunted now? Was her mother out for revenge? An eye for an eye?

Stroke – exhale – stroke – breathe – stroke. Loser. Drunk. Killer. Hunted. Revenge. Oh God. It would never, ever leave him.

Gaby felt in need of a break. They had been making good progress and neither she nor her new buddy had experienced any major mechanical problems. She needed a break.

She swam diagonally across and gently tapped O'Neill on the side. They both trod water and squinted in the blinding sun as they slid back their goggles.

"I need a rest. Do you want to go ahead?" She asked.

"No, no. I'm with you on this bit. Let's take five."

They scrambled up onto their respective pontoons that had been stopped just ahead of them. Gaby slid under the awning and lay back. She reached for neither food nor drink. The reason she needed to stop swimming so urgently was that her heartbeat had suddenly started to race out of control. It was pulsing close to 220 beats per minute. She closed her eyes tight. Please don't let me die. Not now. Not here.

Lenny cast a gimlet eye over the scene and checked the monitor close-up. He was displeased with the cosy twosome. Suddenly five competitors had merged into four. Commercially, it did not make good sense for Gaby to be linking her efforts so closely to O'Neill's, especially this early on. He had woven an entire raft of merchandising sales on the strength of her being projected as a desirable, unattached 'uberbabe'. It was a mistake for him not to have spelled out her obligations to protect that image in her contract. It was a mistake for her to have latched on to Mr Miseryguts. He would speak to them personally at the transition zone. Lieutenant Wheatley would not be able to convey his insistence in quite the right way.

Wheatley himself was having a bad day. His knees still hurt, but on more than one occasion he had felt himself start to nod off in the hazy heat of the helicopter. He began to dream of his Kentucky stud farm all over again. He would be hailed as the most prodigious flat racing trainer in the civilised world. But he would employ someone else to do the training. He had had it up to here with early morning starts, deadlines, crises and generally chasing his goddamn frigging tail.

It had been a bad week. Viv Wheatley had never had a greater sense of his own mortality than at the start of Sport Armageddon when Stein told him the coffee had been poisoned. It had taken him a while to regain his composure and at one stage he thought he was going to have a heart attack. Surely it was not him she was after? He did not have anyone he would describe as an enemy but when you had turned 50 years of age with a career in television, there were bound to be a few people harbouring grudges. Maybe he had been a bit brusque with some outside broadcast production assistants over the years – but Melanie had often reassured him that he was the most popular member of Prime Life's management.

He didn't like the idea of being a target. He would be glad when Sport Armageddon was over.

"Cut to commercial break..." It was Lenny, yet again. Wheatley twitched.

"Cut to commercial break..." Wheatley yelled. Why this time?

"Tell those guys to get the friggin' 'yards to the finish' caption sorted out."

"Get the friggin' 'yards to the finish' caption sorted out," Viv yelled.

Stein had been brutal with any initial teething problems in the transmission of Prime Life's 24 hour output. He had peremptorily ordered the sacking of one of the on-screen graphics technicians when Sport Armageddon was barely six hours old. It left an already overworked department in disarray and it was not clear whether anyone from Atlanta head office could be drafted in to provide suitable cover. Certainly it would cause some disruption for a couple of days. None of this concerned Stein. He would dismiss the whole department as soon as the race finished but right now he needed the production output to be spot-on. He didn't care at all if this meant some poor Prime Life minion going without sleep for three days at a time. The end product was all that mattered.

Gaby Vaughan lay on her pontoon, preparing to die, and listening to her heartbeat thumping an insistent tom-tom in her head. Then, as had happened many times previously, her heart rate began to ease up. In the space of less than two minutes, it was back down to 80 beats per minute. She could not carry on like this. A specialist's appointment was long overdue and would have to be arranged as soon as she had finished Sport Armageddon provided, of course that it didn't kill her first. She opened her eyes to see Jane and Patsy from Team Vaughan crouched over her. She confirmed that she was indeed perfectly fine and spent her allocated 15 minutes gulping specially concocted banana and malt milk drinks and having the hairdryer blasted over the puckered skin of her hands.

Gaby had never ducked a challenge in her life. Off-duty, anyone of her acquaintance would confirm that she was courteous and pleasant company. In competitive mode, there was a streak of determination that rendered her almost schizophrenic. Mostly it manifested itself in a dogged head-down determination. Just occasionally it boiled over into nastiness. She had been known to lash out at helpers like Jane and Patsy without any conspicuous provocation. Her love life had always taken second place to the pursuit of excellence. There had been discarded romances along the way. When she had time on her hands she thought of what might have been. Twenty-four hours in a freshwater lake allowed all sorts of suppressed memories to bubble up. Unlike O'Neill, she would not allow any negative thoughts to fester. Instead she forced her mind to contemplate the future. Right now that comprised of the toughest endurance challenge on the planet. She also wondered what it was that drew her mesmerically to Steve O'Neill.

The camera recorded Gaby's pit stop but it was Brent Ryan's break that was actually being transmitted on screen. Ryan had taken the high-tech route to prepare for the event. His blood had been monitored, his oxygen uptake measured and his heat tolerance improved by using an atmospheric chamber at the University of Colorado. Nothing had been left to chance. Now, as he lay on his pontoon, dizzy with the heat and sheer exertion of trying to catch the Russian, his father rolled back the cuff of Ryan's wetsuit sleeve. It revealed a two inch wide waterproof bandage that he rapidly unravelled. There was a small neat slit on his wrist, which had been incised the previous morning.

Melanie had completed the assembly of a portable drip-feed unit and a tube was deftly inserted into his incision. A sugar solution began seeping into his veins.

"Well I'll be damned!" Rasped Hal 'The Mouth', now up and croaking for his second commentary stunt. "Brent Ryan has gone on an intravenous drip for this pit stop. I have never seen that before. I recall Jimmy Connors opting for one after a tough tennis match at the US Open. Remember these are live pictures of Brent Ryan out in the middle of Lake Okeechobee on Day Two of the million dollar Sport Armageddon. I guess Team Ryan must have figured this all out in advance. Hey, I wonder if his vein leaks when he starts swimming again?"

Melanie had the stopwatch running. Twelve minutes of sugar, six of saline solution drip and then a further eight minutes while the scar was temporarily frozen and re-sealed before he could get back in the water. There was no reason why Hal or anyone else should have known in advance about their high-tech back up, although Lenny would probably cuss her out for not keeping him advised.

The Prime Life switchboard in Atlanta lit up like a Christmas tree. Indignant viewers and fans of Vaughan and Kogo in particular wanted to know whether their heroes would have access to the same facility. If not, why not?

The nature of their complaints was conveyed to Stein in the helicopter later that day.

"Eight hundred calls logged, Chief," reported Wheatley. "All saying pretty much the same thing."

"God bless America's sense of fair play," Stein smirked. "We'd better make sure they all have them for the cycle phase. Don't want people thinking it's an unfair contest, do we? See to it, Viv."

'See to it, Viv' would make a great name for one of his virtual reality thoroughbred horses. It would also be his epitaph. A few quick words from Lenny would lead to many hours of grief and chasing his tail for Viv. Wheatley angrily punched the buttons on his cellular phone.

"Mel, honey. Where d'ya get those intravenous gizmos?"

Stein was having an upbeat spell. He had the overnight viewing figures that covered the opening eight hours of Sport Armageddon. Like the curate's egg, it had certainly been very good in parts. If only everywhere could have demonstrated the impeccable taste and judgement of the good citizens of Columbus, Ohio where the figures for Prime Life were the highest nationally. It was purely coincidental that Columbus was Brent Ryan's home city and where his father was a former city councillor with Senate aspirations. To deny the Ryans high profile in Columbus would be to credit Bill Clinton with only a passing acquaintance with Little Rock, Arkansas.

Florida and Georgia had returned strong provisional numbers but the chosen ones of California, Oregon, Arizona and Texas were tuning in to Sport Armageddon in woefully low numbers. It was time to bully the sales force and get the promotions manager for Prime Life hauling his miserable ass around those key states on a massive subscriptions drive over the next seven days. Stein knew well enough that this would be a critical week for the station's growth and market penetration prospects.

"Give me that mobile phone, Viv."

In a few seconds he was in full on rant mode with the hapless Joe, his sales director back in Atlanta.

"We've got the friggin' best event in the history of US sports here," he trumpeted. "Get your sales guys pushing a deal harder in the West. It's not like this event has arrived by surprise. We've been trailing it on all media for a damn year. If we don't get a subscriptions hike over the next seven days, there'll be a number of your overpaid team looking at situations vacant. Got it?"

There was an inaudible sigh at the end of the line.

"Right you are, Chief." The conversation was over. Stein was not noted for extending unnecessary courtesies such as 'please' or 'thank you' or even 'hello' and 'goodbye'. Joe resumed his scrutiny of the situations vacant page of the executive section of 'Marketing Week' magazine open on his desk. He had been at Prime Life for ten months, which was almost into gold watch long service territory for Stein's senior staff. During that time he endured harrying, threats and unreasonableness as his daily diet from the great Lenny. All the while he and his surprisingly loyal and resolute sales force were putting in 70 hour weeks, doing their bit for Sport Armageddon. He'd had enough. It was time to go. He would certainly not be laying any more pressure on his Western States sales team. He probably would ring National Enquirer with a view to selling his story on 'My Life With Lenny the Tyrant' just as soon as he found a new job. Any job.

Karelov looked back down the channel of buoys as he rubbed more sunscreen on his hands, neck, face and feet. There was no one in sight behind him. He took a swig of one of Nemo's dubious potions and looked up at the helicopter hovering directly above him. He grinned in defiance. He knew perfectly well that Leonard Stein was up there. He waved playfully. This has sure spoiled your script buddy. Only a matter of time before I take your Yankee million bucks.

It was a great sight. He ached. His head pulsed from the heat. He was tired. He needed more rest but however bad he felt, the others must feel much worse. There was only one Sport Armageddon competitor who could actually see the finish area by Pahokee.

"How far?" he asked Nemo.

"About five and a half kilometres."

"How long?"

"About eighty-five minutes."

"Time to go, then." He winked at Nemo, zipped up the hood of his wetsuit and pulled his goggles over his eyes.

Nemo drew near to him in case the long range cameras were rolling. He turned his back in their direction.

"Take this." He pushed a yellow capsule into Karelov's puffy, grizzled paw.

"What is it?" asked Karelov slipping it discreetly into his mouth and reaching for the bottle of water.

"To settle stomach pain," replied Nemo haltingly.

Karelov looked directly into his coach's eyes. No words were exchanged. Karelov turned, jumped into the water as the eco-friendly engines of his support boats chugged into life and eased the craft ahead of him. The first stroke felt terrible. He thought he must have wrenched his arm out of its socket. He also swallowed yet another mouthful of Lake Okeechobee. No matter, he was leading by a very long way. They would have to invent a whole gang of raging crocodiles to stop him being first onto his bike. As he turned his head to one side, he caught sight of the Karelov big game sharpshooter on his perch. 'Cheating damn Yankee conman', thought Karelov and increased his stroke-rate.

Jennifer Kogo had a little time on her hands. Her husband was swimming breaststroke. She was aware that Karelov would be out of the water in just over an hour. The on-board TV monitor also confirmed that Ryan, O'Neill and Vaughan would all hit the edge of the Lake in less than three hours at their present rate of progress.

Hal 'The Mouth' was making it all too clear that her poor husband would be lucky to finish at all. His breaks were becoming longer and more frequent. The last mile had taken him almost an hour to cover. More than 20 hours after the official start of the race, he was still only a fraction over the halfway point.

She had asked him to sleep for two or three hours during the hottest part of the day. He had tried, but after just 30 minutes of slumber, the cramps in his legs and stomach had woken him sharply. After two more abortive attempts to sleep, he had gone back into the water. As his father once told him, the best way to eat an elephant is in small pieces. He was determined to keep edging his way forward.

His belly ached and felt empty. His tongue was swollen and sore from all the Lake water that had flowed over it. His head and neck hurt so much, he could not think straight. He didn't need to think. He needed to swim. It was some while since he had even attempted front crawl but it was time to try and be competitive again. At first, he felt like he had forgotten how to swim altogether but slowly, very slowly, things began to improve. His leg kick got stronger, his breathing became more regular. For one fleeting moment, it looked as if his support boats would need to move up into second gear. He would complete this swim if it killed him.

Hal 'The Croak' was due for a rest break.

"Welcome Back. Let's remind ourselves what the million dollar first prize looks like. It was a cue for the well worn trailer to the tune of 'Who wants to be a millionaire?' to be run. It featured all of the competitors offering a soundbite on what the money would mean to them. Only Leonid Karelov came across as completely honest. He announced that he would spend all the money on himself and probably quite quickly.

Then there was the obligatory shot of a million bucks piled high in ten dollar bills. Finally, they screened a range of useful items that could be bought with a million dollars. On this screening, it was the turn of two executive helicopters to be showcased in all their finery.

The pictures cut back to Karelov in live action. Hal continued.

"Now as the Russian presses on, let's go with him courtesy of the special cameras around the Team Karelov boats."

At that moment there were actually five cameras charting Karelov. Prime Life loved to show off the range of imagery that they could conjure up.

First, the heli-telly shot which confirmed briefly but emphatically that the American was indeed a long, long way behind. Then, by contrast, the underwater shot from the Lake bed silhouetted the relentless swimmer against a bright Florida sky.

The truly special camera was on one of the Prime Life boats. It could be dipped in the water and towed, giving the same eye-level water surface view that the swimmer enjoyed. There were two regular cameras in the boats ahead of Karelov and now, for the first time, a shore-based fixed camera near the transition zone at Pahokee could pick up the action.

Hal 'The Mouth' continued to enthuse about the machine-like power of Karelov's swimming action. Stein's helicopter swooped down to Pahokee but he continued to watch and frown.

He had ordered bodyguards to run in front of each of the competitors from the water to the transition zone and then screen them safely onto their bikes. If the 'Z' woman was down there with a shooter, she was not going to get any stationary targets, although, frankly, Karelov was bothering him more than 'Z' for the time being.

"This guy's gonna spoil the whole goddamn shooting match if he carries on like this." He paused. "Is he clean, Viv?"

"Drugs, you mean? Nope, I reckon he pops a few pills now and again. I've had my suspicions since that Nemo guy showed up. Karelov's also got that gnarly old vein that bulges up all the way down his arm. I read somewhere that if you take steroids, that's one of the telltale signs. Plus, he has that real thick neck hummock and his eyes are too close together."

Stein would have laughed at this rather implausible analysis but he was in a serious mood. A goddamn Commie was dominating his dream event.

"How quickly could we process a drugs test?"

Vivian Wheatley rubbed his chin thoughtfully "Well the doctors here could take a blood sample at any time during the run or bike phase. We could probably get some analysis done in Tallahassee within 72 hours – but you know we haven't written anything like this into their contracts..."

"Screw the contracts. If I tell them to run round with buckets on their heads, they'll do it. Remember, it's a million bucks. Can't we get anything quicker in Miami? In seventy two hours, we'll have lost all our viewers if Karelov carries on like this."

"I'll make some enquiries, Chief."

"Can you get me Melanie on the line?"

Wheatley dialled and passed the handset to Stein.

"Mel, honey its Lenny." He was immediately into unctuous mode. "How are you doin'?"

"Good, Chief. How are you?"

"Great. Listen, between you and me, we are looking to protect the good name of Sport Armageddon by introducing some drug testing when they get out of the water. We'll have to do it for all of them although really we are trying to catch out 'you-know-who' up front. I just wanted to make sure that something like this would definitely not cause embarrassment to our man Ryan. Is he clean?"

Melanie did not know what to say. How the hell did she know? A quick and professional answer was required.

"Chief, to the best of my knowledge he is not a cheat. I have seen nothing dubious," she whispered. "But you can never be one hundred per cent certain on these things. I would be devastated if he were taking drugs."

Sure you would, thought Stein. He was beginning to suspect that his employee was conducting more than a supervisory role with the American boy wonder.

"Okay, that's what I thought. Actually I had him checked out at our vetting stage. We always thought that Karelov was the one drinking rocket fuel. It didn't matter at the time but it matters now if he's gonna spoil our event."

"You know I'm not a fan of his, Chief."

"I know. If he's trying to turn us over, we'll get him. Bye."

The helicopter touched down at the water's edge, where a large crowd had gathered to see the swimmers' arrival. Stein strode briskly across to his waiting 'battlebus'. It was a high-tech mobile TV control vehicle that would be the operations centre for the remainder of Sport Armageddon.

Wheatley scuttled to the medical tent on his good knee and left instructions for blood samples to be taken from each of the competitors as they reached the transition zone. The 'sprint' left him quite out of breath and he could barely raise a hobble to catch up with Stein.

"Go, Viv," shouted someone from the crowd. It made him jump at first because the mad woman was still on his mind but Wheatley gave a cheery wave and drew a round of applause. What a guy! They must have recognised him from some of the Prime Life footage or maybe they knew of him from college football days. He had quite forgotten that emblazoned on the back of his green silk baseball jacket was 'Sport Armageddon. Viv Wheatley.'

Karelov could see the crowds on the shore. Another two minutes would do it. He felt quite comfortable with surprisingly little fatigue, but kept one beady eye fixed on his rifle marksmen. Once they reached the land this man would cease to be a feature of the race. Good. As the TV launch drew alongside he was even inclined to show off a little. He began kicking his legs strongly and increasing his stroke-rate.

"Wow!" exclaimed Hal 'The Mouth'. "As Karelov enters the final one hundred and fifty metres to the shore, he's even managing to up the pace. The man is a torpedo. Let's hope America's own Brent Ryan, who is now almost thirty minutes behind, doesn't get too discouraged by the sheer strength of this Russian."

The last thing Team Ryan was about to do was to let their man know that Karelov was set to commence the bike phase. Brent could not possibly see the far bank of Lake Okeechobee and he was going through a bit of a rough patch.

Melanie leant back in the boat seat and rolled back the hem on her Bermuda shorts to expose a little more already tanned thigh to the rays. Thirty feet behind her was the regular slop-slop splash of the Ryan freestyle. He had slowed quite considerably and the dynamic duo of Vaughan and O'Neill had taken the opportunity to peg back almost eight minutes on him.

He was still moving smoothly but they would all be glad to get clear of the water. Several times, Melanie thought she had glimpsed an alligator breaking the surface near Brent and once she had shouted to the marksman.

He had just laughed, reminding her that they are reptiles that would not venture too far from the shore. She had reminded him that the southeastern edge of the Lake was very near and anyway the whole lake was only 14 feet deep. Of course it could have been an alligator. Hadn't one attacked Karelov?

The other big fright was the thought that Brent might be a druggie. How could anyone else know for sure? Even if he was dosed up to the eyeballs would he tell her, or anyone else for that matter? Drug takers were not noted for their candour and honesty. He would probably admit he was a cross-dressing murderer before he'd admit taking drugs. She guessed that these were shameful secrets known only to the people at either end of the needle.

Melanie also knew that apart from a drugs scam, Sport Armageddon could be blighted at any moment by the woman assassin. She had learnt a little more of that particular episode than she was prepared to let on but only Lenny and Viv knew the full story. The woman had obviously given some indication that she was capable of carrying out her threats. The old stagers at Prime Life would not have been spooked by mere telephone threats. She felt it must be a strangely empowering experience for the woman to put the event organisers on the back foot in such a dramatic way – not that Melanie could condone such crazed behaviour, especially if it was taken to its promised conclusion. Everyone involved in the event was at risk unless and until 'Z' could be outmanoeuvred. She wondered what the woman was like. What kind of experience had triggered off this behaviour? Could love be at the root of all this?

She looked back to the water. Brent was still chugging away. Too slow to be on drugs, too cute to be killed. She smiled to herself. Surely her Brent was not at risk. Surely?

Karelov felt his feet touch the bed of the Lake. He had been nervous over the last few yards because despite all the activity at lakeside, this was where he was most likely to get a well-muscled leg ripped off by a 'gator.

His legs felt unsteady, but in anticipation of a brown adrenalin surge, he skipped through the shallows and on to dry land.

A microphone was thrust under his nose. He was unwilling to pause but took the opportunity to look back across the Lake. Ryan's flotilla was a tiny speck in the distance.

"Leonid, congratulations on being the first out of the water. How do you feel?"

"I feel very good. Very, very good indeed."

"Is it part of your strategy to build up a big lead so that you can control the race?"

"Yes."

You need to say more than that, you Bozo, thought Stein as he watched from his battlebus, speeding ahead on Highway 80.

The TV interviewer pressed on.

"You don't appear to have taken very many breaks at all. Will you be having a nap before you move on?"

"No. Now I must go."

Karelov trotted towards the transition zone, shielded by body-guards and accompanied by resounding jeers from a crowd used to somewhat longer soundbites. They were well aware that Karelov was the villain of this three act drama. Two hundred hours of Prime Life trailers and one swing of a microphone stand had made sure of that.

He unzipped his wetsuit as he ran and stepped into the bike enclosure. There were some screens set up to enable him to take a shower and change into his cycling gear. The sun was intense. Almost 90 degrees. He would just cycle for an hour or two and then take a good rest.

Nemo was already there, laying out his cycling equipment and preparing to give him a quick rub down. Both of them were taken aback to be joined in this inner sanctuary by an uninvited guest. A white-suited figure introduced himself as the event doctor and confirmed that he had been instructed to take blood samples from all competitors for drug-testing purposes.

Nemo and Karelov were dumbstruck. The doctor began to unpack a hypodermic syringe.

"What is this? Is this a joke?" Karelov blurted. "There was nothing of this in the contract. What if I say no? I have no blood to give to you."

"I am told you will be disqualified immediately if you do not co-operate." The doctor was poised with the needle.

"I refuse. You cannot do this." He took a step backward and looked pleadingly at Nemo.

Nemo's mind was racing. After the initial panic, some cold logic started to set in. It was true that Karelov's body was awash with proscribed substances but Nemo had no respect for the usual drug-testing protocol, even unannounced. None of his athletes had taken a hit yet.

Let's see. He had last injected Leonid with erythropoietin (EPO) to increase his red blood cell production, three days previously. It was detectable in the body for only six to eight hours so they were okay on that score. He had finished his dosages of insulin and human growth hormones several weeks previously and had been covertly wearing an epitestosterone skin patch. This ensured that it stayed within the 6:1 ratio with testosterone that was the international limit. Traces of Nandrolone could always be explained away, everyone knew that. That still left the stimulants, which the Russian had been gobbling in tablet form in prodigious quantities. The key ingredient in these was pseudo-ephedrine. Now that might just show up in the test, even though he had taken a couple of masking agents. It was too late now for the emergency swig of vinegar, smear of whisky or shampoo to help cover the trace elements. They would have to take their chances and, if necessary, cite a defence based on regular use of prescribed cough medicine, asthma cures, herbal brews or dental treatment. He would think of something.

"It's OK," he murmured to Karelov.

Karelov looked at him, bewildered.

"It's OK," he repeated.

Karelov sat down. His eyes never left Nemo's. Nemo nodded to him as the doctor plunged the needle into his vein and drew off a quantity of chemicals with trace elements of blood.

It was all over in a moment. The doctor thanked them for their co-operation and Karelov moved swiftly from shower to massage, to bike. All the while he and Nemo kept up a furious whispered argument about the probable outcome of the test. Karelov remained sceptical but was obliged to give Nemo the benefit of the doubt. At the end of the day, Nemo was the best mixer, masker, stacker and barefaced liar in the business. He had no choice but to trust him.

He powered out of the bike area with one support bus, one security vehicle and a Prime Life TV bike ahead of him. Lenny Stein had been very concerned to keep additional traffic to a minimum.

He knew he would pass through the Florida Highways without difficulty. He was less certain of the reception that lay ahead in Georgia. The Press would cover the race from a series of media centres dotted along the route. The first was a makeshift unit in a gymnasium at the quaint waterside town of Pahokee.

Karelov hit the road to the sound of decidedly muted applause as the American journalists looked despondently at the computer graphic showing a 37 minute lead over their man.

By the time Brent Ryan finally emerged from the cool waters of Okeechobee, the margin was somewhat generously estimated at 55 minutes. Gaby Vaughan and Steve O'Neill were put at 48 minutes further back, with PJ Kogo six and a quarter hours down.

As Ryan's flotilla came ashore the chant of 'U-S-A, U-S-A' began to rise. The Floridian audience had no doubts of their country's invincibility. Brent Ryan was an American. It would be his birthright privilege, on behalf of the free world to see off Karelov's challenge on the roads of the Southeastern US. This collective mood changed quite suddenly as they got their first sighting of Ryan. He emerged from the water on all fours and crawled across the shore, retching as he moved. He lay motionless, face down, as the paramedics rushed to him. He was totally exhausted. The drug test doctor decided to wait a while for his sample. He and Ryan's father picked him up and carried him to the cool of the medical unit. He was immediately put on an intravenous drip-feed. Brent was fast asleep before the tube had been put in his arm. Melanie looked on anxiously. Was the American challenge in Sport Armageddon to be snuffed out within the first 24 hours?

She conveyed the grim news to Lenny and Hal 'The Mouth'. Ryan's dramatic collapse was played over and over. "He's OK," 'Hal the Mouth' would repeatedly reassure the viewers.

"It is hoped that he will be able to pick up where he left off after a bit of extra 'R & R'. Brent is noted for his strong cycling."

Stein felt powerless. He knew the ratings would be boosted in the short-term by the spectacle of Ryan's swim. It was classic Ironman strive-till-you-drop stuff but this time it was offset by the sight of a fresh-looking archrival blasting ahead on the bike.

Besides, a brief ratings surge was no good at all if the eventual outcome was the demise of viewer interest in the whole event.

When O'Neill and Vaughan completed the swim, there was not the same obvious fatigue. They did allow themselves a full 45 minutes to recover before pushing out gently on their bikes. Melanie, as instructed, had waited behind and took O'Neill to one side and passed on Stein's personal edict that they should not work together. Lenny felt strongly that the onus was on O'Neill to commit himself to the chase after Karelov. O'Neill's decision to flagrantly ignore this would leave Stein fuming.

Steve and Gaby embarked slowly on the cycle route. They each planned to ride for four hours before taking a major break, but in the incredible heat and humidity they found they were getting diminishing returns on their efforts. After barely two hours they had had enough. The opportunity was there to call up the mobile homes parked ahead of them on the highway. There was one at the disposal of each competitor. They preferred instead to check into a nearby 'Big 8' motel, just west of Clewiston. They were intent on sleep. Brent Ryan slept. Karelov forged ahead. Kogo swam.

PJ had taken one nap break of two hours. He had also suffered the ignominy of another rifle incident, although this time it was for real, as PJ's eagle-eyed sharpshooter took out a cottonmouth water moccasin snake. It was basking almost 20 feet away from PJ. It represented no danger but it was an excellent shot. It broke up the boredom for the marksman and made great television. It scared the life out of PJ who was otherwise in a zombie-like state.

He was swimming for large distances on his back. Progress was painfully slow. Some hours had more rest than action but it was a major triumph when he caught his first glimpse of the shore, way off in the distance. His head ached from the sharp sun. His neck and shoulders seemed locked up. His tongue felt the size of a tennis ball. His stomach was in spasm.

The final hour was the longest of his life. His vision became blurred and monochrome. At times he could have sworn that he was moving further away from the land but very slowly, PJ Kogo was coming home.

It was almost dusk at Pahokee as he entered the final 100 yards. It was more than 24 hours since he had set out. He had slept for barely three of those hours in total. He felt as if he had recycled the entire contents of the Lake. The crowd at the edge of the water was estimated at 6000 – far more than had greeted the leaders. They had watched his exploits on Prime Life, seen him suffering and had come to lend encouragement to the underdog.

The roar began when the crowd first sighted him in the distance and rose to a crescendo as he dragged himself clear of the water. Jennifer dashed away from the support boat to hug him. He stood swaying as he tried to re-orientate himself. It was time to rest. He had conquered his demons. He raised both arms unsteadily above his head, gave a modest bow and then, with as much dignity as his body would allow, walked carefully to the medical unit.

As he entered, he could see Ryan in deep slumber. Who knew what lay ahead for the American but as PJ Kogo showered and took one of the camp beds, he knew that the worst part of the challenge was over for him.

He was asleep within a minute. Four competitors slept but Karelov cycled on through La Belle, halfway towards Fort Myers. Just one more hour towards the million bucks, he decided. All of the Prime Life coverage now centred on him. Meanwhile, his blood sample was awaiting analysis at a laboratory in South Miami.

Stein was almost ready for sleep. He watched the Russian and ground his teeth. This was not good for the race. Tomorrow would require remedial action.

From the Days Inn motel in Belle Glade, Zelda watched intently. It had been a good day's sport for her. They had reacted exactly as scripted to the coffee 'poison' tease but she had a few more shocks in store for the clowns as she closed in for the kill.

CHAPTER ELEVEN

Sport Armageddon Standings 00:00 hours Friday

1st Leonid Karelov (Russia)	106.5 miles
2nd Gabrielle Vaughan (Australia)	60.5 miles
3rd Steven O'Neill (GB)	60.5 miles
4th Brent Ryan (USA)	25.0 miles
5th Philemon Kogo (Kenya)	25.0 miles

VIVIAN WHEATLEY III had overslept. He had suffered the fatal double whammy of switching off his mobile phone but failing to switch on his alarm clock, having quietly slipped into a 'Best Western' near Clewiston. He should, by rights, have been in the TV van following Karelov at the head of the field, but he had had a hell of a day.

It was all very well Lenny barking out his orders and demanding this and that on an instant-fix basis, but it had taken four or five dozen calls the previous evening to set up the level of blood test analysis required. Eventually, he had sent Karelov's sample by motorbike courier to the University of Miami Medical School in Coral Gables. The single in-depth expedited analysis would cost 2000 bucks. Lenny had decided that Karelov's would be the only sample to be tested, although they would keep this information to themselves and maintain the veneer of impartiality.

By the time he had got to bed, having made an about-turn to Pahokee to check on Ryan's health, it was two o'clock in the morning. He had set his alarm for six o'clock, or at least he thought he had. Once again, he had dreamt of kicking back with a cold beer on the verandah, watching the sunset over Wheatley Acres stud farm. Bliss.

When he awoke, it was almost ten-thirty. A blind panic ensued. He plunged into an ice cold shower, forgetting altogether that he still had his underpants on. While he was dressing, he switched on his mobile phone. The message service had twelve new recordings, eight of them from an increasingly irate Lenny Stein.

He rang the Prime Life helicopter and arranged for it to collect him from the back of the motel 25 minutes later. He would need to call Lenny but he could not face doing that on an empty stomach.

He ordered a black coffee and his favourite bear claw doughnut from the motel lobby noting with disgust that the TV was tuned into NBC. He asked the duty manager to re-tune to Prime Life and was immediately updated by Hal 'The Mouth'.

"There's our camera on the edge of Lake Okeechobee where PJ Kogo has been asleep since around eight o'clock last night..."

There's always someone worse off than yourself, thought Wheatley, as he reached for a second bear claw.

"...The Team Kogo advisers have decided to let him sleep to a natural conclusion. This was a monumental effort by the African and his wife Jennifer wants to make sure he is properly rested before hitting the road, although the gaps are now very substantial up ahead. In fourth place, as everyone who was watching earlier will know is our own Brent Ryan. Here's our exclusive footage from four o'clock this morning when America's golden boy kick-started his Sport Armageddon challenge back into life. We understand from Prime Life's representative with Team Ryan that, apart from a headache and sore shoulders, he appears to have recovered well. His plan is to rest each day between 10.00 am and 3.00 pm, wherever possible."

The footage was a gem. To an instrumental of 'Yankee Doodle Dandy', the editing team had spliced together pictures of Ryan staggering in from the swim, followed by images of him blasting along Highway 80 in the pre-dawn darkness. He had taken a couple of breaks but as the action caught up with him live, he was swooping towards the outskirts of Fort Myers.

The coverage then cut to Vaughan and O'Neill. Despite a 'final warning' by telephone from Lenny Stein, they were still sharing the road. The attempt to split them up was not working because every time Hal 'The Mouth', on Stein's orders, had criticised their 'lack of individuality in pursuing such a great prize' the switchboard had been jammed by viewers praising the spirit of their team effort.

They were just heading out south of Naples on the long road that cut the state from west to east through the Everglades. Highway 41 was a monotonous stretch of road that would cover the 150 miles from Fort Myers to Miami.

Stein had commissioned all sorts of film footage to show off in a glitzy light the Collier-Seminole State Park, the Big Cypress National Preserve and Shark Valley.

"Keep the camera work tight on their faces and bodies. Keep the heli-telly shots brief. A lot of these Highways are so goddamn boring, they'll send our viewers to sleep. Be creative in the way you use composite footage. If it looks like any aspect of the race is flagging, cut back to the studio for some musical 'slow-mo' sequences. The viewers love those."

Stein's pre-event briefing had been very detailed in the many suggested ways of keeping the action pacey. It would mean 24 hour days for his editing team but that bothered him not at all.

"And here we see our event leader, Leonid Karelov, still going well as he nears the far side of the Big Cypress National Preserve. He has an estimated three and a half hour lead over the second and third placers." Hal 'The Mouth' had been told not to refer to them as equal second. There would be no ties in Sport Armageddon.

"Let's take another look at some footage of this natural wonderland of woodpeckers, wild hogs, mink and Florida panthers..."

Wheatley's mobile phone rang. The barking noise began as soon as he hit the receiver button.

"Where the hell have you been? Haven't you got any of my messages?"

"My mobile phone wasn't functioning, Chief," Wheatley replied truthfully. "I'm about to board the helicopter. I should be able to get to Miami well ahead of you."

"Well I'm almost there now," spat Stein. "What time do we get those drug test results?"

"I'm hoping we'll have something by 6 pm latest."

"Well get on with it then."

"I'm on my way."

Wheatley ordered another bear claw doughnut and savoured a coffee refill before strolling out to the waiting helicopter. Taking his time when the boss said 'jump to it' was, he reasoned, one of the minor triumphs of an otherwise servile existence.

The Chief had immersed himself in the detail of the race once again, right from the moment he had awoken. Mostly he was spitting out orders to Prime Life officials, working steadily ahead of the race as it rounded South Florida. Always Lenny had one eye on the style of the product being beamed into viewers' lounges. He had a direct line to the control desk when he felt that a change of emphasis, pre-recorded insert or commercial break was required. As he busied himself on these matters, he was ill prepared for one particular incoming call on his mobile phone.

"Yup," he snapped before the receiver even reached his ear.

"It's show time, Lenny. The circus is in full swing."

It was her. He felt the hairs on the back of his neck stand on end.

"Who are you? How did you get this number?" he spluttered.

"I always get what I want Lenny. And you know who I am. I'm the waitress in the competitor's tent. I'm the lady with the rats. I am the one who will destroy your show. Nobody took any notice of me. That was a big mistake but I was only playing with you. Now it's for real. Loverboy dies. It could be today."

"If anyone at Prime Life or Sport Armageddon has wronged you, there's ways and means of resolving these things. You cannot take the law into your own hands. I demand that you tell me what your problem is."

"You make no demands, Lenny. You only watch the circus and wait for Loverboy to die. That is Z's demand. Bye, bye Lenny."

"Wait..."

The line was dead.

Stein rang the operator immediately and asked for the call to be traced. It took 20 minutes to track it down to a public payphone in a shopping mall in Fort Lauderdale.

Stein's heart sank as he realised that she had travelled southeast to be ahead of the field. She could hit any of them within three or four hours.

He was loath to call in the police until he had to. He refused to contemplate the possibility of the event being disrupted by this woman. He was quite certain now that her accent was Californian and that she was in her late 20's or early 30's. He sent bulletins to everyone involved with Prime Life and Sport Armageddon, seeking urgent confirmation if those particulars registered with anyone.

'We cannot rule out the possibility that this is a hoax' he wrote.

Like hell, he thought. This is no hoax.

This is a nightmare.

Vivian Wheatley made a couple of calls during the helicopter flight and then tried to snooze. He awoke as their on-board camera picked up on Vaughan and O'Neill preparing to take a siesta break on the western edge of Shark Valley.

They had not anticipated that so many of the competitors would opt out during the heat of the day. Karelov, Ryan, O'Neill and Vaughan had all elected to take a break around 11.30 am. Kogo seemed impervious to the heat but he had barely begun cycling. He was making good time at last but was still heading west, having just left Highway 27 on to 80, due south of Moore Haven. There was only so much airtime they could give the catch-up endeavours of the game Kenyan. They would probably need to bung Karelov a few bucks to persuade him to keep cycling through the mid-day sun. He was a mad dog, after all.

If Karelov acted true to form, he would catnap for less than three hours. His ability to take short infrequent sleep breaks was already giving him a huge buffer over the rest of the field. O'Neill and Vaughan had cycled quicker than him through the morning but the gap was still more than 70 miles, with Brent Ryan making ground steadily to be approximately 62 miles further back down the highway.

O'Neill and Vaughan had decided that this was to be a four hour stop, with the maximum sleep possible being taken. They advised the Prime Life crewmembers that they would not require the RV's that were parked eight miles ahead of them but would again be dipping into the competitor support budget by taking rooms at a 'Rodeway Inn' just off the main highway.

Steve and Gaby were both suffering. After swimming almost 30 miles and cycling nearly 200 in less than 24 hours, it would have surprised them to have had no aches and pains. Gaby's calves were extremely tight, and her shoulders badly sunburnt. She was experiencing senior blisters on delicate hands that had been softened by Okeechobee's waters.

Apart from his depressed state, O'Neill's back was seizing up and he was getting some sciatic shooting pain down both legs.

None of these problems were regarded as cause for concern by their medical back-up teams who gave running repairs throughout the day, but it meant the two competitors had very little spring in their steps as they dismounted by the Rodeway Inn. There was no point in worrying how this would leave them for the running phase. They could only think as far as the next chunk of cycling action and, for now, enjoy the chance to escape the furnace heat.

Air-conditioned ground floor rooms were provided for them within moments by a receptionist who had been watching them on

TV as they drew near. Patsy rewarded her with some sweatbands and a T-shirt as a souvenir.

O'Neill showered and was given a vigorous back massage by the event physio. It prevented him dozing off completely, but as the physio left the room, Gaby, clad only in a bathrobe crept in.

"Okay if I use your shower? Mine's broken."

"Of course, go ahead."

He lay back in the bed and as he heard the shower jets whoosh into life in the bathroom. He tried to imagine what she would look like naked. Beautiful. It was a struggle to hold the mental image. He was too tired to fantasise, too depressed to sustain pleasant thoughts. He drifted towards sleep – so far towards sleep in fact, that he wasn't quite sure whether he was dreaming when the duvet was disturbed by the arrival of a pert, blonde, tanned Australian.

"Mind if I join you?" she whispered.

"Yes," he slurred.

"What's that, 'yes' I can come in, or 'yes' you do mind if I join you?"

"Do come in."

"Thank you kindly."

He had not troubled to open his eyes. He couldn't. He was too tired for that as well. Anyway the room was in darkness. He wasn't too tired to feel a surge of excitement as their bodies touched. She was naked.

She drew herself towards him and he wrapped his arms around her waist. Her body was warm and tingly and smelled sweetly of talcum powder. Even a depressed man could be in heaven for a short while. Sex was out of the question. They were both too weary for that. Besides this was far more intimate.

"I want you to know that I love sharing the road out there with you," she said softly. "In spite of everything, I'm enjoying it all."

"So am I. It's my pleasure."

"And when we wake up I want you to tell me what it is that's bothering you, OK?"

"OK."

"Night, night."

He kissed her gently on the lips. They were still asleep in exactly the same position when the wake-up call pierced their dreams four brief hours later.

When she came to her senses, Gaby had to grab her robe and hobble back out and along the corridor to take the call for her own room. No point in giving Jane and Patsy in the buses parked out the back any more gossip than they already had.

O'Neill had scarcely stirred as Gaby left the room. The phone rang a dozen times before he jabbed a clumsy hand in the general direction of the receiver. The ringing stopped. Deep inside, Steve knew he had to react. If he continued to slumber it would be disastrous. It was time to wake up. The first few minutes were always the worst, as he sat bolt upright in bed and opened his eyes. He felt terrible and, because it would take him a moment to gather his thoughts, he leant his head against the back wall and gazed at the ceiling. He inhaled deeply and rubbed his eyes. He looked down blearily at the duvet. All at once the bleariness left him. His eyes widened and a resting heartbeat suddenly pounded like a ticker tape-machine. Not two feet from his bare torso and edging his way was a massive furry spider about six inches in diameter. He froze. The beast edged nearer. Suddenly he flung back the cover sheet and dived, screaming, for the door. In a matter of moments, Gaby, Patsy, Jane and the various private detectives and security guards appeared alongside the shrieking man in his boxer shorts.

"There's a bloody tarantula on my bed!" O'Neill announced.

The motel manager had no protocol guidebook to help him deal with such eventualities. He and the detective, along with one of the security guards, gingerly let themselves into the room using the maid's key. The spider was still on top of the bed and, on the manager's emphatic instructions, it was terminated using a very long broom handle.

The manager took possession of a note that lay at the foot of the bed.

'My friend will not hurt you. His poison glands have been removed. He's in town for the circus and the grand finale is fast approaching. Z.'

"I think I'll take that," said the private detective. "I believe we know what has happened here. If you don't mind, sir, we'll clear up and be on our way. I'd appreciate you not mentioning this to anyone."

The manager looked at him quizzically.

"Well...OK, we are a discreet establishment."

The detective rang Lenny Stein's mobile number. It was busy. Stein had a pressing engagement. He was trying to nail Karelov that evening.

Karelov was playing with the traffic on the fringes of Miami, cursing the drivers who seemed surprised to see a racing cyclist on the Old Cutler Road. He felt light-headed, probably caused by the humidity and large quantities of cough linctus that he had swigged all day long. Ironically, he was within ten miles of the laboratory at the University of Miami where, at that precise moment, Vivian Wheatley III was pacing the corridor. He had switched off his mobile phone. He could always blame a technical fault when the Chief got through on the line.

"You told me it would be ready by 6 pm. What the hell are we paying two thousand bucks for? Our managing director will have my ass," he snapped.

The lab technician was unfazed by this latest tantrum.

"As I mentioned just now, Mr Wheatley, some of the tests take time. Our spectrometer is as advanced as any equipment in regular use but some of the diffusion procedures require the plasma to settle before analysis."

"What does all that mean?"

"We should have our final print-out within the next ten minutes. Then I can talk you through the results."

This place was not at all what Wheatley had imagined a drug-testing laboratory to be like. He had envisaged somehow that a blood sample would work its way through a series of pipes around the room and periodically be shaken, probed or put through a hoop. Probably a positive test would set alarm bells ringing and lights flashing all over the place. White-coated mad professors would come streaming into the lab with shouts of 'Holy smoke!' and 'Whoa, we've got a hot one here!'.

There was none of that. From the spectrometer printout just six minutes later, the technician pointed out a few key figures from a massive matrix of data.

"High haemoglobin levels but inconclusive without comparison with the subject's previous read-outs," the technician pronounced.

"Blood doping or EPO?" Wheatley was trying to keep up with the jargon. "Inconclusive on either point. Traces of pseudo-ephedrine. Ratios of testosterone to epitestosterone within acceptable tolerances..."

"Traces of...?" Wheatley had caught what he wanted to hear in the incantation.

"Of pseudo-ephedrine. A synthetic stimulant, found occasionally in ginseng or some prescription medicines, although not generally in these proportions..."

"Great. Could you highlight those figures and fax a full report over tomorrow mornin'. I gotta run."

"Sure."

It was enough. As Wheatley shot out of the door, he was already on the mobile phone to Stein. Lenny greeted the news without obvious surprise or concern. He ordered the Prime Life battlebus to turn around and rang through to Karelov's crew, ordering them to stop their vehicle and wait for him outside the K-Mart store that they were just drawing alongside.

Stein was with them in less than 15 minutes.

"Come with me, you two." He jabbed a finger at Karelov and Nemo and they dutifully trooped after him as he strode into the K-Mart.

They looked an odd group as they walked into the electrical goods aisle, but Stein wanted this conversation away from prying media. Amidst the housewives pushing trolleys, the three men, including one in lycra suit and cycle helmet, were fairly conspicuous. Lenny directed them to the furthest corner of the store.

"You have been taking drugs. We have the test results to prove it. What do you have to say about it?" Stein looked deep into Karelov's eyes. Karelov stared blankly back at him.

"What is this? I take no drugs."

The brotherhood of the needle had one unbreakable code. If ever you should get caught – deny, deny, deny. It was the Goebbels principle that if you told a lie often enough and insistently enough, sooner or later it would be believed. Karelov knew that in Lenny Stein's case, the best that he could hope for would be to muddy the waters a little. He had reckoned without the unorthodox but direct methods used by Stein.

"Listen up, son. I'm only going to say this once. We have just got results from the lab that show beyond any doubt that you have been messing with your blood and that you have recently taken stimulants. Do you understand?"

"I understand but I take only cough medicine for my cough." He coughed.

Stein was only a small man. Probably about 5'8" and a 160 pounds. Karelov was six inches taller and 20 pounds heavier.

The speed with which Stein suddenly lifted Karelov by his singlet and rammed him against the partition surprised Karelov and Nemo, not to mention half a dozen Miami matrons who were not accustomed to grappling matches in K-Mart.

Stein pressed his nose against Karelov's, then moved back an inch.

"Don't mess with me boy. I didn't just come in on the boat. I'm not asking you if you've been on the monkey glands. I'm telling you. Understand?"

Karelov was not exactly sure if his English was good enough to understand the idiom but in the circumstances it was best to agree. He nodded meekly.

Nemo did not intervene. Karelov could look after himself if he needed to and when it came to current possession of the million bucks there was no question who was operating the 'have' and 'have not' positions.

"I have a deal to offer you. I am a fair man," Lenny continued. "I will keep quiet about the positive dope test, if you wait right here in Miami until Brent Ryan has passed three hours north of here. Then you can race full out again. If you win the race you still get the cash prize."

In his mind, he had already resolved that there was no way that this Commie would ever see any of Prime Life's money.

"If you quit or race on before he has reached Delray Beach, I will call a press conference and announce the drugs test results. You got it? It's a take-it-or-leave-it deal."

Karelov nodded.

"Do we have a deal?"

Karelov nodded.

"You try and screw my event one more time, boy and you're dead meat, OK?"

Karelov nodded. Stein released his grip and headed for the exit.

Karelov and Nemo held a hasty tactical meeting. Normal shopping had resumed all around them. They emerged from the K-Mart ten minutes later. Nemo had purchased a pack of frozen peas and an elasticated thigh bandage.

A small press deputation had gathered outside the store, kept back by security guards. Karelov and Nemo walked towards the support van with microphones coming at them from all directions.

"What has been the purpose of this stop? Why did Mr Stein visit you?"

Karelov paused. It would be a rare piece of co-operation with a mid-race press enquiry.

"We radioed Mr Stein to report bad injury to my hamstring. He was worried, of course he was. It looks like I can carry on but I must get treatment immediately."

He held up the frozen peas and bandage. "This will help but I must get special massage and treatment. We rest here until I can go on."

Nemo was already in the back of the van setting up the ultra-sound machine. Karelov limped towards him clutching the back of his leg. He had to try and remember whether it was the left or right leg.

"Sensation!" Croaked Hal 'The Mouth'. "If you're just coming in from work, you join us here live on Prime Life for a dramatic announcement. You heard right there, from Karelov himself, that he has big-time injury problems. Our runaway train has been derailed! Maybe the Russian Leonid Karelov just pushed too hard on the first full day of cycling. He did appear to be in really bad shape as he headed off for treatment. This news will be a great boost to his rivals who have perhaps judged their effort a little better. Let's take a look at where this leaves the chasing pack."

"The competitors know all about the mad woman now. She left a friggin' tarantula on O'Neill's hotel bed, although it wasn't a poisonous one, according to her," Viv announced. Stein was back in the battlebus and addressing his other major headache.

"Oh, God. That's all we need. Did she leave a message?" enquired Stein.

"As always." He read back the transcript of her latest despatch. There was a long, long pause from Stein.

"How are we going to stop her, Viv? She seems to get everywhere."

Vivian shrugged. He was unaccustomed to dealing with crazed psychopaths despite three decades in television.

"I absolutely refuse," Lenny continued slowly, "to abandon this race for one person. Sport Armageddon has been planned for too long. It matters too much to Prime Life. We must double our efforts to trap this woman. We need to find out more about who she's after. Ask O'Neill whether it could be him and why. Let's double the number of security guards so that the competitors are protected whenever they're not cycling or running. There needs to be a constant guard on their support vehicles or motels, whenever they're resting. That's when they're most vulnerable."

Then he added almost inaudibly, "If she harms Sport Armageddon or any part of it, she destroys me. I'll get this bitch."

Wheatley nodded.

"And get some surveillance photography done of the people in and around the event. She's in amongst us, Viv."

CHAPTER TWELVE

Sport Armageddon Standings 00.00 hours Saturday

1st Gabrielle Vaughan (Australia)	·	303.5 miles
2nd Steven O'Neill (GB)		303.5 miles
3rd Leonid Karelov (Russia)		285.0 miles
4th Brent Ryan (USA)		248.0 miles
5th Philemon Kogo (Kenya)		219.0 miles

WHEATLEY awoke at five-thirty the next morning.

He switched on the TV and tuned in to Hal 'The Mouth's' stand-in for the graveyard shift.

"Let's take another look at the current standings as the ultimate challenge of Sport Armageddon enters its eightieth hour of competition. It's boiling up for an incredible day. Our leader Gaby Vaughan is neck-and-neck with Steve O'Neill. Despite taking an overnight sleep, they are both through West Palm Beach and heading for Jupiter County on the beautiful scenic route of Highway A1A. Look at those fabulous sunrise shots out across the Atlantic and you can also hear the great support they are getting from enthusiastic early bird spectators."

Stein had arranged that each Florida County would provide three busloads of supporters to be deployed at strategic in-camera vantage points along the route. They would be in position roughly 12 times in any full day, for which privilege they were to be given two packed meals and paid 15 dollars by Prime Life. They were mostly high school students but they were very much motivated by the once-a-day cash prize of 100 dollars for the loudest cheerer and the most colourful outfit-wearer. This was the second stop of the day for this particular group. Their enthusiasm remained commendable. Lenny Stein lived in hope that their presence would encourage Tour de France-style spectator picnicking out on the course. Even though the route was subject to last-minute change, and the weather was not conducive, there was some evidence that the live audience was picking up.

The commentator continued.

"But now this is the really exciting news as we cut to Brent Ryan. America's great hope has ridden through the night to reach Boca Raton, just south of Delray Beach. He is just twenty nine miles down on the leader, which is a great boost for his many fans.

"But if you thought that was good, just check this out. PJ Kogo the man who struggled so badly, with the dreaded swim has made it to Hollywood... Hollywood, Florida that is. He's twenty seven miles north of Miami and, as our caption shows, that puts him twenty nine miles behind Ryan.

"And I'm hearing on my headphones that we have news of Leonid Karelov, our long-term leader who has been sidelined since yesterday afternoon with a serious injury to his left hamstring. It looks like he's ready to get back on his bike. We're looking at pictures of his support vehicle bringing him back to the exact place where he had to quit last night."

Karelov had not slept well. He and Nemo sat wordlessly in the back of the van. Karelov's supposedly uninterrupted sleep had been anything but smooth. He knew more about drugs than he let on to Nemo because he had a vested interest in not destroying his body before he could enjoy the million bucks. They very rarely spoke of such matters. The less information passing between them, the less likely it was that a third party could prove anything. He did know that the old guy was particularly determined to get his hands on some of the new RGR-13 synthesised blood that was being clinically trialled on cancer patients. Sometimes Karelov felt like he was a scientific experiment for Nemo and even Karelov shuddered at Nemo's long-term plans to get into gene manipulation as the ultimate body enhancement process. The governing bodies in every sport in every nation would need to take DNA samples from every child at birth to be able to validate any alleged changes in an athlete's genetic fingerprint. How likely was that? None of the emerging nations were capable of such screening, none of the developed nations would have the desire and it would only need the American civil liberties lobby to cry foul and the medicine men would be two decades ahead of the clean-up operation. Nemo wanted a piece of that action.

"It's the ultimate, Leonid. No test could ever detect a DNA enhanced gene, designed to improve your sport. You would need no more injections after that." Nemo was extremely excited by the prospect. Karelov hoped to be profitably retired before the crazy Pole got his hands on his genes.

The downsides of Nemo's chemistry lessons were not discussed. Karelov had to reflect on such possibilities during his quieter moments. He did not see how insulin injections could do any harm because it was also produced naturally in the body but he had a little dangerous knowledge of EPO. Regular users of EPO had such 'thick' blood that they had to get up in the night and walk around, to prevent it settling around their joints and vital organs. The previous night he had suffered his recurrent nightmare about his veins sludging up completely and inducing a fatal heart attack. It had happened to a number of Europe's top road cyclists although it was not widely reported. Ever since Nemo had explained how EPO worked, Karelov had been a little unnerved by its possible side effects.

Karelov was not a timid man. He feared no one. But death was right up there with losing a million dollars as something that frightened him. In reality, Karelov was also a little bit afraid of the idea of the 'Z' woman. With a life like his, enemies were an occupational hazard. Too numerous to mention. He just could not get his head around the idea of an avenging woman. Then he remembered his own banshee experience. Long before his inept firestarting episode in Berlin, he had undertaken a similar, more successful piece of insurance arson, for Guido as always, on a nightclub in St Petersburg.

Karelov had been the junior partner in this particular criminal escapade and watched in awe as the basement premises went up in a whoosh of flames at the hand of a seasoned pro. It would have been the perfect scam of its kind but had a horrible flaw. Although it was 4.30 am and deserted in that quarter of St Petersburg, the building still had one occupant – a young go-go dancer. He feared it might even have been one of the girls he had smooched with when they cased the joint at a party the previous night. She survived the inferno but sustained disfiguring burns to her hands and face. Karelov had felt sick at this subsequent discovery. He heard that the girl was American and had received extensive plastic surgery paid for by her previously estranged family. Her father, it was rumoured, had also employed a private investigator and offered a large reward to track down the arsonists. He believed he was a prime suspect and received some very odd telephone calls. For a long time afterwards, he, Guido and their gang kept their distance from their local mafia contacts. A sharp knock at the door in the dead of night was never a welcome sound in that part of the world. He never knew the American dancer's name. He had never seen her. He prayed that he never would. Surely this could not be 'Z'?

Karelov's van would be back at the K-Mart in a couple of minutes. By then the goddamn Yankee golden boy would be on the outskirts of Delray Beach and he could start chasing them properly again. If he had to, he would cycle and run right through to Atlanta without a moment's rest. This time no one would stop him.

"So as Karelov gets set to hit the road again with that heavy strapping on his injured thigh, it means that all the Sport Armageddon competitors are in action at the same time and they are all within two and a half hours of each other. The following messages on

Prime Life come to you courtesy of Boccarelli Pasta, silver medal sponsor of Sport Armageddon, the ultimate challenge. We'll be right back as the action hots up in Florida..."

Well at least that much is good news, thought Stein. The race was nicely poised just as the scenery was about to go boring again. It was possible that by breakfast time, the gaps might concertina down to less than an hour, which would be pretty exciting and good for ratings, but Lenny had a logistical problem to add to his other worries.

The passage of Sport Armageddon through the state of Florida was not in doubt. He had secured compliance and approval wherever it was needed. Georgia would be different and despite Prime Life's status as an Atlanta-based company, the State Government had resolutely refused to give formal consent of any kind. The whole event was viewed as a poor taste publicity stunt. Prime Life's lawyers had looked into the options in great detail. Provided the route was chosen carefully, especially avoiding the Interstate Highways, the event could only be halted if it represented a security risk or was likely to create a public order problem. It might mean the competitors having only one support bus each that would have to drive ahead at intervals and park up. It would probably mean Prime Life having to use the heli-telly and fixed camera positions more than bike or van cameras. Stein would have to tread carefully.

The chances of the event finishing, as planned in Peachtree Road between the Hyatt and the Prime Life HQ in downtown Atlanta were also looking slim. Lenny decided to call up his lawyers to check out the possibilities and to have Viv arrange a face-saving alternative. When he thought of how many of his and his company's taxes were going to a city that was turning its back on him, it nearly made him spit. He had Georgia on his mind. It made a change from Karelov and the 'Z' bitch.

O'Neill and Vaughan were enjoying sharing the lead. The fatigue was coming at them in waves, but every once in a while there was a lucid interval where they could both savour the experience. Sunrise was one such occasion. It would herald the return of their mutual enemies, the heat and the humidity, but it also meant barely more than five hours to siesta time. The long haul north on A1A would be draining and would then be followed by the Orlando Chicane, a massive loop back towards West Central Florida. There was no point thinking of that. It was best to take things in one hour segments. As they cycled, O'Neill's melancholy persisted. At times he could hold down a conversation. At others, he stared heavy-lidded at the asphalt until he nearly drifted into a trance. She was coming for him. Marie Bowen's mother was closing on him. An eye for an eye.

"So, are you goin' to tell me what's botherin' you? I guess it must be connected with the spider you received." He had been dreading the question. He had planned to avoid discussing it or to pretend that there was nothing troubling him but you could not gloss over the sort of encounter that had befallen them in the previous 24 hours. She wanted to know. He had never discussed the full story with anyone.

"It was a long time ago," he faltered.

"OK."

"But it still preys on my mind."

"Mmm."

And with that, O'Neill found himself telling a woman of less than two weeks acquaintance exactly what it was that was driving him mad. He told her about the car accident, the inquest and the court case and the guilt that never left him. He talked for longer than he could ever remember and all the while, Gaby listened, never questioning, never letting her attention wander. She knew he needed her just to share this unburdening. As he spoke, O'Neill was embarrassed to feel tears rolling down his cheeks. The emotion just poured out of him but as he kept talking and describing his feelings, he felt a sense of release. It took more than 30 minutes to purge himself.

The Prime Life cameras had mercifully been concentrating on Ryan and Karelov during this breakfast time period.

"...And that's why I think I'm the intended victim of this woman who's been making the threats. What do you think?" asked O'Neill.

"I doubt that, mate. This is going to be some jilted woman. You're letting this get to you too much. I'll tell you what I reckon. One of my dad's former doctor colleagues now has a practice in Tampa. He's into psychological and psychiatric matters. I'm not saying you're a case for a shrink but he was going to meet me in Tampa anyway, so why don't I see if he's free towards the end of today or tomorrow so you can have a proper talk with him?"

An hour beforehand the idea of a couch session with a psychiatrist would have mortified O'Neill, but opening up had been therapeutic. He agreed to talk. He felt comfortable with Gaby, valued her support and accepted her judgement. She understood what made him tick. He could not remember feeling so strongly about someone for many years.

Brent Ryan was thinking that perhaps he had overdone it. His overnight cycling had powered him back into contention but now a rest was long overdue. The weight of expectation from the American viewing public was beginning to sap him. On the morning before the race began, Stein had taken him to one side and indicated that he had a sports management company in place that would handle Ryan's commercial interests when he won Sport Armageddon. When he won? Death and taxes were the only certainties in life.

As the hype of the build-up had continued it had increasingly become his duty, and not just his ambition, to deliver a win. He needed a rest. Just 30 minutes more of cycling and then he would take a nap. He shouted his intentions to Melanie and his father as he passed the support van parked up in a rest area. They smiled and waved and carried on feasting on their blueberry muffins. He had given exactly the same indication an hour ago, and the hour before that, and the hour before that. They knew full well that he would probably not allow himself a break until he could tap the leaders on the shoulder.

The women in Brent Ryan's life had come and gone, like leaves falling from a tree. He could not even remember all of their names, although he never forgot a body. There had been so many one night stands through college that he could have filled the Orange Bowl with his 'amores'. The threat that hung over Sport Armageddon from this one crazy woman bothered him greatly. Time was something that was in plentiful supply during long hours in the saddle and he had wracked his brains for an episode that could have made him the sitting target. There was one.

It all seemed so long ago. It was from his days as a rookie high school quarterback in Columbus, Ohio. The team had made the regional final thanks to Ryan's 50 yard touchdown pass in the last minute of the play-off. In the dying seconds of the game there was an off-the-ball skirmish between Brent and the opposing team's nose-tackle, which had resulted in the latter sustaining two broken ribs. Both players were banned for five games. It meant that Brent missed the final. As a full-time student it was hard for Brent to avoid the build up but his mood became progressively more sullen and irritable. Under pressure from his classmates, he found himself drawn to one of the many pre-arranged parties on the eve of the game. There was some illicit alcohol available. Ryan had no head for it. Pretty soon he was hitting on one of the cheerleaders who had joined them. Her name was Suzy. She was fifteen years old and very flattered by the attention from one of the pin-ups from the grade above hers. What happened outside, just before her parents arrived to collect her, was the subject of some dispute. Ryan's recollection was hazy but he remembered a lot of groping around. Suzy's was vivid. Her old man wanted him charged with date rape and unlawful sexual intercourse. He kicked up a hell of a stink. Most of the school got wind of it, but despite threats, the girl's family never progressed to a formal complaint with the police. The word was that Suzy went hysterical every time the subject was mentioned. The whole family moved away the next term, ostensibly on a business relocation. He never heard from Suzy Harper again. The family moved to California. Maybe she was back East to visit him now.

"Sonofabitch. Get me Alred on the telephone." Stein flung down his edition of the Jacksonville Bugle in disgust.

'Secret Shame of Armageddon Russian' ran the headline. 'The Bugle can exclusively reveal that Leonid Karelov, the early leader of the Sports Armageddon event, faces criminal charges in Germany in connection with an alleged arson attack that caused property damage running to tens of millions of dollars. Detective Inspector Klaus, the head of the investigation team in Berlin, indicated that it relates to an insurance scam...'

"This is the press truck on the 'phone, Chief." Wheatley passed Stein the receiver. "It's Doug Alred."

Stein grabbed the handset. "What the hell do you think you're playing at Alred? Don't I feed you enough useful titbits to stop you raking this sort of stuff up from Europe? I thought you were one of us. We go way back."

"It's in the public interest, Lenny," replied Alred, well accustomed to Stein's outbursts. "I think our readers have a right to know if one of the competitors is from the wrong side of the tracks."

Lenny subscribed to the view that there was no such thing as bad publicity. In the year leading up to the start of Sport Armageddon, he had tried to cultivate the right image for all of the competitors. Any whiff of unscripted scandal could have led to a raft of sponsors withdrawing their cash stakes. Now it suited him fine for Karelov's hat to get blacker and blacker. As a matter of general principle, however, he did not much care for investigative journalists. He also did not like one of his supposedly tame scribes sniffing around the event. You never knew what they would dig up next. The trouble was that journalists always had the last word.

"Anyway Doug, if you keep going off at tangents with your write-ups, you'll find yourself excluded from a few parties. I would hate to see you on the margins buddy. OK?"

"OK. Bye."

By mid-day, Steve O'Neill and Gaby Vaughan were asleep for the mandatory two hours. They intended that two such breaks in every 24 hour period would see them through. The sleep had been preceded by an upper body massage and they were both linked to their new intravenous drips of saline and sucrose, replenishing the body's diminished stores. The tubing that protruded from their wrists was somewhat inconvenient, so too was the high-level fatigue. In spite of that, they had still managed to weave another motel subterfuge enabling them to share a bed. It was less easy than before because of the security guard assigned to each door. Fortunately a partition fire door between the rooms was easily opened after removing the glass panel. Gaby laid out the lignocaine and xylocaine sprays and Ibruprofen tablets that would keep saddle sores at bay. For the same purpose, she had three new pairs of cycling shorts to be worn at the same time. A fresh pair of cycling shoes a full size larger than normal had arrived. Her feet had begun to swell with the heat and the relentless effort.

She rested alongside O'Neill who was already starting to breathe deeply as he plunged towards REM sleep. His body would shudder every few seconds, as the overworked muscles found it hard to come to terms with the rest period. Even though he was barely conscious, he instinctively wrapped one arm round her – the one without the IV tube. She smiled as his body twitched with mild cramp. She could love this man.

A little way back down the road, another Sport Armageddon competitor's bed was being shared. Brent Ryan still felt that he had some reserves of sleep stored up from his marathon sleep in Okeechobee. He therefore proposed to use his bed in the support bus for its most popular purpose. To clear the way for a little mattress mileage, he had dispatched his father to buy some whole-wheat pancakes. His father had thought this to be a ridiculous request when they had a truckload of his preferred regular pancakes and waffles. He was mindful that all of the competitors' nerves were stretched to breaking point and did not want to provoke him also. The slightest irritation or inconvenience could send him into a towering rage. He duly trooped off with Dr Psyche, in search of more pancakes.

The security guard was ordered to stay at least 30 feet from the bus. "Keep an eye on the road, please. I just need some space to myself." As the guard took up position, scanning distant horizons, Brent turned to Melanie, "I do need my calves massaged a bit more though." He winked. "The Doc normally does it but he's busy."

During her time at Prime Life, Melanie had done everything she could to avoid becoming a trollop. She had fended off unwelcome advances from Stein, Wheatley and Karelov. Now, in full view of the Prime Life cameras, she was about to disappear into a curtained van that contained nothing more than a bed, in the company of a hunky man wearing only a clean pair of shorts. What would her Aunt May in Kansas think?

It was expected to be up to two hours before she emerged but speculation would prove to be more exotic than the reality. She had carefully massaged Ryan's calves and he had asked her to minister similarly to the front of his thighs. After barely three sweeps of her gentle hands, Ryan had had enough foreplay and pulled her down on top of him. She stifled a shriek as he expertly unbuttoned her blouse and unclipped her bra with one hand. Years of practice made perfect. Rather more slowly, he slid his hands to the backs of her thighs and put a thumb inside the waistband of her panties. Then...nothing. Melanie lay still and lifted her head away from his chest. He had fallen asleep!

Fearing the return of the pancakes, she knelt up and carefully re-arranged her clothing and smartened her hair. She draped the blanket over Ryan and kissed him on the cheek. She could love this man.

As she stepped back out of the bus, Melanie could afford a smile. She nodded solemnly to the security guard and made a point of walking into camera shot but away from the vehicle. She would probably still get a Christmas card from her Aunt May in Kansas after all.

Only Karelov and PJ were still cycling, rapidly embellishing their reputations as the human dynamos of Sport Armageddon.

For PJ, all was not quite as smooth as it seemed. He had some painful problems with saddle soreness that would literally bring tears to his eyes when he remounted after a break. Earlier that day he had received confirmation that the death threats were coming from a Californian woman in her late twenties. It was Sonia. It had to be. He was filled with despair. But why had she tormented O'Neill? He had not been able to bring himself to tell Jennifer that he thought he might be the ultimate target but he was trying to stay alert to any danger. It was not easy because he had also experienced his first fatigue-induced hallucination. He had imagined that there had been a corpse lying in the road at one point and taken evasive action. Hal 'The Mouth', for it was he, had picked up on it.

"Boy that was a bad swerve there by the Kenyan. He must have come across a patch of oil or some mud on the road because he moved about six feet out towards the median. That could have been nasty but it looks as though he's OK and the charge continues for the little man from the Rift Valley. He's still in last place but he's nearer than ever before to the racers up ahead. If he maintains this momentum, we could have him and Karelov in the lead before the end of today. It's been a brilliant, brilliant fightback. We're going to go to our hourly news desk update now. Join us again right after this…"

Zelda lay in her motel room, just south of St Augustine. It was mid-afternoon but she had the curtains drawn. She was gathering her thoughts, in preparation for a final strike. She reached into her holdall and pulled out a dog-eared wallet of photographs. She had gazed upon them thousands of times. It was almost a daily ritual but increasingly it angered her. As she leafed through them she stopped, as always, at the photograph that upset her most. It was a form of self-torture. The photo, complete with amateurish red-eye images, was from a party many years previously. A group of obviously drunk young revellers were gathered around the camera grinning and pulling faces. All except two, Zelda and Loverboy who were on the brink of a discreet kiss. They only had eyes for each other. That evening had been tumultuous. It touched emotions that she had never reached before or since. Before the following morning the lovers had gone their separate ways never to see each other again – until now.

The anger bubbled uncontrollably again. Zelda grabbed a ball-point pen and stabbed repeatedly at the wretched photo. With each stab came a cry of suppressed pain but she could not exorcise the anguish completely. She got up and paced around the room trying to settle her breathing. As she slowly regained her composure, she found that the sobs were gradually replaced by halting laughter.

She would know true happiness again and it would be very soon. It was almost time to stop the circus and eliminate Loverboy.

Karelov was sidelined on the A1A near Fort Pierce. He had encountered a torrential thunderstorm. Cycling was out of the question as the water curtain hurtled down. He had tried that and almost lost control. The forks of lightning that accompanied it were none too reassuring either. It would pass soon enough but Karelov loudly cursed the fact that his support vehicle had travelled so far ahead up the road. By the time he had caught up on foot, globules of rain, the size of a Mekon's head, were stinging his eyelids. He ripped off the spoof thigh bandage that was sodden. It was time for that injury to be cured. The RV was required to park up while Karelov was on board, so instead of passing through the storm in four or five minutes, Karelov had to bide his time and make a change of clothes while 20 precious minutes elapsed. He watched the small TV monitor in the RV.

Hal 'The Mouth' brought the standings up-to-date.

"Well, we have temporarily lost our picture of Team Karelov near Indian River, as one of those famous Florida flash storms hits this section of road. Only PJ Kogo is in action. Everyone else is taking 'five', enforced or otherwise."

"Goddamn Kenyan," muttered the cheerless Russian.

"Brent Ryan has moved to within a few miles of the lead and we know from your calls that it would be popular if America's representative could lead the event through Central Florida."

"Goddamn Yankee," hissed Karelov.

Hal continued. "Gaby Vaughan and Steve O'Neill are still tied for first place. They are expected back out on the road any minute now and should be the first contestants to head west on Highway 528 towards Orlando. Let's take a look at the background to Florida's Turnpike Road and how the small rural town of Orlando has become the holidaymaking capital of the world, despite its nearest beach being fifty miles away."

"Goddamn Brits, Aussies and Yankee Disney." Karelov was in no mood to be delayed further in his quest for a million bucks. The rain was easing. He was on his way again.

Lenny Stein perused the latest TV audience figures with a measure of satisfaction. In Europe, Japan and Australia, the transmission of Sport Armageddon highlight packages every hour was proving to be much more successful than anticipated. Zing Cola was happy enough with the commercial exposure that Sport Armageddon was bringing to the brand. Around two hundred Prime Life viewers, mostly good ol' boys from the South, had rung the Sport Armageddon hotline to complain that the criminal Karelov should be thrown out of the event on his ear. That was gratifying. Stein knew that he needed to keep hyping and tweaking his event. If Sport Armageddon stood still for a moment, it was dead. His viewing figures, especially on the East Coast of the US were good, but he could do better yet.

O'Neill enjoyed the cathartic experience of talking to Gaby's childhood friend, the Doc. By the time they reached Winter Garden, they had been overtaken by Brent Ryan. Karelov was very close behind. It was therefore only a quarter of an hour's break in the Highway Rest Area while Steve dosed up on bananas but it was enough. The Doc was a kindly man in his fifties, with big features and crinkly skin. His eyes stayed fixed on O'Neill while the latter explained his broodiness and contemplation. The Doc then asked lots of questions about his job, his social circle, his eating and sleeping.

"You know, Steve, you will be okay with all of this, but you're not going to shake it off or clear your head without a bit of help. It's taken root like paranoia. I would say that you are suffering a touch of clinical depression. Deep down, I think you know that you have nothing to feel guilty about but you should have talked this one out long ago, mate. And I don't reckon that the nutter who has been making all these threats is the victim's mother, so unless you've jilted a psychopath in the past couple of years, I think you're in the clear. Anyway, do you feel a bit happier about life today than you did yesterday?"

"Yeah. It has helped to get if off my chest."

"Well, good. That's how these things get worked out. It's time to put it behind you and start living. To help you a bit, I'm going to prescribe an anti-depressant called Prozac. Have you come across it?"

Steve vaguely had.

"It's the wonder sunshine drug, right?"

"That's right. Alberto Salazar rescued his running career with it. It helped him win the Comrades Marathon in South Africa."

"I remember that. So it's one for athletes?"

"Of course. It's legal for sports drug testing."

"Any side effects?"

"Nope. Just give it a go. It's your best hope of emerging from the fog."

"I'll give it a try, although my routines are a bit unusual right now. Thanks Doc."

"No problem. Now it's time to race. You have a big bad Russian bearing down on you."

O'Neill headed for the van to see if Gaby was ready to hit the road again. His sudden return caught her by surprise.

She was lying on the floor of the van with her feet elevated and propped up on the window rim. Her eyes were squeezed tightly shut. She had two fingers on her neck, checking her pulse. It was 190 beats per minute. This was the worst turn she had ever had.

"Are you OK, love?" O'Neill was worried by the pained expression on her face.

"Sure," she lied. "Just give me a minute to change into some clean shorts and I'll be right with you."

It must have been a further two minutes after Steve stepped away before her pulse began to calm down. 180-150-130-110-90-70. It was back down to normal in another 45 seconds. Scary, but not quite scary enough for her to speak to the Doc about it. She would leave that until after Sport Armageddon was over. She would have more time then. Now there was a mission to be completed.

A bead of sweat dripped off Vivian Wheatley III's nose and splattered onto the sheet of letterhead in front of him. Damn. He screwed the sheet into a ball and tossed it over his shoulder where it joined six other similar failed missive missiles on the floor. He was trying to compose his letter of resignation to Prime Life and he could not get into the flow at all.

'Dear Lenny' had been dropped in favour of an altogether starchier and more formal 'Dear Mr Stein'.

'It has been my privilege and pleasure to work with you these past two decades' ...had been substituted by 'It is time for me to move on. I wish to retire...'

It was no use. He would just have to tell the man in person. After all the running around over the previous two years, recruiting and filming the competitors, arranging and measuring the route, finding and sweetening the sponsors, and now ducking from some crazed witch, Wheatley had just about had his fill of Sport Armageddon.

He had run himself ragged over the past two days with the friggin' emergency drug testing. No man had ever got a result through quicker. And now, on top of everything else, he was tasked with dealing with the Georgia authorities, in whose jurisdiction Sport Armageddon would arrive in just a few days. At that moment there was half a chance it would be halted on the Florida-Georgia border. He was wrestling like crazy with the red tape, greasing up to politicians and what thanks did he get for it? Damn all. His other management colleagues appreciated his efforts but Lenny could not care less about him. That stud farm in Kentucky was looking more alluring than ever. It was nearly midnight. Viv started to dial Stein's number and then cancelled. He switched off the phone and tossed it across the room. He would sleep on his decision and speak to the aforementioned Mr Stein on the morrow.

While Wheatley had been smoothing the pathway up ahead, the event had drawn huge crowds of curious holidaymakers as it skirted the south side of Orlando and headed for Tampa on Highway 17.

Tampa had been confirmed as part of the race route only after a summit meeting with city councillors in the final few days before the race started. It was financially important to get the Gulf Coast capital onside. How Stein would love to have told them, just after the contract had been signed, that the race was always secretly scheduled to pass through Tampa anyway.

Karelov had overtaken O'Neill and Vaughan without so much as a cheery wave as they sped west of Kissimmee. Brent Ryan had built up a big lead over the Russian. PJ 'no-rest' Kogo was still in fifth.

At midnight, when every competitor was on the road, Ryan was just south of Bushnell, still 20 miles clear of Karelov, much the same gap as when the big Russian had resumed the chase that morning. This angered Karelov, who was slamming the pedals as if it was the final day of competition. Stein loved it. All the other racers had to be told to look like they were working flat out. Karelov did not need to be told. He was putting every atom into it. O'Neill and Vaughan were nine miles back and Kogo, long overdue a rest, was only five miles behind them, west of Plant City on 92.

All five competitors were within 34 miles of each other and the American superstar leading. This was surely the stuff of dreams for Lenny Stein...

CHAPTER THIRTEEN

Sport Armageddon Standings 00.00 hours Sunday
1st Brent Ryan (USA)   688.0 miles
2nd Leonid Karelov (Russia)   668.0 miles
3rd Gabrielle Vaughan (Australia)   659.5 miles
4th Steven O'Neill (GB)   659.5 miles
5th Philemon Kogo (Kenya)   654.5 miles

LENNY had to believe that the increased security measures were sufficient to keep the mad woman at bay, but until he had eliminated her from the equation, it was an uncomfortable feeling.

The overnight viewing figures were as good as Stein dared hope. What was unexpected was the speed at which the competitors were powering through the cycle phase. Prime Life's pre-event planning had assumed an average cycle speed of no better than 14-15 miles per hour and complete rest for between four and a half and five and a half hours per day. Even the most leisurely competitors – currently Vaughan and O'Neill – were resting for less than four and a half hours per day and averaging between 15 and 17 miles per hour. It didn't matter when they got to Atlanta. For the moment it would be sufficient that they got to Atlanta at all. The fitness displayed in such cauldron-like heat was awesome. But then, as he had told Doug Alred, he always went for the best, and these guys had been handpicked as the world's finest ultra-endurance athletes. He should probably give Wheatley some credit for that. Wheatley? It was nearly seven o'clock in the morning. Where the hell was the idle slug?

He rang the 'memory' one number on his phone.

There was no answer. Stein knew where Wheatley was staying, so he rang the motel number. The motel room phone rang for a full minute before a conspicuously bleary voice replied.

"Mornin', Chief."

"Mornin'. How d'ya know it was me?"

"You're the only one with the motel number and I didn't figure the front desk would ring me this early."

"Right. You still in bed?"

"Nope. I've been up and about for a couple of hours now. Making a few calls to the team, you know," he had no compunction about lying to the Chief. The Chief could repay that particular compliment in spades.

The Chief, of course, knew full well that he was lying but could not be bothered to argue the point.

"You know Karelov's taken the lead again overnight."

"Has he? I mean, yeah, right."

"I wasn't expecting this to happen. I need to think what we can do. He's paid the penalty that I imposed and I'm a man of honour. I guess we'll just have to wait and see what happens."

"Sure, we could always try another drugs test."

"Nope. We'll just wait and see what happens."

The phone went dead. Wheatley switched on the motel room TV. He did not feel motivated to bust a gut on Prime Life's behalf. He rang room service and ordered bacon, hash browns and four eggs over easy. Becoming suddenly conscious of his strict dietary regime, he cancelled the side order of coffee and doughnuts and substituted a Zing Lite instead.

Eventually, after slightly too many musical trailers of Karelov and Ryan filmed during some separate pre-race visits to Walt Disney World, Hal 'The Mouth' cut back to the live action.

"And those are the same two fun-loving guys who are currently slugging it out for a million bucks on the mean streets of Central Florida, as the battle of Sport Armageddon continues. If you're just joining us, it has been a night of steady progress and the second coming of Leonid Karelov. Now seemingly free of that troublesome injury to his thigh, he passed Brent Ryan while the American was taking a nap, southbound on Highway 441 at Gainesville. The time was a quarter after four this morning, as we watch the replay of the very wide overtaking manoeuvre by Karelov. If you're thinking you can hear an exchange of greetings between the two of them, you're right, but I won't repeat it. No love lost there.

"And the caption confirms that on Day Four of Sport Armageddon, it could still be anybody's race. Karelov is now estimated to be seventy-five minutes clear at Belleview. O'Neill and Vaughan are still locked together at Orange Lake a further forty minutes down and the Kogo machine still keeps chugging along. His rest almost exactly matched the Brit and the Aussie but he's now just three miles down, south of Micanopy."

PJ was feeling quite pleased with the low-tech nature of his Sport Armageddon cycle challenge. He would get there on his own terms. He had not made as much use as the others of the IV drip. He decided after the second session that it was not for him. Similarly, he was the only competitor to eschew the use of a heart-rate monitor. His diet was heavily reliant on traditional Kenyan maize dishes and sweet tea. Jennifer's hands were enough to keep the shoulder and neck tension tolerable and three pairs of cycling shorts were the best he could muster to muffle the pain of saddle sores. He had used his ingenuity throughout the contest. During the swim phase the air had been warm but the Okeechobee water was very cold. He had kept his core body temperature within acceptable limits by having Jennifer pour hot water down inside the neck of his wetsuit every time he took a break.

Now he began the breakfast cycle session with another Heath-Robinson piece of innovation – the PJ Kogo ice hat. In place of the standard issue cycle safety helmet, he had substituted an outsize baseball cap packed inside with ice cubes, inside perforated polythene. The ice would slowly melt in the heat of the day and help keep him cool. When pictures of it appeared on Prime Life, it caused a stir. It looked cumbersome but within a day, most of his rivals would follow his lead and adopt a similar natty line in headwear.

PJ was on a roll. The only dark cloud in his personal blue sky was the 'Z' woman. PJ was certain that his one night stand was coming for revenge. Every time he thought of it, he looked over his shoulder. Usually, a race could suppress all other emotions but riding in fear of his life was one way of staying alert.

Ryan's approach to the event was extremely high-tech by contrast. He was using every type of sophisticated back-up that he could lay hands on. Prime Life had placed the 'Zing Cola' minicam on his bike. It was a tiny camera on the handlebars that could be operated remotely to show the view ahead or behind or catch a close-up of his face at crucial stages. It was disconcerting to have such a stowaway on board but he was paid handsomely for the privilege and was the last person to complain about extra attention. He wasn't happy to relinquish the lead again to Karelov but was fully confident that victory in the long run would be his alone. He just needed to maintain his composure and good things would happen.

More bad news was about to befall Lenny Stein. Doug Alred had been at it once more. The morning's Jacksonville Bugle did not arrive until after lunchtime but it brought confirmation that his loose cannon had fired off again. This time, God knows how, Alred had delved sufficiently into Steve O'Neill's background to justify an 'Armageddon Scot in death crash riddle' headline. The article went on to quote from the coroner's observations at the inquest and details of the magistrates' court acquittal. Alred was careful to make it clear that no blame was attached to O'Neill, although the roadside breath test was mentioned. The headline was just about the most incriminating aspect of the piece. Stein didn't object to the article. In some strange way, it invested O'Neill with a bit of colour and character, of which there was no extraneous evidence. Stein did very much mind, however, that Alred was operating out of control. Something would have to be done about it.

The Prozac was working wonders for O'Neill. It was only Day One of his rehabilitation but he felt completely rejuvenated. It was as if he had emerged from a tunnel. He could not believe he had let himself get into such a state.

It had gone on for so long and miraculously appeared to have been righted by a couple of friendly faces to talk to and a dose of pep pills. Wheatley quizzed him briefly later that day about the Alred article, which had been syndicated in a number of evening newspapers. A day or two previously, those revelations would have been a horrendous setback to his equilibrium. He would have been reaching for the hemlock at the first opportunity. Now he was able to deal with it calmly and rationally, accepting that by fully objective standards he had been examined and cleared of wrongdoing and guilt. He felt ready for anything.

Since midnight, just before Stein retired to bed the previous evening, some more heavy thunderstorms had been forecast for Central Florida. The road conditions were likely to be treacherous. If the pattern of the first few days was followed, only Karelov, Kogo and possibly Ryan would cycle through the noonday heat and humidity. Stein sent out a directive that the spare bike cameras should focus on Kogo as the competitor of the day. He had closed down the gap on the rest of the field to a tantalising distance and was a firm favourite with Prime Life's networked viewers around the world.

By the time the storms broke, in dramatic fashion, Karelov had put a vast amount of tarmac between himself and Ryan. It had been an awesome display of endurance sport by the Russian bear and Hal was back in the saddle to see it.

"I cannot believe the power this man is generating. He's like a machine. There's no sign of the leg injury that humbled him back in Miami. He is making light of these long straights on the north-bound section of Highway 17. In the background, you can see

Lake Monroe. The big crowds of Orlando are thirty miles back down the road and we estimate that the gap back to Brent Ryan, currently resting, must be more than sixty five miles. The American is still north of all of the Central Florida Lakes, with a six mile lead over Vaughan and O'Neill. PJ Kogo is still just about three miles off the back.

"We can also see signs of heavy clouds and a serious electrical storm rolling towards Karelov to the north of Lake Monroe, and at this point we'll leave him and cut to this incredible game of catch-up which Kogo is playing with the field. I know PJ has a lot of fans out there, and here he comes, past the southwestern edge of Ocala National Forest. Let's ride with him now..."

Karelov could see the storm approaching like a curtain. The daylight turned to darkness and lightning streaked through the sky. When the rain began lashing down he was ready for it. He had changed to a lightweight Gore-Tex suit and wore a visor to protect his eyes. The support vehicle had been ordered to park eight miles further up the road, where the storm was likely to have cleared. He was going to ride this one out. He put his head down – metaphorically and physically – and began hammering the pedals even harder. No way was that dumb jerk Lenny Stein going to stand in the way of him getting to that million bucks. He would ride and run all day if need be. The weather was appalling but he let out a roar as he psyched himself up and blasted on through the torrential downpour.

He cursed again a few moments later as a Q-Haul van veered perilously close as it passed him. It nearly knocked him clean off the bike. The bike was fitted with two powerful lamps front and back. The guy was going too fast. Was he a lunatic or something? Goddamn Yankee. He sped on and peered through his streaming visor as his speedometer clocked up another mile. Only Karelov was tough enough to knock out 14 miles per hour through this rain. He grinned as he thought of the marshmallow soft American, probably holed up in his caravan with his wimpy team. At this rate Karelov would be in Jacksonville before he knew it. He gritted his teeth and ploughed on.

Up ahead he could make out a Citgo gas station. The next stop after that would be the link-up with the support bus. He would probably take a Snickers Bar and a banana when he stopped. He liked Snickers Bars.

Leonid Karelov had no chance of avoiding the Q-Haul van as it pulled out into the road from behind the gas station fence. It hit him full on from the right hand side and flung him out across the carriageway towards the median. Although he was wearing a protective helmet, the impact of the landing on the road knocked him out cold.

The next car on the scene braked late and narrowly avoided running over the prostrate Russian. He lay like a broken doll across the fast lane, his mangled bike next to him. No one from the gas station knew of his presence and the Q-Haul van had long gone. By the time an ambulance had been summoned by the car driver, they were joined by his support bus and a Prime Life film crew, who had hurried back down the southbound carriageway when Karelov had uncharacteristically failed to arrive at the rendezvous.

The hospital emergency staff were concerned at the potential seriousness of the head injuries. Karelov was conscious but incoherent by the time he was admitted to the casualty department. Nemo trotted alongside the stretcher, weeping and bad-mouthing the goddamn Yankees. Several film crews and reporters were held back at the main entrance. It was high drama and once the storms had passed, Lenny Stein himself arrived at the hospital.

"This is a terrible setback for Sport Armageddon," he announced solemnly to the waiting media after he had visited Karelov. "I know that Brent Ryan and his fellow competitors would have wanted to beat Leonid fair and square but this turn of events has been extraordinary and tragic for our race leader. His injuries, apart from cuts and bruising, are a fractured thumb, concussion and a cracked wrist. He is feeling very sorry for himself but is talking about rejoining the event. The doctors have said that that is out of the question but he is a strong-willed man, as we all know. We shall have to wait and see."

"Is there any news of the driver of the vehicle which hit him?" Doug Alred, as always, led the inquisitors.

"None at all. It makes me very angry to see a hit-and-run like this. Leonid has described the vehicle as a removal truck or similar. He wasn't sure of the size but nobody else at all saw it. There must be hundreds of those things hired out in Central Florida each day. The police offer little hope of catching the driver and, as you know, it wasn't captured on TV. It's a tragedy but it leaves Brent Ryan in the lead and the other three competitors within a thirty minute time span. It's an unbelievable event. God knows what will happen next."

Doug Alred pressed on. "Is there any suggestion of foul play – that the collision was not an accident and that someone did it deliberately?"

You're trying my patience, thought Stein. Why do you have to go rummaging around every little incident and hype up the negative?

"None at all." Lenny affected stoicism worthy of a Watergate witness. "The weather conditions were atrocious, visibility virtually nil and the driver would not be looking out for a cyclist on the highway. It looks like it was just plain bad luck."

Lenny watched with interest as the interview he gave was played again for the umpteenth time in the eight o'clock news bulletin on Prime Life. The crash had been a ratings magnet. It was a bizarre incident although there was little sympathy for Karelov, who, by common consent, had again 'got what was coming to him'.

American spectator interest was restored and this was evident when Brent Ryan led the remaining competitors on their circuits of

Daytona racetrack. The timing was impeccable. He cycled on to the arena at a quarter past five that evening, to a tumultuous reception from the working population of Daytona Beach who had dropped by on their way home. There must have been ten or twelve thousand fans who began their own 'U-S-A, U-S-A' chant as he poured on the pace round the purpose-built lap. Vaughan and O'Neill would arrive barely 12 minutes after Ryan had left to head north on A1A but already the number of spectators had dwindled to a few hundred. Viv watched incredulously on the battlebus monitor. The Chief had drummed it into him countless times over the years that Prime Life's viewers wanted American winners, seeing off the best of the rest. You could never, ever under-estimate their partisan nature. Wheatley was not sure exactly what lengths the Chief would go to in giving the viewers what they wanted. He had grave doubts about the Karelov hit-and-run.

O'Neill led Vaughan by a bike length through the departing crowds of American supporters. Their police outrider had to switch on his klaxon and flashing lights to ensure that they had a clear passage. There were plenty of wolf whistles and leering looks for the pert lady in pink. In the bars of Daytona Beach many beer pundits would conclude that O'Neill was as mad as a hatter for cycling in front of her when he could have been savouring the rear view. The reality was that O'Neill, still high on Prozac, was coaxing her through a bad patch. Gaby had toiled for the last 36 hours, hoping that the feeling of extreme fatigue would pass, praying that her heart palpitations would not return.

A couple of times, she had nearly fallen asleep on the bike. It was only the pain of her aching thighs after 900 miles of cycling that kept her awake. Nine hundred miles. Good grief! It was a ludicrous event, with perhaps the worst of all yet to come. She knew her performance was going down well in Australia. The men there thought it was a hoot that their top Sheila was holding her own against the best men in the world and they loved the way she looked. The syndicated viewing figures were terrific. Up to three and a half million viewers for the nightly highlights programme on terrestrial and cable TV combined. And that from a country with a total population of 17 million.

She looked at Mr Sunshine just up ahead. Would they keep in touch after Sport Armageddon was over? Would they date properly? She hoped so. She had fallen for this thin little man in a really big way. And best of all, she discovered that he had a terrific sense of humour, now that he had snapped out of his long-term downer.

She begrudged the circuits of Daytona raceway. She wanted to press on to Jacksonville. They had completed just five full circuits when PJ Kogo cycled onto the track just behind them. There was a tremendous cheer for the African, which he acknowledged with a wave and a grin. Instead of trying to overtake them, PJ cycled alongside the Brit and the Australian for the remainder of their laps. Stein would not like it, but what the hell, they were all in this together and their common enemies were distance and the heat.

They had not seen PJ since he headed in the opposite direction on the shores of Okeechobee.

"Long time no see, PJ," greeted O'Neill in his new upbeat manner.

"How are you, my friends? And do tell me, where does it hurt most?" They all laughed.

A comparison of notes revealed that the legs, apart from the two Australian ones, were pretty good, and mostly it was saddle soreness and tightness in neck, back, shoulders and triceps that was making them reach for the Ibrufen. Gaby had the record for the number of pairs of cycle shorts being sported all at once. She was wearing four pairs for that session. Yes, she confirmed, they were all pink, and yes they were keeping the sores at bay. PJ resolved to double his quota of leg garments.

They discussed how far Ryan had extended the lead, all believing that their running strength would boost their prospects over the final competitive phase. They also discussed Karelov, and agreed how risky it had been to try to cycle through a heavy storm.

"I guess he's lucky to be alive," pronounced Gaby.

"Do you think it was the 'Z' woman?" Asked PJ.

"I doubt it," said Gaby "And if she's in the grandstands here, we're rather vulnerable, don't you think?"

There was no reply from the other two.

"Karelov's not finished yet, you know," declared O'Neill, hastily changing the subject. "I reckon we haven't seen the last of our Comrade."

"He is one very tough man," agreed Kogo. "But surely he would not be very wise to cycle and run after that."

Nemo had wiped away his tears and now concentrated his efforts on healing his protÈgÈ. The medics at the hospital in Lake Monroe did not welcome Nemo's presence at the bedside. It was fair enough that he had ordered them to put Karelov's wrist in a special lightweight fibreglass cast but a nurse had reported her suspicions that Nemo was slipping tablets to Karelov, which had not been prescribed by the consultant.

At around eleven o'clock that night Karelov awoke from a deep sleep.

"How do you feel?" Nemo immediately asked in Russian.

"Like I have been hit by a truck," replied Karelov dourly. "I ache all over and my arm and head are very sore."

"Could you carry on?"

"I want to, but I'm not sure if I can." It was rare for Karelov to have doubts.

"You can," urged Nemo.

He led Karelov carefully out of bed and slowly into the bathroom. Nemo ran a hot bath, which he infused with several large capsules of what he claimed were herbs. The water fizzed and bubbled and gave off a pungent smell. Karelov struggled to ease himself into the bath but instantly felt his beaten-up limbs begin to soothe.

"I give you massage and you take these," said Nemo, handing him five tablets of assorted colours and shapes.

"What are they?" asked Karelov.

"They are special. You can still win, Leonid."

"Then let's go, my friend."

At 11.45 pm, Karelov discharged himself, without formality, from the hospital. He walked stiffly across the car park to the support van that Nemo had primed for his return. The driver winked at Karelov. The man was barking mad.

"We go again," said Karelov, as the van headed back to the Citgo gas station with a replacement bike on board.

"Sensation!" Bawled Hal 'The Mouth's' stand-in as Prime Life's cameras captured the restart.

"We have all five competitors back out on the road again, as the million dollar prize looms nearer. Sport Armageddon is still anyone's race."

Lenny Stein rued the fact that everyone except Karelov passed through St Augustine during the hours of darkness. It was one of the oldest settlements in the continental United States and they had recorded acres of promotional footage in conjunction with the tourist authorities.

The leading four riders had taken at least two hours sleep between midnight and four o'clock, but they had still whizzed through town in the small hours, way ahead of forecast. So much scenery, so little daylight, so few viewers.

Lenny had rung Melanie at midnight to see if there was any chance of Ryan taking a break so that his arrival in the Jacksonville Beach transition zone would coincide with the breakfast time viewing and peak crowds.

"I can't believe you asked me that Chief. We're only forty-two miles from the Beach. Sure, he's going to take a two hour nap. But even so, he'll be there by six o'clock at the latest. This is sport you know; you can't regulate it to suit the programming schedules. It's unpredictable."

Where the hell did she develop a mouth like that? If that was what hanging around with old Golden Groin Ryan was doing for her, he could transfer her back to the studio before her sassy little ass touched the ground.

"No, you're quite right honey. It would be against the spirit of the event for me to intervene. It's great for the ratings to have one of our own boys in the lead though. Reckon he can keep it goin'?"

"Sure, Chief. He looks great."

I bet he does, though Stein, and if I find out that you've been in for too many close-up looks, we'll have to have one of our little chats.

"OK, keep up the good work, 'Night honey."

"Night, Chief."

He wasn't too concerned. Vaughan, O'Neill and Kogo were all on course to complete the cycle a little after eight o'clock, which would keep the beach breakfasters happy and make great television. As for Karelov, well it was anyone's guess whether he would even make it to Jacksonville at all. The man was a cadaver on wheels.

For a corpse, Karelov was actually cycling rather well. The first 30 minutes from Lake Monroe towards De Land bore all the hallmarks of a mistake. His wrist, thumb and head were so painful he thought he would scream. He could only grip the handlebars with one hand and the aerodynamic crouch position was a thing of the past. In those first 30 minutes, he wobbled a mere six miles up the road. Then, slowly but surely, some of the aches and pains began to ebb. Perhaps it was a question of the circulation getting going in his body. More likely, it was Nemo's magic pills starting to take effect. He clung to the thought that most of the others would be taking their two hour break so he would surely claw back some ground before dawn. He had lost a front tooth in the crash. It would require some orthodontic work to be paid for out of his million bucks, but for now he concentrated on the effort of edging north on Highway A1A. He was in no mood for smiling anyway. To take his mind off the discomfort, he tried to replay the truck incident in his mind. Whichever way he looked at it, there was one inescapable conclusion. Someone had tried to kill him. Was he riding back toward a million bucks or into the lair of the mad woman? Would she finish him off if she got a second chance?

Ryan showboated the final two miles of cycling between the beaches of Ponte Vedra and Jacksonville. He hit 20 miles per hour, whooping loudly to the clusters of spectators, mostly the payola student busloads.

The transition zone had a hastily convened party atmosphere. Hal 'The Mouth's' deputy was doing the honours as MC and 'YMCA' was thumping out of a pair of huge speakers as Brent Ryan shot down the temporary ramp from the boardwalk onto the beach itself. Eighty metres of duckboarding marked the final stretch of the Bike Ride from Hell. Fans, students, holidaymakers and nosey rubberneckers lined either side, two deep in places.

The DJ was yelling so loud into the microphone that none of them could understand a single word he was saying. It didn't matter. The excitement in his voice transmitted everything that was necessary and the crowd applauded, cheered and shrieked as if it was the Second Coming.

Melanie was laughing out loud in the Team Ryan bus as they drove parallel on the boardwalk. Sometimes she felt so proud to be an American, they were so...enthusiastic. If enough of them grouped together they'd cheer the opening of a box of Wheeties.

Ryan entered into the spirit of it, dismounting from his bike at speed, as camera flashes lit up the dawn light.

He snapped free the disc release on his cycling shoes and trotted towards the shower cubicle, planning a rapid massage, change of clothes and refuelling.

It was precisely eight minutes later when he emerged – ice hat, wrap-round shades, singlet, trunks, two pairs of socks and heavy duty Puma running shoes. Sadly, the brief trunks highlighted mahogany tanned thighs but also a welter of heavily creamed saddle sores. He didn't care if it looked unsightly. The sunshine, sea air and absence of a saddle would clear it in no time.

His first 800 metres on the concrete promenade were covered in less than four minutes. This was an error of judgement. He had practised the bike-run transition endlessly. He had received lengthy seminars about the way running would impact upon muscles that were still in cycling mode. He knew that the energy release and metabolic functions differed slightly. He knew that he would generally run the second half of an Ironman marathon quicker than the first. All that knowledge helped him not at all. He felt like a yachtsman stepping ashore after a year at sea. Co-ordination and rhythm were terrible.

"Do I look like Pinocchio?" he asked Melanie as soon as the crowds began to thin out and they were clear of the omnipresent film crew.

"Well you have got rather a long nose."

"Ha-ha. No, I mean do I look like I'm running normally. I feel like crap."

"You look like you're going too fast. If you keep this up, we'll be in Atlanta for lunchtime."

It was something for him to wrestle with for the rest of the morning but despite his misgivings and pace judgement errors, Brent Ryan actually handled the transition phase considerably better than all his opponents.

Steve O'Neill and Gaby Vaughan arrived at Jacksonville Beach less than two hours later. The Australian was still struggling and they agreed, as they swept through the still air of the beach, already toasting the sun worshippers with a 90 degree reading, that they would take their time on the changeover. They thought 20 minutes would be time enough to get some IV fluid into Gaby, who was feeling light-headed and queasy.

The Prime Life medic deftly inserted the tube into her wrist, once she had showered and was receiving a synchronised leg massage from Patsy and Jane of Team Vaughan. As a matter of routine, the medic also recorded a pulse.

"Jeez...You're at 160 beats per minute but you stopped cycling ten minutes ago." The medic feared she would have to implement her trauma unit procedure right there on the beach.

"No, no. Check again," said Gaby unclenching her fist as she felt the racing heartbeat slow up.

The medic furrowed her brow.

"Oh...it's 90 beats per minute. I must have miscalculated before. Perhaps the leg massage prompted a false reading. It looks like you're recovering OK."

Gaby wondered whether she should tell her. Whether she should mention that this event was making a mess of her heart. Whether she was dying in instalments. She said nothing, gave her a warm smile and closed her eyes.

"Thanks, Doc."

It was 35 minutes before the two amigos set off on the third and cruellest phase of Sport Armageddon. They demonstrated their respect for the distance by walking and jogging the first three miles, desperately seeking their running co-ordination.

During their stopover, the PJ Kogo cabaret show had hit the beach, literally.

PJ had zipped onto the duckboarding to another rapturous

reception, less than ten minutes behind the dynamic duo. He had hurried to the Kogo team tent, determined to set off in second place on the run.

He was underway in barely three minutes but it was a short-lived bid for glory. His co-ordination had completely deserted him and he fell flat on his face. Three attempts to get going brought the same result.

Jennifer rushed to prop him up.

"You've either pulled a muscle or your legs need charging up. Let's get back to the tent."

PJ could have wept. All that effort to catch up and now he was going to be pummelled until he could remember how to run. And how long would that take? Jennifer handed him a mug of sweet hot tea.

"It's OK, honey. You're still hanging in there. Let's just be cool."

Karelov was still creaking up Highway A1A north of Ormond Beach – an estimated six hours behind. He was thinking murderous thoughts. He should have belted Ryan harder with that microphone stand. He should have socked Stein in K-Mart. It all helped detract from the gnawing pain in his head and arm. Slowly, the miles were clicking by. He was coping with the heat and he did not feel tired. With his powers of concentration, he could blot out any doubts, any pain, any fear, and any mad assassins. They would hear again from Leonid Karelov.

Stein was glad that the gaps between the leaders were bridgeable. There was still plenty of spice in the head-to-head contest and an American leader, thank God.

He turned to the Jacksonville Bugle with interest and was staggered to see that the turncoat Doug Alred had written another critical piece that covered all of the back page and part of the front. There was nothing specific this time. He just seemed to have taken all of the negative features aired previously and rehashed them. He also questioned the ethics of the whole Sport Armageddon project.

'Many experienced endurance pundits feel very uneasy about the selection of the five competitors, arbitrarily and without reference to national federations,' he wrote. 'The race itself is not sanctioned by triathlon's world governing body. The accident to Leonid Karelov throws into question the safety aspects of an event held round the clock on public roads with such a big prize at stake. Inevitably, risks will be taken. No wonder the State of Georgia is indifferent towards the event.'

"Bastard!" cursed Stein unable to comprehend the formerly loyal Alred's quest for the hidden agenda of Sport Armageddon.

Alred himself had spent very little time in the Prime Life press bus during the previous two days. Away from the event, he was hitting the telephones hard as he uncovered murkier aspects of the event's organisation. He was preparing a major feature on Stein himself. Early research suggested that Sport Armageddon was merely the culmination of a progressively sleazy career curve in sport pro-gramming.

"It's a story that needs to be told," he confided to his Editor that evening. The deadline for the following morning's Bugle had passed without incident and they were relaxing with beer and chicken wings at the 'Hooters' restaurant in Jacksonville Landing. The establishment overlooked the St John's River and afforded some great views upstream. The Editor, as ever, was more impressed by the contours of their waitresses clad in skimpy orange lycra shorts and a low cut white T-shirts.

"Did you see that one?" he interrupted Doug and nudged him as an improbable bust, in need of cantilever support, jiggled past. From beneath a peroxide mop, Tiffany, as advertised on her badge, winked and flashed the most tip-winning of smiles.

"What a babe! She's gorgeous." The Editor winked and waved back. Two pitchers of Bud had completely neutralised his sense of decorum and dignity.

"Sorry Doug, what were you saying?"

"That I used to be on good terms with Lenny Stein but that what I have seen of this event makes me sick to my stomach. Stein is a bully and a conman. You and I have watched enough football and baseball to know that this race with five deluded athletes flogging themselves to death for the sake of a bigger share of the cable audience, bears only a passing resemblance to sport."

"But the public loves it."

"The public loves what it has been trained to love. There has been some masterful hype. For God's sake, it's a triathlon with five people in it. That would normally rate a zero audience. They watch to see Gaby's tushy and to see whether the damn Russian gets his comeuppance from the American boy wonder. They watch to see why black men can't swim. They watch to see if someone keels over and dies. They..."

"OK. OK. So it's an illusion. So are Tiffany's breasts, but where's the harm in it?" quizzed the Editor.

"The harm in it is that it's a fraud. What you see is not what you get. The race is manipulated more than most people could possibly imagine. We even think there's at least one serious death threat been made against a competitor and no one has notified the police." Alred's eyes were aflame with the injustice and hypocrisy of it all.

"Then you're right. It's a story that needs to be written. Now let's get off the case and enjoy a few beers. OK?"

"OK."

The Editor knew how to relax and Doug was a willing pupil. Several more foaming pitchers were brought to them, clutched to the ample bosom of Tiffany.

They reminisced about football, blondes, the scrapes they had got into over the years and good times had by one and all. Before they knew it, the clock chimed for one o'clock in the morning. Alred explained that he had to rejoin the race west of Savannah, which would require an early start that morning. The Editor offered him the spare bed in his suite at the Jacksonville Hotel, just across Main Street Bridge. The offer was gratefully accepted and they bid a soft focus farewell to Tiffany and her bosom buddies. The Editor tried some blatant groping, which she deftly side-stepped and they swaggered out into the night air towards the riverside walk. As they reached the edge of the buildings on the Landing, the sound of two gunfire shots rang out. Doug Alred crumpled to the ground. He had been hit twice. The Editor immediately snapped out of his drunken stupor and dived for the railings.

After less than a minute of the deathly silence that ensued, the Hooters waitresses led the charge out of the restaurant, without pausing to think that they might themselves be running into sniper fire. Tiffany made the 911 call before rushing outside to find the Editor cradling Doug's head in his hands as blood poured from his shoulders and chest. He was barely coherent.

"The psycho... it's that psycho..."

He slipped into unconsciousness as the anxious wait for the ambulance began.

It was a great way to sober up, thought the Editor as he paced the hospital accident and emergency waiting area. He was onto his fifth cup of black coffee. His mind was turning cartwheels. His conscience was asking why he had dived for the railings as soon as the first shot struck Doug. He had seen Alred recoil before he had plunged for cover. At the same time there was a sense of relief that his self-preservation instincts remained intact, despite the equivalent of eight pints of beer.

The Bugle's news reporters were already speculating on possible motives for the attack, on behalf of their colleague. There had been no positive sightings of a gunman and no clues beyond the fact that the shots had been fired from the riverside car park, possibly from a range of 60 yards. It was a time of night when few witnesses were expected.

Doug Alred's life was not in danger. He had suffered a crushed collarbone and heavy loss of blood. Bizarrely, he appeared to have been the subject of marksmanship of a deadly kind with both bullets striking his upper chest at the same height and distance, either side of his sternum. His collarbone had fractured at two symmetrically opposite points. It was a professional hit.

His fellow journalists at the Bugle were more than suspicious of a Lenny Stein connection with the shooting although they dared not hint too strongly at this in their write-ups. The alternative theory: that someone had a grudge against everyone linked to Sport Armageddon, was also floated.

Stein himself paid tribute to 'a popular and hardworking writer, whose quest for the truth knows no bounds'. Lenny would later remark to Wheatley that it could easily have been the 'Z' woman's handiwork but Viv detected none of the usual alarm or bewilderment transmitted by the Chief when the madwoman's name was mentioned.

It was true that Doug Alred's periodic sorties into investigative journalism occasionally made him enemies. It was also plausible that one of these had carried out a reprisal and the possibility of a random attack could also not be ruled out. It was an extraordinary end to an otherwise routine day for Sport Armageddon.

Brent Ryan had slowed considerably from the opening miles of his run phase. The hot asphalt pounded feet that had previously sat comfortably in pedal clips for almost five days and caused severe blister problems. Each time he felt a hot spot developing, he had stopped for treatment. It had not prevented egg-sized blood blisters developing on both arches.

"You're limping. You gotta take a break." Melanie had urged just before noon.

Ryan was reluctant to pause completely, even in the heat of the mid-day sun. Progress was so hard to come by that he needed every minute he could get. The adjustment from 14 miles per hour on the bike to five or six miles per hour on the run was difficult to take. He was still on the road at midnight nursing a 39 mile lead, as well as monster blisters. He was having to grind out every step of it.

The move to running did Gaby no favours either. She had walked and jogged most of the daylight hours after their customary two hour siesta. Steve O'Neill was cranking out five and a half miles per hour like a man possessed. She stayed two steps behind, head down, teeth clenched.

"Steve, I'm really not sure I can carry on with this," she announced during the late afternoon, as they headed north on Highway 17 past Woodbine. The support vehicle was parked four miles ahead. Lenny Stein had given precise instructions about not cluttering up the road as they tiptoed through Georgia. Gaby flopped down onto the grass verge and began to weep.

"You can't quit on me now. We've come too far." O'Neill sat down beside her, his gold racing lycra soaked with sweat. "Don't lie down, you'll seize up. Come on let's walk a little bit."

"I'm telling you, it's no good. I just can't carry on. I ache all over. I can't run another step." She lashed out with her fist as he reached over to help her up.

A Georgia State patrolman drew up alongside them.

"Everything alright, ma'am?"

That brought her to her senses. She wasn't going to give the State any reason to prevent the race going ahead. There had to be five of them on the roads.

"Just getting ready for a little walk, officer." She managed a weak smile as Steve lifted her to her feet and helped dry her eyes. They began walking slowly with one arm round each other's waists. The cop advised them to stay close to the kerb and he sped off.

"Regular honeymoon couple out for a stroll, aren't we?" laughed O'Neill.

A busload of cheering student fans of Gaby roared by.

"I'm sorry about that. I'll be OK if we can just walk a while. How far back is PJ?" asked Vaughan.

PJ was much further back than he would have liked. Hal 'The Mouth' duly pronounced that PJ had 'bonked' when he set off on the run.

"A clear case of 'hitting the wall'," declared Hal. "We've seen it so many times before in the New York and Boston Marathons. A competitor can just run right out of glycogen, the body's natural energy stores. PJ is lighter than any of the other four and more at risk. This has set his challenge back quite considerably."

Even when he did get running it was very spasmodic. The lack of co-operation from his body was upsetting PJ.

When Karelov passed him just before midnight, it was his lowest point since the swim ended in Pahokee but he resolved to hang in there and see what the new day might bring.

As the sun rose after the first 24 hours of the run to Atlanta, Karelov's mood changed. His bony injuries had subsided to a dull and manageable ache. He had adapted his already low-slung running action to minimise impact on his upper body. The cracked wrist moved scarcely at all. It was not pretty but it was relentless. He had caught the African. He would catch them all, even if they broke his legs.

He had noticed that the effort of running was affecting his body very differently from the cycle phase.

"Come here, my friend," he beckoned to Nemo during one of his rare pit stops. They wandered away from the roadside to avoid the prying microphones of Prime Life. It was an unnecessary precaution because the early morning viewers would be unlikely to latch on to too much of their Slavic patois blend.

"Why do my legs cramp so bad?" demanded Karelov. "Is it because my blood's too thick?"

It was a fair point. EPO-enriched blood coursing through the veins might produce a heightened tendency to muscle spasm. This would not have previously been apparent during the cycling, where the legs were not supporting the full body weight. Nemo scratched his head.

"I give you massage. We need to clear lactic acid out. Blood no problem."

"What about the heat? When it gets about ninety degrees, my blood feels like its boiling over. A million bucks is no good to me if I die."

"You will not die, Leonid. But you need to keep pulse down. If it gets above one-fifty, slow down. Better to move steadily. Need less rest."

Karelov looked carefully at Nemo once more. They had been through a great deal together. He had always felt that he would trust the old man with his life. Now that was about to be put to the true test, for it was the muscles and blood which Nemo had designed that would see him through the final three days of Sport Armageddon or see him to his grave.

As his calf massage was completed, he set off back on the road. The statistics that had been generated for the first 24 hours of the run from Jacksonville to Atlanta showed that Karelov had covered 21 miles further than anyone else.

He was only running fractionally faster than Ryan but whereas the American had taken three hours sleep, no one could remember Karelov taking any rest at all. The old war-horse was clawing his way back into contention.

Lenny Stein had stayed out of sight for a complete day after Doug Alred's shooting. He took great pride in the rising audience figures and relief from the fact that stringent security measures had kept the mad woman out of sight and out of mind for 48 hours.

Prime Life had established a loyal TV following. As they neared Savannah, the Sport Armageddon fans were voting with their feet and flocking to Highway 17 to witness good old Brent Ryan was giving the rest of the world a real beating. Stein contented himself with beating up his lieutenant.

Wheatley's mobile sounded. He had grown to hate the noise.

"What's the news from our friends in Atlanta?" No introduction necessary.

"We're doing OK so far, Chief. I reckon there's enough registered voters watching us on the Highway and on TV that they don't dare throw us out completely. As long as we keep the support vehicles from crawling, we're alright."

"And what about the finish?"

"Well now, that is a problem."

"Tell me something I don't know, bozo."

Only three more days of this, thought Wheatley, and one more pay cheque, then I'll stick his mobile phone where the sun doesn't shine. Meanwhile politeness remained the order of the day.

"There's no way we can finish in downtown Atlanta. The Governor has already issued a statement saying pretty much that he'll tolerate us as we head across Georgia but there's no way we can interrupt the city's traffic flow."

"But that's not the point," interrupted Stein. "We have to finish somewhere high profile and draw the eyes of the world to Sport Armageddon. I haven't invested so much time and money for us to crawl off to some goddamn corner and slope away. We need impact and hype. What about finishing alongside Stone Mountain or the Braves Stadium?"

"I've already looked into those places, Chief. Stone Mountain is too quiet. Braves Stadium is too busy. It's right beside the freeway. We have to come in on the smaller roads and find somewhere where we can put up a finish gantry real quick."

"We'll sort something out. You've got two days."

The phone went dead. Wheatley poked his tongue at it. He wished he hadn't. It was a childish gesture that was captured for a worldwide audience. A camera swept across the inside of the Prime Life battlebus at that very moment, supposedly offering its viewer's a behind-the-scenes look at the TV coverage of Sport Armageddon.

"Well that was the Sport Armageddon event manager, Vivian Wheatley, taking everything in his stride," chuckled Hal 'The Mouth'. "He's busy clearing the logistical operations that will give all the contestants a clear run through to the State capital. Let's see how the race is shaping up."

Wheatley's phone rang again.

"Do that once more and I'll skin you," a familiar voice announced.

The Chief must have had access to a television, wherever he was.

Hal 'The Mouth' continued. "We can see that, as we near 11.30, Brent Ryan is still hammering towards that million dollar prize. He's now on the outskirts of Savannah, about to turn west on the last big sweep of the race as Highway 80 will lead him through Macon and then on to the finish in Atlanta."

He nearly said 'downtown Atlanta' but had been warned that it was about at the same odds that the race would finish downtown as those for Vivian Wheatley III winning the Hawaii Ironman. Hal, who had long harboured dreams of a high profile job with one of the big networks, delighted in the rising audience figures and envisaged himself broadcasting to millions more Americans. Hal loved to showboat.

"Good morning, if you're just joining us. Let me remind you that, in the ultimate contest, it's America all the way. Brent Ryan has lost a little ground after that mid-morning rest but he's still thirty miles ahead of Gaby Vaughan of Australia and Britain's Steve O'Neill. They, in turn, are thirty-two miles clear of the remarkable Leonid Karelov of Russia, who suffered concussion and cracked bones on the cycle phase. PJ Kogo is six and a half miles behind him. You can see from the heli-telly split-screen that the fastest runners at present are Karelov and Kogo. The race is boiling towards a great finale."

Ryan just had to take a break. He had indicated to his father a couple of hours previously, that he would need less than the planned four hours sleep but that he wanted to use a hotel bed instead of the van and that, above all, he craved the soothing luxury of a hot bath. An en-suite room at a small guesthouse, near City Market, complete with wrought-iron balconies was duly booked. It was right on the race route.

Brent slowed to a walk as Dr Psyche pointed out the hotel less than a block ahead. As he ventured onto the sidewalk, a dozen or so of Lenny's hired supporters flocked towards him. They had been cheering him from the roadside all the way from Jacksonville. Inevitably, they were almost all teenage girls who had a collective crush on him. He kept walking as he wearily and illegibly signed the proffered autographs books.

"Here's a good luck card. I know you can win", said one, as she thrust an envelope in his hand.

"Thanks," he said, looking up briefly to see an attractive brunette in dark glasses, and Zing Cola crop-top with matching shorts.

If you just had a little more energy Brent old boy, you could really live the rock-star-on-tour life, he thought to himself as he walked wearily through the hotel lobby.

His bathtub was already running and he left instructions to be woken at half past two before closing the door behind him. He was alone at last.

As he undressed, he tore open the envelope that the girl had handed him. It was quite a thick greetings card, probably one of those with a musical tune inside.

He looked at the front of the card. 'The circus is in town' it said on the cover. It looked like it was homemade. He began opening it a split-second before the alarm bells rang in his head. He just barely had time to read 'Loverboy must die for 'Z'' on the inside page, before the card began to incinerate in his hand. It had been set off by some kind of chemical trigger mechanism as he broke the seal. It burned spectacularly and quickly. Before he had time to get his senses round what was happening, it was all over. He looked at the charred remains at his feet. He did not need to think too long and hard about this episode. It was the nutter and it was him she was after.

He rushed to the door and yelled for his father.

"Right," said Lenny when he had absorbed the latest news. "She may have pushed her luck too far this time. If she was wearing official merchandise and was with one of our busloads, she was probably there first thing in the morning when they set off. And if she was, my instructions were for all those guys to be photographed as a group. Check it out, Viv. We may have got her."

Sure enough, by mid-afternoon, Stein had his first picture of Zelda. The woman who handed over Ryan's card had enrolled as a Prime Life cheerleader the previous evening under a false name and with a false driver's licence. They had already investigated that. In the group photograph, she made no attempt to look away. She grinned straight into the camera – no sunglasses. It was almost certainly a wig but her features were sharp and distinct. Either she was taunting them, as if it was all some deadly game, or she wanted to be recognised.

Stein felt that he had started to get control of the situation at last. He passed the enlarged photo to all of the teams, with offers of lavish rewards to the security guards and private detectives. He was sure that they could track her down and identify her, without the need for any potential disruption of the race by the police. Everyone involved with Sport Armageddon scrutinised the photo closely. One person recognised Zelda immediately.

Vivian Wheatley had received formal written confirmation that Sport Armageddon would be an unwelcome gatecrasher in Atlanta. The Governor of Georgia, Jim Sims, had let Prime Life know, in no uncertain terms, that the passage of the event through the state would be tolerated all the while that it presented no public order or road safety problem. It would be a different story if the race entered the zone still sometimes referred to as the Olympic Ring, a four mile diameter loop around central Atlanta that had hosted nine Olympic competition venues in 1996.

Governor Sims advised that Georgia State Troopers would continue to monitor the progress of Sport Armageddon and that, if there was any likelihood of disruption or if the event came within that zone, everyone involved would be arrested. It was an uncompromising edict, which Lenny Stein would probably accept as a challenge. It served, however, to spark off an idea in Viv Wheatley's mind for an inspired choice of finish-line venue. The more he thought about it, the more perfect it was. In fact, it was so great that he would make sure that the credit for the idea was his, and his alone. It would also be good sport to tease the chief. He punched the speed dial number into his phone.

"Stein," barked Stein.

"Chief, it is I, Vivian. I do believe I have come up with a finish-line site in Atlanta. It's a classic – a high profile, main thoroughfare. It's controversial but probably won't lead to any arrests."

"OK, OK. Where is it?"

"I couldn't possibly tell you over an open phone line. It is a place in Atlanta which you know very well indeed, but for security reasons, I ought to keep it to myself at this time."

"What? Don't be a wise-ass. If I don't get to know, who the hell will?"

"Exactly. I must keep it to myself for the time being. Bye."

"What?"

Deep joy. During Viv's final 48 hours as a Prime Life employee, he would enjoy all the petty triumphs he could possibly score over the little tyrant. He reached to his top pocket for a slender cheroot of a cigar. As his checkout time drew nearer, he would graduate to bigger and bigger cigars to celebrate in style. Even a finely honed clean-living athlete like him needed a little luxury now and again.

Brent Ryan was running scared. Scared of the opposition. Scared of the 'Z' woman. Through the city limits in Savannah, it had seemed like everyone in the world knew his name. He had tried to scrutinise the faces in the crowd but it was a scary exercise. She could be anywhere. He had previously upped his cruising speed to nine-minute-miles as he endeavoured to surf the wave of applause and goodwill. Now all of that good news was a long way behind him. True, he had increased his lead by a further three miles as he headed out on Highway 80 towards Statesboro, but the long lonely stretches gave him ample time to rue the sudden change of pace. His body did not like it and was sending frequent grumbling messages.

Dr Psyche had prepared him a stack of morale-boosting MP3 music tapes. He had played them to death. Neil Diamond's 'America' was cued for the umpteenth time.

"We've been travelling far..."

The rest of the field was beginning to bunch behind him. Melanie had been giving him regular updates all the time that he was extending his lead. Now she had fallen ominously silent.

The biggest gap in the entire race was between him and the

Vaughan/O'Neill combo in second. Kogo and Karelov were closing fast. They might even be working together. Hunting as a pack and he was the prey. He felt a ripple in his left calf.

"In the eye of the storm...
Freedom's light burning warm....
Every time that flag's unfurled...
They're coming to America."

A roadside sign showed 'Atlanta 252 miles', It was a major psychological breakthrough to see the finish line signposted for the very first time. Dr Psyche had realised it too. He waited beneath the roadsign, pointing upwards.

"Pathway to greatness," he bawled as Brent chugged past, managing half a wan smile.

It was too serious now to goof around. He needed to guard every yard of his lead. He would rather die than be caught.

"Free, only want to be free...
Hang on to a dream."

A 34 mile lead could be lost in the time it took to take a nap, and Karelov and Kogo did not seem to need rest. Karelov. He hated the guy. He was a machine.

His calf bubbled suddenly and painfully.

God, no! He dropped to the verge and began to massage his leg to relieve the spasm.

"My country tis of thee
Sweet land of liberty..."

Tears welled up. This could blow it all. Dr Psyche, arrived, panting. "Cramp?" He enquired, and immediately began manipulating

Ryan's left foot.

"Yup, I felt it pulling."

Dr Psyche was not a medic, but prodded around the offending limb, unable to pinpoint a tear.

"Reckon you might have got away with a warning shot but it's caused by dehydration so let's get you on the IV for thirty minutes."

He led Brent to a bus parked 50 yards ahead. Melanie trotted back and offered a consoling arm. Brent's father had the saline drip rigged up and inserted the tube the second he stepped inside the van.

"Sensation!" shrieked Hal 'The Mouth'. "Ryan looks to have been pole-axed by cramp. This will be worrying news for his legions of fans. He is nearly six hours ahead, but even at this late stage, a setback like this could be curtains. The chase is hotting up. We cut to PJ Kogo after these words from our sponsors..."

PJ's rhythm had been a long time coming but now he had it. He felt as if he was hitting a gear that none of the others had at their disposal. He was able to crank out seven miles an hour for long spells right through the heat of the day. Jennifer was delighted that the potency that he had displayed for most of the cycle ride was back at last.

As they too headed northwest on Highway 80 at seven o'clock in the evening, she was thrilled. And not just because her husband was giving an excellent account of himself and impressing her fellow Americans with his dignity and fortitude. She had news for him.

PJ liked to take his pancakes on the hoof. He would walk steadily, munching away and swigging tea or electrolyte drinks. Jennifer would usually accompany him on these 15 minute strolls. She liked early evening best. The Prime Life cameras would generally lose interest at that point and cut elsewhere, unvariably to Ryan for the benefit of the peak domestic TV audience. The privacy was most welcome and on this occasion she could contain herself no longer.

"It's going really well at the moment, honey," she whispered.

"Yes, I believe I can still win. There is still time." PJ had a confident gleam in his eyes. He had put 'Z' out of his mind.

"Is there anything that could possibly make you go any better?"

"I don't think so. Not now that my legs have stopped wobbling. I have a blister and my shoulders ache but it all fades when the blisters are bandaged and you massage my shoulders. I feel very good indeed. I have got used to the tiredness."

"Well, you know I've been feeling a bit queasy at mealtimes? It's not a bug. I took a test today. There's three of us walking along here." There was a long pause as the penny dropped. PJ stared at her.

"You're pregnant? Oh my dear God!"

She nodded. "It's about seven weeks. Congratulations. You're going to be a dad."

PJ was speechless.

"I had a suspicion a week or so ago. I've been getting a metallic taste in my mouth and stuff like toothpaste and wine have been making me feel sick."

PJ's composure was coming back.

"This is fantastic news," he beamed as he gave her a hug. "You are such a clever woman. But you must sit down and take a break. You should not be rushing about."

"I'm OK. I'm OK, honestly. A bit of sickness never hurt anyone. Now we must keep this news to ourselves. It will be our secret for another five weeks. Come on, there's still four people ahead of you. You're racing for three, you know." She took his empty cup and headed back towards the bus with a wink as she left him.

"This is fantastic news. Just watch me go, Jennifer."

PJ resumed running at speed. A belch, which almost provided an action replay of his tea, persuaded him to slow down fractionally. A bit of sickness never hurt anyone. Nothing could stop him now. PJ was floating on air.

Karelov was still grinding it out, feet hardly leaving the ground, minimal arm swing, thanks to the fibreglass cast. There was a rhythm of sorts but it was more funeral march than foxtrot.

"Gap now on TV," shouted Nemo. "Ryan forty-eight miles ahead, Vaughan and O'Neill twenty-two miles ahead, Kogo three miles behind. Kogo run very good."

"Pill," mumbled Karelov. It was a request not a comment on PJ. Nemo dutifully jumped from the van and trotted alongside Karelov. When he was sure the Prime Life camera was off, he slipped the big Russian two red tablets at the same time as a large bottle of water.

Karelov discreetly swallowed the tablets, his eyes never wavering from the horizon ahead. He would not need to rest for more than an hour all night long. And that, as he had already calculated, would bring him right back within range of the sweet smell of a million dollars. The American was a long way clear but Karelov would bet his last nickel that Sport Armageddon would still have a worthy Russian winner.

As they neared their midnight break, O'Neill and Vaughan discussed the extraordinary way that the race was panning out.

"Patsy and Jane have been watching the pictures of Brent. They say he's got problems with his calf and he's having to baby it along. He's in real trouble. That's why we're closing him down. We haven't speeded up that much," declared the petite Australian. She was wearing a pink cotton sweatsuit to keep her body temperature constant in the cool night air. O'Neill wore the equivalent concoction in gold.

"Never mind about him. What are those two behind us on? I thought they were dead and buried. I'm afraid we're going to have to take a much shorter nap tonight. This whole thing is getting very serious now."

CHAPTER FOURTEEN

Sport Armageddon Standings 00.00 hours Wednesday
1st Brent Ryan (USA)   1284.0 miles
2nd Gabrielle Vaughan (Australia)   1260.0 miles
3rd Steven O'Neill (GB)   1260.0 miles
4th Leonid Karelov (Russia)   1239.0 miles
5th Philemon Kogo (Kenya)   1234.0 miles

THE pressure was mounting. Lenny Stein had not slept well. He did not know if he was chasing Zelda or she was chasing him but he would not lose. On the small matter of his other confrontation, he had consulted with his lawyers far into the night. The Jacksonville Bugle was trying to drag him and his great event into the squalid business of Doug Alred's shooting. Around breakfast time that day, the Editor would be served with an injunction. That would shut them up for a few days. Stein was a veteran of defamation actions. As a regular tactic, he would issue proceedings very quickly and then wait for the heat to die down before quietly withdrawing. It was expensive but it generally served its purpose and bought some respectful silence. He observed that Wednesday's faxed copy of the Bugle was notable for its complete lack of criticism of the event, at last. They knew they could not afford to take a hit. He should have been a riverboat poker player. When it came to brazening out these sorts of face-offs, nobody could play a duff hand better than Lenny Stein.

He had certainly squeezed maximum value out of the gamble that was Sport Armageddon. He perused the overnight figures with further satisfaction, as Hal 'The Mouth' brought the breakfast time updates.

"If you're just joining us, the most important point to take on board is that every one of these athletes is displaying stamina and staying power that is quite out of this world. After a solid seven days of battling in the furnace heat, all of them are still hammering out a fantastic pace off just an hour or two of sleep. The most that any of them slept last night was eighty minutes and we're not aware that the old fox Leonid Karelov took any rest at all. They are so far ahead of schedule that this could actually be the last full day of competition. Brent Ryan is leading the pack on the road between Wrightsville and Irwinton.

"Now I know a lot of you, joining us on our first phone-in this morning, would like to know where exactly the race will finish. We are thrilled to see so many of you Sport Armageddon fans out on the roads, getting behind all of our contenders. The exact venue in Atlanta will remain a secret, I am told by our course director, Viv Wheatley, until the leading contenders are nearing the Atlanta Metropolitan area. Stay tuned."

It was very likely that Stein and Wheatley would spend almost all of the remaining frantic hours of Sport Armageddon ensconced together in the Prime Life battlebus. It suited Vivian Wheatley. He had had quite enough of belting around between car and helicopter. It did not suit Lenny Stein quite as well. Wheatley was still acting like the cat that had got the cream, nursing the secret of where Sport Armageddon would finish. It was driving Stein to distraction. They had been through the gentle pleading stage. They had been through the threats stage. It had become very tiresome.

"Is it Atlanta Beach?"

"Nope – too far out."

"Is it Lake Lanier?"

"Nope. You're getting colder."

"Look, I'm ordering you to tell me where it is. It's my event. If you don't tell me, I shall knock your teeth down your throat."

When Wheatley laughed, this only enraged Stein more. Viv knew he could not sack him before the race finished. He had no one left who could mastermind the rest of the route and he certainly could not do it himself. Wheatley played it for all it was worth.

"You'll know in good time, Chief. Don't let it upset you."

"Just remember one thing, Viv," Stein said quietly without looking up. "Three people have crossed me so far – Karelov, Alred and the 'Z' woman. The first two have already been hospitalised..." He let the full implications of this pronouncement hang in the air for a few moments. Control was everything.

Stein's mobile rang. There was silence at the end of the line. He could sense her. His palms were clammy immediately.

"Yes." he said hoarsely.

"Comin' to get Loverboy. The time is now. Death on wings. You know it's showtime, don't you, Lenny?"

"Look... What is it that you want? Who is it that has upset you? I'm sure we can sort something out. If it's money you want..."

"Money means nothing at all. Money is not king. Power is queen. You know it's not money, Lenny. It's retribution. An eye for an eye. Zelda will close down your circus."

Wheatley knew who was on the line from the moment the Chief picked up the receiver. He was feverishly dialling the operator on his own handset to try and trace the call while she was on line. He signalled to Lenny that he was on the case.

"Lady, if you make one more attempt to interfere with this event, I will hunt you down. You cannot expect to get away with behaviour like this. You will be brought to justice." When cornered, Stein always favoured attack as the best form of defence.

There was a manic cackle on the other end of the line.

"You have no idea, Lenny. I'm coming to get you. You can run but you can't hide. You will never, ever catch me. It's all over. Bye, bye Lenny."

The handset was replaced. Wheatley leant back in his chair and exhaled slowly. His heart was pounding. Control really was everything.

"Chief, we've got a trace on it. It looks like downtown Atlanta.

A payphone. They can get us confirmation within an hour," announced Wheatley.

"An hour may be all we have if she's in Atlanta," Lenny replied carefully. "I reckon we've used up all our warnings. She's coming in for the kill...I wish I knew who she's hunting."

"Chief, let's call in the police."

"No, we can still deal with this but we must identify her before she strikes. We are not going to interrupt Sport Armageddon now and nor is anyone else. Double the security guards on each of the competitors." He paused. "And you'd better put two more outside this bus."

Brent Ryan's calf was still troubling him.

"You need to manage this situation," Dr Psyche advised. "You still have a good buffer between you and the pack and maybe only a day and a half for them to get back to you. Let them do the chasing and the worrying. We know that you can run between five and six miles an hour without it breaking down and we ought to be able to keep the pit stops brief. Steady and sure has got to be the strategy. Think of it like pouring a glass of Guinness. If you do it nice and evenly, it's full in no time. If you try and rush it, everything will froth up and you'll have to wait for it to settle. Stay in control of your destiny. Stay on the pathway."

Ryan did as he was told. He could not believe his body could have betrayed him so treacherously but then, as he was only too painfully aware, he was exploring uncharted territory. Lesser mortals would have seen their muscles turn to liquid in this heat, he reminded himself. If he was still moving, with all that fatigue in check, and only a dodgy calf to show for it, he would be a worthy winner of Sport Armageddon. He thought of the million bucks and forged on grimly. Melanie looked back over her shoulder for the Black Widow. Hell hath no fury, she thought. This woman must have been seriously jilted and her Brent was as likely a target as any for the assassin's strike. Despite her fear, Melanie wanted at least to see her coming for him.

O'Neill reflected on the last two weeks of his life and thought, not for the first time, that someone up there was steering him through it. He might stumble but he never fell. Just when the black shroud of depression had threatened to envelop him, he had been reprieved. Just when his life was chugging into a cul-de-sac, along came this race and this little Aussie and gave him something to be grateful for.

He looked across at the petite power-pack alongside him. The event, which had ravaged most of the competitors, had left her ravishing. During the race Gaby must have lost ten or twelve pounds in weight, but she still radiated health and vitality.

The two weeks that they had been together were so intense that they would be worth two years in any regular courtship timeframe. He adored her.

His only remaining grey cloud was the 'Z' woman. If she wasn't Marie Bowen's mother, why had she left a tarantula in his motel bed?

He and Gaby were both experiencing the sort of tiredness that would need seven days solid sleep to rectify. He felt protective towards her.

"How do you feel?"

"Not too bad," she lied. An hour previously she had called for a pit stop to cover another bout of heart palpitations. She was also getting chest pains. "How about you?"

"Reasonable." He could put out a white lie too.

Steve O'Neill was becoming flustered by the heat. Occasionally he would go light-headed and disorientated with black-and-white vision. That was when they would slow to 13 minute miling. He put it down to the lack of sleep and less time spent on the intravenous drip. It was all getting very torrid. They were fighting like mad to get back on terms with the American and yet, with every mile, they were being caught from behind. And nobody seemed to be taking proper breaks any more. Would they have to just keep right on going all the way to Atlanta? It was now signposted at 198 miles. Another psychological barrier breached as they toiled through the early afternoon heat. In just over a day, they could be there. O'Neill pressed on. With a gap of only 19 miles up ahead, the prospect of a win was realistic. He and Gaby had already agreed that they would split the prize money. Now they had to reach out for it.

America was taking Sport Armageddon to its heart. For Stein, with all five starters still within 40 miles of each other, it was a broadcasting and orchestration masterpiece. He knew he had cracked it when Governor Sims declined to intervene or block the race. His backroom team would have worked out the pros and cons and the implication on his electorate. All this for a one-off event, created by a regional cable TV station. Well, not for much longer. Stein would enjoy playing hardball with the big hitters in television. He never understood the phrase 'not in your wildest dreams' because his dreams were wilder and more ambitious than any man alive.

PJ's feet were still not touching the ground. The news of Jennifer's pregnancy was a bolt from the blue but it thrilled him. It put the image of himself as a sniper's target to the back of his mind for a while. When he refocused on the event in hand, he could not understand why he had still not caught Karelov. The gap remained at just over two miles. He was flying, and yet making no headway on a man running with one arm and fractures.

The good news was that both of them were gaining on the top three. It was out of the question for PJ to work with Karelov, even when he caught him. Besides, he wanted that million dollars for his family. The sun had not yet set. By this time tomorrow it could all be over. He felt a pang of urgency and cranked up the pace quicker still.

"Stay with Kogo," Stein yelled at his director. "You can see he's really going for it. Do a split-screen with him and Karelov and then use the heli-telly shot showing the gap."

The production director was heartily sick of Stein's frequent interventions. The director found that he, and what was left of his team, produced the best footage when left to their own devices but Stein's meddling was a fact of life for anyone who banked a Prime Life pay cheque.

Lenny's mind was racing ahead. The security guards would need to take care of 'Z'. He had just one last chance to ram the success of this event down the viewing public's throat. A great final 24 hours had to be topped by a great presentation of awards and press conference.

"What's the plan for the awards ceremony?" he asked Wheatley.

"Oh, its all in hand, Chief. We'll have the million dollar stack of notes on display just behind the finish line. Then we've got some fireworks and celebrities and stuff."

In reality, the only firework that he had planned was his own on-air resignation and the only B-list celebrity would be the chintzy Mr Leonard Stein.

The Chief would be left high and dry with nothing – nothing planned or organised beyond the first finisher crossing the line triumphantly and, hopefully, alive, at Viv's special finish location. He felt all his weariness and worries ebbing way at the mere prospect of retirement from Prime Life.

Wheatley squeezed his way through the banks of monitors and mixing desks on the Prime Life battlebus and eased himself into the front passenger seat. He opened the window, put his feet on the dashboard and lit a medium sized Havana cigar. At the same time he cracked an ice cold smile.

Twenty-four hours to the finish and Karelov was on autopilot. The mixture of toxins coursing round his veins and the sleep deprivation were leaving him in zombie mode. Several times he suspected that he had nearly nodded off to sleep while still running. On one occasion, he veered towards the middle of the road when he thought the conifers at the roadside were on fire. It was a subliminal message from his Eastern Europe arson days. PJ was not the only one to experience hallucinations.

None of it was slowing him down at all. The competitive streak ran very deep.

"You need pill, Leonid?" Nemo whispered.

"Pill for what?"

"Pill to stop pain. Help you keep going."   "OK."

The Russian was a creature of the night. The fears that he harboured over an EPO-induced coronary disappeared with the cool of sundown, although they were counterbalanced by a logical belief that the killer woman was more likely to strike at night. It was his time. He was still surviving on virtually no rest.

"Nine o'clock leader board coming up" shouted Nemo from the Team Karelov bus.

"Damn Yankee approaching Macon, now only fourteen miles ahead. He looks bad. Englishman and Australian girl look very bad too. They are only eighteen miles up the road. Kenyan still two miles behind. You can win Leonid. You can win it, man."

Vaughan was feeling terrible. At this time of night her body craved a rest and yet, to win they might need to keep going right through to Atlanta. She was alternating between chronic fatigue and lighter spells when she merely felt exhausted. Her heart flutters had not returned that day but the chest tightness would not shift. There ought, she concluded, to be 100 different words to describe the varying degrees of tiredness, rather like the Eskimos who have dozens of different words for snow.

"You must go on, mate," she finally announced to O'Neill who had also been toiling in silence.

"What's wrong?"

"I know I said we should carry on right through, what with there only being a hundred and sixteen miles to go."

"A hundred and fifteen."

"Right, but if I don't take an hour's sleep now, I'm just about going to die right here. You go on." There were tears in her eyes.

"No, I need the rest too. We're in this together. Call up the bus and we'll both take exactly an hour."

Hal 'The Mouth' was relieved that Sports Armageddon was reaching its conclusion. If his voice went any croakier he would need to commentate with hand signals and subtitles. He could not believe the event was moving to such a dramatic finish. Who would have credited this scenario when Karelov was so far clear on the bike in South Florida? If he hadn't had the hamstring injury setback and the bike crash, he would surely have dominated Sport Armageddon. He was closing fast, back in fourth place and grinding out the miles but Hal's money was still riding on the man in Zing green.

Patsy and Jane could not rouse Gaby at the end of her one hour sleep.

For a dreadful moment, they both feared she was dead. She might as well have been. It was a very deep sleep. Only the smelling salts and the trusty wet flannel slap on the face routine finally brought her round. It was probably a mistake to have stopped, she agreed, as she and O'Neill shuffled into the night like pink and yellow sleepwalkers, searching for a rhythm, feeling worse than ever.

Stein would have no trouble staying awake. He watched the monitors intently, proud of his creation. One hundred miles to run and still anybody's race. The areas around each of the competitors were as safe as he could make them. Zelda would have to perpetrate a highly risky drive-by shooting if she was to pick anyone off and that, Lenny concluded, just wasn't her style. He would not get mad, he would get even. Surely she could not get to him now? The competitors were close to breaking point, but it made for classic television. He had made his event as impregnable as humanly possible, and it was still on course for a classic finale. No one could have stage-managed it better.

CHAPTER FIFTEEN

Sport Armageddon Standings 00.00 hours Thursday

1st Brent Ryan (USA)	1402.5 miles
2nd Gabrielle Vaughan (Australia)	1386.5 miles
3rd Steven O'Neill (GB)	1386.5 miles
4th Leonid Karelov Russia)	1380.0 miles
5th Philemon Kogo (Kenya)	1378.0 miles

STEIN did not sleep at all as his monster careered towards its conclusion. Atlanta could not help but admit the competitors into its City Limit.

People power demanded to see how the drama finally ended. Lenny was in overdrive but he was not about to let anyone at Prime Life rest on their laurels. A dog-tired technical crew soldiered on.

Out on the course, a sharp-eyed bodyguard, assigned to Team Kogo was about to make a name for himself. He radioed in to the battlebus to report that a red Mustang had driven past them three times in the previous 15 minutes. He had noted it because it was the same as his wife's car and he also reported that the woman driver did not look across at Kogo, although she must have been following PJ or the event itself to have overtaken them so frequently.

"If you see her again, pull her over for questioning," Stein snapped.

He bellowed across to the mixing desk for them to replay the last ten miles of pictures to see if the woman and her car showed up on screen.

It was a painstaking task but Lenny stayed at the technician's shoulder for a full hour as they carefully replayed all of the videotape footage. Lenny would stay there for as long as necessary. Time might be ebbing away for 'Z's victim. She had to be intercepted. His pulse quickened as a slow-moving red Mustang eased past Leonid Karelov. The pictures had been recorded just 20 minutes previously.

"Stop the tape," he yelled. "There! It's her." He was jabbing a finger at the screen. "Can you enlarge this?"

The technician zoomed in on the figure in the driver's seat and paused as the grainy image filled the screen.

She wore a headscarf and horn-rimmed spectacles. She appeared to have long straight dark hair. It was a woman in her late twenties or early thirties. Stein recognised the angular features without hesitation. It was Zelda.

"Jesus Christ. It is her. Get the licence plate of that car."

Within minutes all of the teams were told about the sighting and security outriders were briefed. She had gone too far this time. Lenny Stein knew that a high-powered rifle shot from one of his guys could pick her off before she could even breathe in their direction again. It had taken a long time to overcome the bitch but Lenny was getting that winning feeling again. It was a feeling that was reinforced when there were no further sightings of Zelda or her Mustang anywhere near the fortified Sport Armageddon positions for the next two hours.

Zelda drove slowly into the parking lot of the car rental company at Hartsfield-Atlanta Airport. She pulled off the dark wig and spectacles and put them carefully into a carrier bag. She handed back the keys to the waiting clerk at the reception area and strode towards the short-term car park at the airport terminal to collect her own blue Mazda sports car. It was time.

Brent Ryan suffered a catastrophe during peak-time breakfast viewing. He had permitted himself half an hour of hypnosis with Dr Psyche at around three o'clock in the morning, realising that conventional sleep was out of the question. In the hours before dawn he had succeeded in extending his lead over Vaughan and O'Neill to 19 miles. With 75 miles to go as they passed between Jackson and McDonough on Highway 23, it was beginning to look like an unassailable lead.

The busloads of students, many of whom had followed the event from Pahokee, were also beginning to get demob happy. They lined up alongside the Highway and whooped and cheered for all they were worth. Lenny had doubled the prize money for the most enthusiastic supporter on the final day.

Hal 'The Mouth' had abandoned all thoughts of saving his larynx and was in home straight overdrive.

"Just look at the waves of supporters lining the route. The people of Georgia have really taken this event to their hearts. What a fantastic finale for Sport Armageddon. We could never, in our wildest dreams, have imagined it being this close on the final day but it's still Brent Ryan of the USA in the lead and he picks up the pace in response to the encouragement."

Ryan had been running on the sidewalk. He stepped off to return to the main highway. Of all the millions of footsteps, cycle rotations and swim kicks he had taken, this millisecond contained the fatal flaw. His left calf muscle pulled suddenly as it recoiled from the extra impact of stepping down. He shrieked and crumpled into a heap, clutching the offending muscle.

Dr Psyche was parked almost half a mile up but saw it instantly on the TV monitor and began running back down the road.

"Sensation!" Bawled Hal 'The Mouth'. "That problem calf which Brent Ryan has been nursing along, has given way on him. This could be a dramatic final twist to his quest for the million dollar prize. Our close-up shows the agony etched on his face. Let's hope he can continue. Remember, he is still almost three hours clear of the field."

Dr Psyche knew it was bad straight away. The calf muscle was freeze sprayed, injected with painkiller and bandaged tightly. Dr Psyche's eyes were misting up with tears as he watched the distraught Ryan. He knew they had to patch him up so that he could walk to Atlanta, if necessary. The tears were rolling down

Melanie's cheeks as she held Ryan's hand. She did not really care how Aunt May in Kansas would construe that. If this was how cruel sport could be, she would apply for a posting to 'home shopping' when she returned to Prime Life.

The medical treatment took 20 minutes before Brent rose to his feet and took weight on the leg.

"Oh God. It's horrible."

"You need to move about on it for a while, Brent. It gets the painkillers circulating. It will get better. Let's walk," suggested Dr Psyche.

So they walked. Very slowly. Three of them with arms round each other's shoulders. Ryan in the middle, Dr Psyche on the left and Melanie on the right. The accompanying race officials warned that they risked disqualification if they offered such assistance for more than a mile. Ryan's father skipped on ahead, urging, cajoling and encouraging, trying all the while to hide the fact that he was shedding a few tears, too.

The burning pain eased marginally at the end of the mile of walking and Ryan declared that he was ready to try to run.

They backed away from him and he set off. Tiny steps, great discomfort, and minimal speed. So be it. If this was the way fate decreed that he must complete the course, he would do it. He was still holding pole position for the million bucks after all. The crowd loved it and Hal 'The Mouth' loved it. Stein didn't like it very much because he feared this would play into Karelov's hands but he knew it would transfix the viewers to see someone toiling away like this, so there was always a silver lining.

Vivian Wheatley III had had a few beers for breakfast. It would be his final day in Lenny Stein's acquaintance and retribution was uppermost in his mind. He breezed into the Prime Life battlebus parked on Highway 23, north of McDonough.

"Mornin' Chief," he slurred. "Have we caught the witch yet?"

Stein eyed him quizzically. He could not possibly be drunk at this hour of the morning. He must be working too hard. There's a first time for everything.

"I'm just taking the chopper into Atlanta to set up the finish area," announced Wheatley. "I just wanted you to know that however this ends up, you've hit the big-time, Chief. I've bought you a present to recognise the achievement of Sport Armageddon. Promise me you'll wear it the rest of today."

He solemnly handed Stein a ten-gallon Stetson, a magnificent cream coloured hat with a band made up in the five competitors colours of Sport Armageddon – Zing green, fuchsia pink, burnt gold, Kogo blue and Russian red. On the front was a large label that pronounced 'I Am A Winner'.

"Why, that's very kind of you, Viv. You shouldn't have."

"The pleasure is all mine, Chief. May I put it on for you?"

The Chief nodded.

Wheatley solemnly placed the Stetson on Stein's head. As he did so, he carefully put a much larger adhesive label on the back of the hat which read, 'I AM THE WORLD'S BIGGEST JERK'.

"Looks great, Chief. Check the reflection in the monitor."

"Hmm, that does have a certain style. Thanks Viv."

The technicians bit their lips. Wheatley made his exit.

"I'll phone through the finish route as soon as they hit the City Limits. Good luck everybody. Let's make it a good one."

As he walked to the helicopter, Vivian Wheatley lit up a very large Havana cigar.

Stein wondered if he had been unduly harsh in his dealings with Wheatley in recent times. They had come through a great deal together and Viv's loyalty could never be questioned. If he had behaved unreasonably towards him it was the stress of the event and the death threats. He decided he would give him a modest pay rise when it was all over, even though he had been very churlish over the business of the finish-line site.

Vaughan and O'Neill knew only too well that they were gaining ground on Ryan very rapidly. If only they had been in better condition to take advantage. Their conversation was virtually non-existent as they stayed locked in their own little worlds. Tense, tired, disorientated and dogged. As they approached noon, O'Neill spoke.

"This is about the time that we would take our siesta. I know it's off the agenda today but God knows, I'm really hurting here. We've got Ryan twelve miles ahead. Karelov and Kogo are only three miles behind but if I don't take a breather I'm going to fry."

"I'm glad you said that. I need to stop a while. Let's get to the van."

They flagged the support buses over. Patsy and Jane sprinted towards Gaby as if it was a one minute break between boxing rounds. She had felt a flicker of heart palpitations, so Steve's offer of a pit stop was very timely.

The ice packs came out. Patsy and Jane worked very swiftly. The sweat-soaked clothing was changed inside the vans. Blisters were treated, legs and shoulders massaged. Electrolyte fluids were swigged and energy bars devoured. Both of them also opted for a cool, fresh pair of disc running shoes and they sat alone inside the van to change them. The pit stop had taken eight minutes but it was all they could spare.

"There's something I need to say," said O'Neill, before they set off. "We've been through a lot together here. I feel as if I've known you all my life. Whatever happens today..." He faltered. "Will you marry me, Gaby?"

He was on one knee. She was transfixed and for a moment, lost for words. He looked deeply into her tired eyes. They never wavered.

"Well for crying out loud. I never expected this. Just what do you expect a girl to say at a time like this? The answer's 'yes', by the way."

He laughed and they hugged each other for a precious minute and said nothing.

"We gotta run, buddy." Gaby whispered eventually, not wanting to break the spell.

When they resumed the chase it was at an increased speed.

Hal 'The Mouth' was intrigued.

"That pit stop appears to have breathed new life into Steve O'Neill and Gaby Vaughan. They have really started to turn the screw on the final run-in to Atlanta. They were off the road for almost eleven minutes and that has enabled Brent Ryan to hobble almost a mile further down the road. Karelov and Kogo have closed much more than a mile from behind. If they keep this speed up, I don't know if Ryan will be able to hold them off."

Zelda drove past two of the competitors. She refused to look to her right as she passed. It was not necessary. She had a mission to complete. They were not part of her realm anymore and soon she would despatch Loverboy to another world.

Karelov was still pumping out a relentless ten minute mile pace. There were times when he felt he might be able to press on a fraction quicker but he still had nagging doubts about how his bloodstream would react to a higher pulse on the run. Better to be a live millionaire than a dead hero. His present rate of progress would claw all of them back before they reached Atlanta. Every now and then the flesh around his joints would tighten. He had definitely taken his last course of EPO. There was no way he was going to jeopardise his health beyond the end of this race. His steely gaze remained fixed on the tarmac six feet ahead.

"Very good Leonid," shouted Nemo as the Team Karelov bus

passed on his left-hand side. "You can win, Leonid."

Nemo held up a chalkboard with the current standings as Ryan neared the southeastern edge of Atlanta, with less than 40 miles to go. It read:

'USA + 12
GB/AUS + 5
KEN – 1'

He pondered it. Did that mean Brent Ryan was 12 miles ahead of him or 17? He had seen the pictures of Ryan when he stopped to change his singlet in the van. The sissy boy was really labouring. Karelov would take him and the goddamn Yankee million bucks. No man could stand in his way now.

Kogo could not comprehend the way this monster run was developing. Why was he not closing in on Karelov? He could not run any quicker and it was good enough to outpace everyone except Karelov.

It was not as if Kogo had taken any long breaks either. He was fuelled by pure adrenalin and emotion but even when he put in a fast half hour section, he never even caught sight of the big Russian.

"Jennifer, are you sure he's still a mile ahead?"

"Yes, we go past him every time we drive ahead to park up. We're on very friendly terms with Mr Nemo."

"So, why do I not ever see Leonid?"

"I guess he's just a master at holding you at bay. He must speed up every time he sees our bus."

"He is a ghost runner, this Karelov."

"Don't worry honey. You're both very close to Ryan and he's virtually walking. There's still time for you to win this PJ. Keep working hard."

"OK. I go. Rest with our baby."

The van drew away and PJ upped the pace another notch.

Vivian Wheatley III was starting to feel the pressure. It was now half past one. It would take the competitors four and a half hours to reach his designated finish zone. The Prime Life helicopter hovered over an upmarket residential area in the northern suburbs of Atlanta.

He had radioed through to his ground trucks to start heading for Buckhead. He was no more specific than that, so the precise venue remained his very personal secret.

The cheerleader buses that had supported Karelov and Kogo through McDonough were also dispatched to Buckhead. In an hour and a half he would go live on air to confirm the venue. Team Ryan and Zing Cola were already protesting that they needed to have precise details of how far was left to run. Wheatley was satisfied that the mileage calculations were correct.

He telephoned the Prime Life battlebus and verified their calculations.

"I make it twenty-three miles to go for the leader. Do you agree?" The graphics complier agreed. From his eye in the sky, Wheatley would only need to fly back for a couple of minutes and he would be able to see all five competitors. It was an incredible finale. What a way to go.

O'Neill was really struggling. He feared he was on the brink of major heat exhaustion. He had been violently sick during the previous mile.

"Maybe its nerves, darling." Vaughan had reassured him.

Steve was scared. He had not even been able to keep down the melted water from an ice cube in his mouth. There was no time to go on the drip and the sun was at its most deadly.

A pump spray of water from the passing Team O'Neill bus soaked him, cooled him and offered temporary relief. His thinking was still clear enough. They had less than the marathon distance to go. After almost 1500 miles, another 22 surely wouldn't hurt, especially when the big prize was dangling just up ahead.

Ryan was like a wounded animal scuttling to his lair. The American had no strength left and the pack was closing. The fear of failure now drove him every bit as much as the will to win.

"We can definitely do this," O'Neill announced to Gaby through gritted teeth. They upped the pace very slightly and, as Gaby fell in step, she felt a familiar fluttering in her chest.

Stein watched it all from the battlebus. His event was a triumph and had a life of its own. Sport Armageddon was now beyond his control but his previous interventions had ensured that the American viewers had stayed enthralled. The sponsors were happy. The concept would grow bigger and better. He would invite every nation on earth to send a representative. They would swim Lake Michigan, cycle to Washington and run to New York. He would sit at the top table of TV sport. In the history of broadcast innovation, the name of Leonard Stein would...

The telephone rang.

It was her. No. No. Not now. Not here.

"The circus is over. Bye, bye, Lenny."

His blood chilled. Where the hell was she? He could see all five competitors on the bank of monitors. She could not possibly get to them. Was it him she was coming for?

Zelda knew exactly where the target bus would park up. It wasn't even a calculated gamble. She had watched the patterns emerge. She had driven this final stretch of road a dozen times, weighing it all up. Above all, she knew Loverboy. She was still inside Loverboy's head. At least one of the vehicles, apart from Loverboy's, would park at this recreational area, probably several at the same time. It was the only suitable stopping place for ten miles.

Zelda had been parked at the rear of the near-deserted rest area for more than an hour. In her hand she watched a miniature television, counting down the final mile as Loverboy moved ever nearer. This would be Loverboy's last halt of the whole race. The final pit stop of all time. She stared intently at the point where she knew Loverboy's vehicle would be. She was inside Loverboy's head and for just a few moments more, Loverboy was inside her head. The roadside lay-by was the other side of a thick barrier of conifers. It could only be reached from the parking lot by crawling beneath the trees. The security men would be scanning the highway for red Mustangs. She was on their blind side. The curtain was about to come down on Loverboy's circus.

Zelda stayed calm but her breathing quickened as she watched a convoy of support vans and the Prime Life battlebus pull into the lay-by in quick succession. Just above the dense foliage, she could make out the precise position of Loverboy's vehicle. It was time to kill.

Carefully she fastened the cuffs and collar of her black jumpsuit and reached into the holdall on the passenger seat for the bomb. It was a Russian-made terrorist device. It weighed less than five pounds but it was a high-density explosive. The casing was magnetic and could be easily fixed to the underside of a van. The detonator was remote controlled and could be triggered from 300 yards away. She would watch the curtain come down from the comfort of her car. But first the little beauty needed to be put in place.

She walked quickly to the perimeter. There was a hedge at right angles to the conifers separating the parking bays and this screened her from the rest of the car park. She was 60 feet from Loverboy's bus and could hear Stein's voice coming over the security guards' radio receivers.

"The mad woman has rung again. Keep your eyes on anything suspicious in the passing traffic. Don't take any chances."

The security guards positioned themselves front and back of the buses scanning both carriageways.

The van was parked right up against the conifer hedge. The foliage was so deep and dense. The security guards all had their backs to it. She had always been one jump ahead of the whole circus but now it was time to end it all. Loverboy had broken her heart. There could only be one solution. It was written. It was now. Time to die. Time to die.

Zelda estimated that she would have three minutes to plant the device, and then three minutes to detonate. Loverboy was still three quarters of a mile up the road.

She dropped down onto her stomach and began creeping towards the van. Her focus never left Loverboy's van. Time to die. Time to die. This was her mission. She could hear the music deep inside her head reaching a crescendo. She could hear the voices chanting, demanding a kill. Tears rolled down her cheeks but Zelda made no sound as she slithered towards her prey.

A decade of brooding and festering for revenge could now be unleashed. She sought absolution. There had been so many highs and lows. Time to die. Time to die. So many bouts of loneliness and depression but the point of release was very near. Less than 60 feet. An eye for an eye. Her pulse was racing. Loverboy must die. She edged forward another couple of yards. That she might live. Fifty feet. She had planned these moments for so long. Zero option. Bye, bye Loverboy. Showtime. Forty feet. Time to die. Time to die.

Zelda died instantly when the explosive device that was still strapped to her body detonated early. When the explosion came it could be heard a mile away. The device was capable of killing a platoon of soldiers but in Atlanta it killed just one person.

The police forensic team would subsequently determine that an unknown assailant was within 12 yards of three of the Sport Armageddon vehicles on the outskirts of Atlanta before being killed in the blast that was triggered by a sophisticated limpet bomb. The support buses and personnel were shaken but undamaged.

Vivian Wheatley saw the whole thing from the Prime Life helicopter and Lenny Stein was almost knocked out of his seat by the fallout. It did not take long to work out what had happened and they feared the worst. It was a massive relief that there was just one unknown casualty, but there was no injury to others and the support vans were able to flee the scene immediately on Stein's orders.

Wheatley surveyed the aftermath and was at a loss for words. Stein wasn't. "We have been spared from the forces of evil," he announced, sounding strangely religious in his relief. "We can explain it all to the police later. In the meantime we've got a million dollar race to complete. Now, for God's sake, tell me where you've put the finish line." A near-dance with the devil had not deflected him from his other priorities in life.

It was back to business for the last time for Vivian Wheatley III.

"West Paces Ferry Road," he replied quietly.

There was a long hesitation as the imagery appeared to Stein.

"The Governor's House," he breathed. "That's brilliant, Viv."

"I thought so too."

"Will they allow it?"

"They're too late to stop us, unless they work out that the explosion was associated with Sport Armageddon. The gantry is already in place and there's a crowd of about five hundred even before we've formally announced it. I've radioed the team vehicles. It's from the south west, clockwise along Forest Parkway, Camp Creek and Fulton Boulevard. The on-screen distance of eighteen miles remaining for Ryan is correct."

If the Governor of the State of Georgia, James O Sims had been at his official residence on West Paces Ferry Road, Buckhead at that very moment, he would have seen a deputation of his state troopers nervously monitoring the assembly of a simple finish line gantry for Sport Armageddon and fearing to intervene. The bush telegraph was working overtime as people arrived in droves. It was not very long before a makeshift public address system relayed Hal 'The Mouth's' commentary and the familiar chant of 'U-S-A, U-S-A' rang out.

Melanie had no fingernails left. There was already a rumour over the walkie-talkies that the 'Z' woman had died when the bomb went off near the buses. Dear God. Had it been meant for them? Dr Psyche's palms were clammy with sweat and Mr Ryan Senior had his fists clenched. The bus was parked on Camp Creek Parkway, west of Hartsfield International Airport. There was a small group of spectators waving the stars and stripes as they looked back down the road for Brent. He had nine miles to go with a lead that was being whittled away all the time. At last, Brent came shuffling around the corner. It was nearly six o'clock in the evening but the sun was as cruel as ever.

Ryan looked ghastly. He had taken all the painkillers the doctor had been permitted to prescribe – and a few more for good measure. His face was contorted in agony. He was hardly taking any weight on his left leg. It was a grotesque parody of a run. And yet, incredibly, there was still no one in sight. They cheered for all they were worth but he was too far gone to notice them.

Dr Psyche and Brent's father set off in the Team Ryan bus. Melanie had been instructed to wait behind and check the gap that he held over his relentless pursuers. She waited anxiously by the Prime Life bus. She had started the stopwatch as Brent had passed.

One minute zipped by then two, three, four, five. She began to breathe again. Suddenly O'Neill and Vaughan appeared. It was a shock because, compared to her Brent, they appeared to be sprinting. Their faces were grey with the tension. They passed her six minutes and 55 seconds behind Ryan. With nine miles to go, would that be a big enough gap? Melanie buried her head in her hands. Surely life would not be so cruel as to rob the American viewing public of its favourite winner in the final hour of a nine day race?

She began making calculations of their relative speeds. If Brent was still running 13 minute miles, they would only have to run 12½ minute miling to catch him.

Midway through her calculations, a square-jawed, one-armed bandit called Leonid Karelov hoved into view. Another shock. He was only nine minutes ten seconds down on Brent. No sooner had she noted that than she could hear Jennifer shouting back to PJ from the Team Kogo bus. She could tell without checking that he was within three minutes of Karelov.

"Let's go," she shouted to the driver.

How on earth could Melanie break this to Brent? It was as if the other four had all been taken to the City Limits together and told to give chase. It was impossibly close.

Hal 'The Mouth' had been ordered by Stein not to mention the explosion.

"Sensation," he bawled, his voice nearly at meltdown stage. "All five competitors are now clearly visible from the same heli-telly camera. Watch as we pan back from Ryan all the way to Kogo. Suddenly the longest triathlon in history and the race for one million bucks has come down to a seven mile dash. Was there ever such a race as this?"

"Stay with Ryan and Karelov," shouted Stein in the fraught atmosphere of the Prime Life battlebus as it parked at the rear of the Prime Life building in downtown Atlanta.

"This is the big one," he announced to no one in particular.

"America versus Russia, East versus West, Good versus Evil. They're both pushing themselves right to the edge."

Ryan thought Fulton Industrial Boulevard would never end. He was beyond pain now. He just wanted the waiting, the feeling of being hunted, to be over. If they were going to pass him then so be it. He had no more left to give. He dared not look back for he knew exactly what he would see.

"Five miles to go, baby," screamed Melanie as the green battle-bus came by again. His father gave a thumbs up.

"Pathway to greatness!" screamed Dr Psyche.

There was a frenzy at the finish area, as a crowd of more than 4000 jostled for position behind the crush barriers directly in front of the Governor's house.

"Have you got the Governor's permission for this?" a cop asked Vivian Wheatley III.

Wheatley had erected a deckchair on the sidewalk on a prime spot by the finish line. He was drawing on a colossal Montecristo cigar and swigging Dom Perignon from the bottle.

"Nope. Not exactly officer."

"Well I'm afraid I will have to ask you to disperse."

"Bit too late for that officer. I think it might be safer to let it all pass off quietly. It'll be all over in a few minutes. Then you can take it up with the organiser, Mr Leonard Stein. He's the chief of Prime Life TV, you know. He can tell you all about that explosion out at the rest area that you'll have heard about. It was his choice to have the event finish here. I should think that Governor Sims will be appalled, and rightly so."

The officer looked away. The crowds were still pouring into West Paces Ferry Road from all directions. They seemed peaceful enough. The old boy was probably right. A watching brief might be best.

Overhead, the Prime Life helicopter whirred ever closer.

A loud cheer went up at the sound of Hal 'The Mouth's' disembodied voice. He announced that Brent Ryan of the USA was still in the lead as they crossed Marrietta Boulevard. He was less than two miles away.

It was right at that moment that Brent Ryan relinquished the lead which he had held since they were cycling towards Cape Canaveral.

He was passed swiftly and decisively by O'Neill and Vaughan, one on either side. Gaby offered words of encouragement. Neither of the other two spoke. They were all on autopilot. They had been told about the bomb but it registered little with any of the competitors at this stage. Their minds were taking their bodies to places where they had no business going. It had been like that for most of Sport Armageddon but now they were all running on empty. It was only the most deeply ingrained basic competitive instinct that was keeping any of them going.

"He's not managed to hang on," Gaby announced looking back at Ryan. "We're leading. We're going to win."

O'Neill said something unintelligible and moaned in discomfort. They could not possibly raise the pace another notch. It was a game of survival.

The crowds grew thicker and the applause louder. It echoed around their heads as they struggled to focus. O'Neill began to drift away from the kerb and stumbled momentarily.

"Keep going, baby. This is West Paces Ferry. We've done it. We're on the final stretch."

Jane and Patsy had told them that the final run-in was precisely one mile and Vivian Wheatley had thoughtfully placed a large 'One Mile To Go' sign at eye level.

A mile can mean different things at different times. Right now it was a mile too far for Steve O'Neill.

Concentration gone, legs turned to mush, he began to sway and lose momentum.

He stumbled, Gaby reached out to support him and they paused. His head was tilted back and he was murmuring incoherently. She wrapped an arm around his waist. Then, locked together, they staggered on. In this desperate fashion, they managed to progress for a full 400 yards...

"Get in close, get in close." Lenny Stein was out of his chair and shrieking. "This is pure theatre. I love it."

The camera zoomed in on O'Neill's suffering.

They had slowed to a walk. Steve was bent at the waist, head bowed, almost unconscious, kept upright only by Gaby's steadying arm.

She looked ahead. The finish line and one million bucks were just round the next corner. They must be only about 500 yards away. It was agony but they were still travelling together.

At that point, O'Neill collapsed completely. The paramedics who had moved towards them from the finish line, dashed the final few yards.

He was sprawled across the roadway, face ashen, eyes rolled back, limp as a sheet.

The paramedic took a pulse.

"Christ," he said. "His heartbeat is very weak. Get the defibrillator."

He slapped an oxygen mask on Steve and put ice packs on his head and chest. O'Neill was drifting away.

"Get an IV drip," shouted the medic.

A small crowd had gathered round the unconscious O'Neill. Gaby wept. Vivian Wheatley rushed onto the scene, took one look at Steve and sobered up. He had recruited him to the event all those months previously and hadn't mentioned 'death' as a finish line bonus.

In the distance, the wail of an ambulance could be heard. The helicopter hovered low overhead.

"Stay in close," shouted Stein. "This is incredible."

In the midst of this pandemonium, a runner appeared. His support team had made him aware of the collapse of O'Neill and his mind had locked onto the unclaimed one million bucks. It was Karelov.

He scuttled by on the far side of the road, unnoticed by most of the spectators. Stealth and surprise were still part of his armoury.

Vivian Wheatley III spotted him.

"The bastard cheat!" He spat.

"Look, there's nothing you can do here," he said to Gaby. "It's a medical thing. Finish the race and come back. We can't have Karelov winning."

Gaby looked up to see Karelov disappear round the corner. Her place was with Steve but, after a moment's hesitation, on legs that could barely move a few minutes earlier, she set off in pursuit of Karelov.

The Russian could sense the chase and scampered still quicker. She must have been 40 yards down with less than 300 yards to go.

The crowd, aware of the life-and-death drama being played out round the corner, roared her on. This served only to galvanise the Russian further. One hundred and fifty yards to run and the gap was still 20 yards.

The Australian's eyes were shut tight, holding back the tears, shutting out the torrent of emotions. Arms pumping, every atom directed to the effort. She wanted to win this thing for her and her man. But there was no time left. The sands had run out. Karelov was galloping towards the finish gantry. She was just two strides down. Thirty yards to go. It was too late. It was impossible. The line was upon them. In desperation, she made a dive for it. At that moment, Karelov looked back for the first time to see who it was in such hot pursuit. That fatal hesitation would cost him one million dollars. As he twisted his torso to look, the flying figure of Gaby Vaughan edged by and won by the narrowest of margins.

Geoff Wightman

There was no time to celebrate. Gaby turned to speed back to the paramedics. O'Neill's heart had stopped beating and they were trying to kick start it with the electrodes. Two attempts had produced nothing on the monitor...

Sport Armageddon

EPILOGUE

FROM the moment that Sport Armageddon was conceived it had paid scant regard for human mortality. It had taken the challenge of physical endurance right to the very brink. During the race itself, the shadow of death had been glimpsed on several occasions. There was indeed to be one more fatality on that dramatic final evening in Atlanta. It happened as the frantic team of paramedics tried to revive Steve O'Neill. The cause of death was clinically recorded as coronary thrombosis. It was a massive heart attack, although mercifully the victim would not have suffered. But it was not O'Neill who died that day. It was not Vaughan. It was not the long suffering Karelov nor the plucky Ryan. The proud PJ Kogo, who had spent the entire race playing catch up, would also live to behold his newborn son. The casualty was Lenny Stein himself, whose hypertension and bloodlust at last got the better of him. A body awash with bile and driven to a frenzy finally gave out as he collapsed in the TV control room.

On West Paces Ferry Road, O'Neill's heart sparked back to life at the third time of asking and the paramedics could begin to weave their magic.

A routine police investigation of the bomb explosion failed to reveal anything more of Zelda. Her Mazda sports car was registered in a different name. There was no other identification present. It was as if she was a ghost. A full six months passed before anyone plucked up the courage to empty her trailer at the park and no connection was made between the dead bomber and the trailer park oddball. Zelda simply disappeared off the face of the earth with almost no one any the wiser about the woman or her crazed motives. Only her true intended victim knew what drove her.

Steve O'Neill decided to move to Australia permanently and travelled out to Sydney at Christmas to prepare for the happy couple's St Valentine's Day wedding at Bondi Beach. The more he got to know Gaby Vaughan, the better he liked her.

"We'll be proud to have you as our son-in-law." Alistair Vaughan declared. "You two seem so comfortable with each other. It's a great match."

Gaby's heart palpitations had not troubled her since that fateful day in Atlanta. It was, she had come to the conclusion, something brought on by a long-term anxiety – but it was history now.

In late January, she was accompanied by her mother for a final fitting of the top secret wedding dress. "You'll probably work out what it's like. We've got no secrets," she whispered to O'Neill as she left. "Dad's dying to play you at golf this afternoon, so you'll need to get some clubs. There's a spare set in the loft."

It took O'Neill 20 minutes of rummaging around through packing cases before he found the battered golf bag. It was propped against a cardboard box marked 'University'. O'Neill could not resist looking inside. It contained files and textbooks from Gaby's days at the University of New South Wales. It also contained her graduation yearbook. He had recently seen some family photos confirming that at 21 she did indeed look just as fabulous. He began leafing through it.

'This had been a highly successful year for UNSW', wrote the Dean of Social Sciences in the introduction to the yearbook. 'With students from twelve different countries, it has been a tremendously rewarding experience to have been on the teaching staff.'

O'Neill turned the page to see individual photos of earnest young geography students. A large snapshot fell to the floor. On the back was scribbled 'eve of graduation party'. There was a group of intoxicated young revellers, celebrating their last night as undergraduates. At the back he recognised Gaby, seemingly oblivious to the camera in a passionate embrace with the classmate on her right. He recognised the mystery person immediately and froze. It was now such a familiar face, the sharp angular features had not changed at all, but the neatly written dedication underneath was the real killer:

'You are my true Loverboy, wherever you go, whatever you do, I will be there. All my love, Zelda.'